DEAD ENDS

ALSO BY S.L. MENEAR

The Jettine Jorgensen Mystery Series

Dead Silent

Dropped Dead

Dead Ends

Dead Reckoning

The Samantha Starr Thriller Series

Flight to Redemption

Flight to Destiny

Triple Threat

Stranded

Vanished

Trapped

Life, Love, & Laughter: 50 Short Stories

DEAD ENDS

A JETTINE JORGENSEN MYSTERY
BOOK 3

S. L. MENEAR

ePublishingWorks!
love what you read

Book design by eBook Prep and cover by Patti Roberts.
www.ebookprep.com

Released: April 2024
ISBN: 978-1-64457-737-0

ePublishing Works!
644 Shrewsbury Commons Ave
Ste 249
Shrewsbury PA 17361
United States of America

www.epublishingworks.com
Phone: 866-846-5123

For Mary Lou Benvenuto

ONE

Her home stands silent,
while the killer lurks within,
watching and waiting.

A suffocating sense of impending doom engulfed me as I gazed at the medieval weapons mounted on a twenty-foot-high wall in the great hall. Ancient people were slaughtered with these brutal arms centuries ago, so why worry now? Heavy rain pelting the oceanside windows of Valhalla Castle, built by my great-great-grandfather from Denmark over a hundred years ago, intensified the dark energy flooding the room.

Was my unease caused by an overactive imagination or inherited intuition? As the raging storm pummeled the castle, my thoughts drifted to the family patriarch.

My ancestor, a wealthy industrialist, designed the mansion as a monument to his Viking heritage. The four-story stone fortress, which looked out of place in tropical Florida, had ramparts and parapets along the roofline and turret towers rising from the four corners. His six-acre estate covered the northeast end of Banyan Isle, an exclusive residential barrier island near Palm Beach.

Sixteen years ago, when I was twelve, my father inherited Valhalla Castle and a hefty trust fund to maintain its splendor. He also inherited the family business, Jorgensen Industries, which had grown into a multinational aerospace corporation.

I spent my childhood living in the Nordic stronghold with Native American art added, thanks to my mother, a Cherokee Shaman of the Wolf Clan. My favorite was a life-size painting of her outfitted in buckskin with flames rising from her outstretched palms and wolves standing guard beside her. A tall, lithe beauty with long black hair, golden skin, and gold eyes, she could peer right into a person's soul. I was fortunate to look like her, except I had my Danish father's blue eyes.

Although I inherited a bit of Mother's *Aniwaya* (Wolf) Clan intuition and connection to the spirit world, my parents gave me the Danish name Jettine. An only child, they called me Jett, and I basked in the warmth of their love until two and a half years ago when their corporate jet crashed into the ocean near the Bahamas, killing them and the crew.

At that time, I was serving overseas as an intelligence officer in the U.S. Navy. Their loss shattered me, and except for their funeral, I avoided our home until January of this year—too many painful memories. By then, I had accumulated two months of leave that I had to take before deciding whether to renew my Navy contract.

I inherited the castle, the trust fund to maintain it, and Jorgensen Industries. The company had good people running it, which allowed me the time and space to decide what to do with my life. That was when I experienced vivid dreams and haunting messages from beyond that implied my parents were murdered. My best friend, Gwen Pendragon, a detective with the Palm Beach Police, had been my next-door neighbor since we were twelve, and she helped me investigate the accident.

After my leave ended, I left the Navy and focused on helping people get justice. Not wanting to be constrained by the rules police officers must follow, I planned to open the Valkyrie Private Detective Agency as soon as I finished my P.I. apprenticeship. During the interim, Edith Pickering, a wealthy Palm Beach octogenarian, convinced me to host Mystery Fest at Valhalla Castle as a favor to her and a way to raise money for my favorite local charity.

Edith was president of Mystery Lovers International, an elite club for fans of mystery novels and real crime stories. Their annual conference was held in a different country every year, and this year was the USA's turn. The macabre appeal for MLI holding the event in my ancestral home was that many people had met violent deaths here during the past six months. Although some might believe otherwise, the carnage was never my fault.

The castle was similar in size to a small luxury hotel with more than enough bedroom suites for the twenty guests and two bodyguards attending the mystery event. Extra staff and security were hired for the multi-day gathering to ensure all would go smoothly.

My unflappable house manager, Sophia DeLuca, the daughter of a New York Mafia *Don*, would be a huge help. Despite our age difference—I was twenty-eight and she was sixty—we had become close friends. Four-foot-ten with an hourglass figure, Sophia was a force of nature who had been deliberately widowed twenty years ago.

The twenty-two guests would arrive later this morning from Europe, Great Britain, and several states in the USA, with Edith being the only local member.

During an earlier visit, Edith confided, "MLI members are in their sixties and older, but they're quite active, especially at night, if you know what I mean." She winked. "Most of them only see each other once a year at this event, so what happens at Mystery Fest is like that saying about Las Vegas."

She went on to explain, "The conference entails lots of socializing and lavish evenings with fancy dinners, dances, and a Hitchcock movie night. The days offer panels and workshops focused on solving fictitious murders, studying real crimes, and learning about unique murder methods and unusual killers."

"That will keep your members busy."

Never one to miss a chance for a fundraiser, Edith added, "I convinced our members to socialize with local dignitaries and wealthy donors at a charity polo match on your beach the third morning of the conference. A hundred tickets at two thousand dollars each will pull in a hefty amount for your women's shelter."

"Thank you, and it sounds exciting. I've never seen beach polo."

"It's not uncommon around here. I recently attended Singer Island's annual polo exhibition. It's always great fun with a VIP tent for spectators."

"How do they manage to play in the sand with that hard little ball?"

"They use an inflated one about the size of a soccer ball." She peered over her designer glasses. "The beach matches are strictly for entertainment and charity."

"I'll look forward to it. Thanks for arranging the event."

"My pleasure, and no worries, the Mystery Fest schedule has been carefully planned." Edith waved goodbye, saying, "I'm sure you'll manage just fine, dear."

I couldn't help thinking, with so many wealthy, entitled A-listers and their huge egos, hosting the conference might not be as easy as Edith implied.

My thoughts returned to the present as another blinding bolt of lightning pierced the early morning sky, followed by booming thunder as loud as a mortar attack. The tall windows shook, and the great hall's iron chandeliers clinked and rattled.

My *Aniwaya* intuition triggered another internal alarm. Goosebumps prickled my skin as a tidal wave of imminent disaster loomed over me.

Who or what was coming?

TWO

The rain stopped, and Sophia and I spent the morning checking in guests. After all the members of Mystery Lovers International were settled, they gathered in the great hall under the vaulted ceiling and iron chandeliers.

I didn't consider myself tall at five-nine, but next to Sophia, I felt like an NBA player. Her diminutive stature belied her fearless and feisty personality. She livened up any situation and made me smile, but for now I concentrated on keeping a poker face in front of the elite guests.

She elbowed me. "I rarely meet age-appropriate single men worth dating, but this event is a chance of a lifetime." She nodded to her left. "That Italian count with a handsome bodyguard is quite the hottie."

I followed her gaze to the elegant, silver-haired gentleman in a navy silk suit. "Count Aldo Medici. I read his bio. He's seventy and a widower who owns several vineyards." Lowering my voice, I said, "You're both Italian. He might be the one."

"When he checked in, I showed him to his room and casually pointed out mine as we walked past it." Sophia grinned. "Aldo invited me to join him on the terrace tomorrow night for drinks after dinner."

I couldn't help smiling. "Well done you saucy little temptress. I assume you said yes."

"I did, but I'm keeping my options open. That Spanish prince isn't bad either." She nodded in the direction of a dark-haired gent who was five-ten and sixty-five with a hunky bodyguard.

"Ah, yes, Prince Gaspar Borbón, fifth in line to the Spanish throne. His bio said he's single, but I think he's a player. See the way he's eyeing the women?"

She nodded. "I read up on all the European guys attending Mystery Fest. They're rich, single, and sixty-five or older—just my type, except maybe that German, Baron Klaus von Helsig."

"I know what you mean. He has the finesse of a sledgehammer, and that monocle makes him look sinister." I scanned the faces. "What about Lord Edmund Helmsley? He resembles Sean Connery and his bio said he's seventy and a member of parliament."

"Nah, Italians and Spaniards are more fun."

After counting heads, I said, "All the guests are here. I'd better get started."

I stepped in front of the massive fireplace where a life-size painting of my late parents hung above the mantel—I missed them every day. My blond father stood beside my raven-haired mother, her warm, golden eyes gazing down on us.

Addressing the group, I said, "Welcome to Valhalla Castle. I'm your hostess, Jett Jorgensen, and this is the house manager, Sophia DeLuca."

The oak interior wall, covered with Nordic paintings and mounted with numerous medieval weapons, faced the windows on the ocean side. "This wall holds many authentic weapons wielded by my Viking ancestors."

An elegant senior raised her white-gloved hand. It was world-famous mystery author Lady Amelia Ainsworth. The guest of honor, she was a short and wiry seventy-year-old spinster with cropped white hair and twinkling blue eyes. She tapped an empty spot on the wall with her fancy lion's head cane. "One of your weapons is missing, dear. What was it?"

Surprised, I stared at the empty space. "A Viking battle axe."

Sophia nudged me and whispered, "That wasn't part of the program."

I replied under my breath, "It was there before the guests arrived." Forcing a smile, I continued, "The castle map you were given at check-in shows the highlighted rooms reserved for your panels and work-shops, including the great hall we're in now, the ballroom, dining room, drawing room, and a media room with stadium seating. Your guest suite is either in the south or north wing, and an elevator is located behind the twin staircases on the north side. The printed schedule of events lists when and where drinks and meals will be served, either on the oceanside terrace, in the dining room, or in the ballroom. Any questions?"

Russian Oligarch Natalya Petrov raised her index finger. "*Da*. Miss Jorgensen, will you be available to discuss the murders and other unusual events that took place here in the past six months?" She spoke in a deep voice with a barely discernable Russian accent.

"Please call me Jett, and yes, I'll spend time chatting with everyone during cocktails and meals."

Sophia nudged me and tapped her favorite watch. It had a Mona Lisa face and a multi-colored Murano glass bezel. "Time for lunch."

"Ladies and Gentlemen, please follow Sophia through the French doors onto the covered terrace where lunch will be served. Chef Karin Kekoa was trained at Le Cordon Bleu in Paris, and I know you'll enjoy her fine cuisine." I gestured toward the tiled terrace, which overlooked the sparkling blue Atlantic Ocean.

Between the castle and the sea, massive banyan trees shaded the broad lawn, and palm trees and hibiscus bushes with pink flowers lined the border along the sandy beach that spanned the eastern coast of Banyan Isle. An Olympic-length infinity pool bordered the north end of the oceanside terrace beside the ballroom.

Guests sat at four round glass-top tables for eight, with an empty seat or two at each, so I could join them as I moved from one group to the next.

I settled at Natalya's table first. At sixty-seven, she was a fit, statuesque, dark-haired beauty with cold gray eyes. Former KGB, if there was such a thing, she was widowed four times and joined the private sector after she inherited her father's vodka empire at age forty.

"Ah, Jett, so good of you to join us." She gestured to her right. "Allow me to introduce Baron Klaus von Helsig."

"A pleasure, Jett." The bald, robust sixty-five-year-old kissed my hand. He stroked his silver Van Dyke mustache and beard and studied me with his racy blue eyes, sans monocle. An inch or two taller than I, Klaus had a barrel chest and an intensity that reminded me of a charging bull.

I smiled as Natalya introduced me to the famous mystery author, Lady Amelia Ainsworth, who had drawn attention to the missing battle axe. Natalya continued around the table, introducing Count Aldo Medici, Prince Gaspar Borbón, Lord Edmund Helmsley, and last, Fiona Campbell, a curvy whisky heiress with red hair and pearl-framed glasses that showcased her expressive green eyes. According to her bio, Fiona was five-foot-two and a sixty-six-year-old widow. That covered the European contingent, including the two bodyguards who stood a few feet behind their charges, surveying the area.

"Jett, is it true numerous people have died here in the past six months?" Natalya took a sip of chardonnay.

"Yes, but several were dead before they landed on my property." I swirled my iced tea, dreading this topic.

"How was that possible?" Prince Gaspar asked.

"A serial killer dropped them out of an airplane." I bit my lip. "Each body was meant as a message, but I didn't understand what he was trying to say."

"Quite unusual." Lord Edmund took a sip of wine. "I also recall reading the Mayor of Banyan Isle was poisoned in one of your guest bedrooms."

"Another serial killer did that." I glanced at their shocked faces.

"Jett, are you saying serial killers murdered all the victims?" Lady Amelia asked.

"No, the majority of deaths were violent gang members who attacked my home because a former member took refuge here." I paused. "My security guards are retired Navy SEALs, and they shot most of them."

"With all those sudden deaths, your castle must be loaded with ghosts." Natalya fixed her gray eyes on me. "How many have you seen?"

I drained my iced tea. "No ghosts, but my mother was Shaman of the Wolf Clan, and I inherited some sensitivity to spirits from her. I believe it was she who influenced my dreams and guided me to investigate their fatal aircraft accident."

"Oh my, what did you do?" Fiona asked.

"I dived on the underwater crash site and discovered they were murdered by an explosive device. Turned out my parents saw something that could've implicated the killer in an earlier murder."

"I read you shot him in your bedroom after he sneaked in and tried to kill you. Is that true?" Count Medici asked in a deep voice with a sexy Italian accent.

"Yes, he fired and missed, which gave me a chance to return fire. A local police detective shot him in the back the same instant I shot him in the head."

"The killer died in your home, so his spirit might still be here," Lady Amelia said. "Have you had any contact with him since that night?"

My stomach churned. "I've never attempted to contact him. He was a monster."

"Surely you've heard from the late mayor?" Lord Edmund asked. "Perhaps he doesn't know who killed him or why."

"I've never tried to contact anyone who died in this castle because once I open that door, it may never close." I sighed. "The spirit world was my mother's area of expertise."

"Well, dearie, we're all from countries much older than yours, and ghosts come with the territory." Fiona finished her wine. "Nothing to fear, mostly, and you might learn something astonishing. We should hold a séance here."

"Jolly good idea, Fiona." Lord Edmund turned to me. "Let's schedule one."

15

Lady Amelia joined in, "It should be conducted at midnight for best results. I'll check with Edith and see which night works." She glanced at me. "That is, if it's all right with you, Jett."

I didn't want to disappoint my guests, so I said, "Fine by me. Let me know which night you choose."

Texas oil billionaire Dina Fenton, slender and seventy with short, bleached-blond hair, waved at me from a nearby table. Her ten-carat diamond lone-star ring flashed in the bright sunlight as she waved me over and asked, "Have you found the missing weapon?"

"No, I'm afraid its disappearance is a complete mystery." I answered a few more questions, excused myself, chatted with another group, and ensured the rest of the day ran smoothly, despite my intuition warning me otherwise.

———

The guests enjoyed cocktails and an early dinner before retiring, tired from traveling. After I turned in for the night, my *Aniwaya* senses kept me awake with those annoying warning bells still ringing inside my head.

I grabbed my cell phone off the nightstand and called a security guard on duty outside. "Everything all right out there?"

"Yes, Miss Jorgensen. All is well. Is there a problem?"

"I'm not sure. Please do a walk-through on the main floor and the upper hallways, then call me."

"Right away, Miss Jorgensen."

Forty-five minutes later, he called. "Everything looks normal. Should I continue my rounds outside?"

"Yes, and thank you for checking."

My seven-month-old Timber-shepherd puppies snuggled beside me and calmed my jangled nerves.

I switched off the light and hoped for the best.

THREE

L ightning flashed and thunder boomed as loud howls echoed from the south wing of the castle's first floor shortly before 8:00 a.m.

I turned and peered down the hall. "I thought the dogs were right behind us."

Sophia grabbed my arm. "It's never anything good when they do that."

I tilted my head and listened. "Sounds like they're in the study. We'd better go check before we greet the guests at breakfast."

Rain pelted the tall windows as we hurried past the music room. The Atlantic Ocean was only fifty yards beyond the castle, but the heavy downpour obscured the view. Sprawling banyan trees in the backyard lurked in the shadows like giant sentinels in a horror movie, and inherited intuition tingled my spine like a harbinger of the grim reaper.

Nice way to start the second day of a mystery lovers' conference.

Sophia and I followed the dogs' wails to the study. Inside, one of the British guests, Lord Edmund Helmsley, lay sprawled on the oak floor with the missing Viking battle axe buried in his skull. A pool of fresh blood formed a halo around his head.

I turned away for a moment and sucked in hallway air, fighting the queasiness brought on by the coppery scent of blood mixed with the odor of his body fluids.

Sophia and I weren't the sort of women who panicked over a murder victim. We'd seen plenty of bodies during the past several months, but the grim sight was distressing.

Attempting to ease the tension, she quipped, "The good news is we found the missing weapon."

"The blood hasn't congealed." My heart pounded as I scanned the room. "The killer might still be in the castle. We need to protect the guests." I pulled out my cell, my hand trembling. "Hold the dogs while I call Mike."

The dogs stood outside the blood pool, which had not spread far enough to stain the vibrant-hued Persian rug beneath my mahogany clawfoot desk.

Sophia grabbed their collars. "Brace yourself. Every major news network will jump on this, and it'll become a media circus."

"We'll worry about that later." I hit speed dial for my new-old flame from six years ago, Detective Mike Miller of the Banyan Isle Police. Despite the tense situation, my breath caught when I heard his deep voice.

"Good morning, Jett. How's the mystery conference going?"

"Not well. One of our guests was just murdered in the study, and we're worried the killer might still be here." My stomach churned, and my heart hammered my chest as I backed farther away from the grisly scene.

On his end, a sharp intake of breath was followed by, "Are you sure it was murder?"

"The axe embedded in his head leaves little doubt. Please come."

After a sigh, he launched into full-on cop mode. "Don't touch anything, and don't allow anyone to leave the premises. I'll be right there with several patrol officers."

The rain stopped, and the morning sun flooding in through the floor-to-ceiling corner windows bathed the massive oak bookcases in a golden light, softening the murder scene.

I dialed Tim Goldy, who was CEO of Trident Security, the

company that protected my home and grounds. "Tim, I should've added interior guards. A guest was murdered this morning. Mike wants my property sealed off, and I need my guests and staff protected."

"I'll call the guards on duty outside and have them get right on it, Jett."

The police station was only a five-minute drive from my house. As I pocketed my phone, loud sirens blared outside. Not long after that, Mike strode into the study.

Thirty years old, he had dreamy brown eyes that usually lit up his handsome face, but the murder sent him back to his former tall, dark, and brooding persona.

He pulled out his electronic tablet. "Jett, what can you tell me about the victim?"

I turned away from the body and took a deep, calming breath. "Lord Edmund Helmsley was seventy, a wealthy widower from London, a member of parliament, and on the short list to be the next prime minister of the UK."

Mike groaned. "Then what was he doing here?"

"Helmsley told me Mystery Lovers International was his one guilty pleasure. He enjoyed attending Mystery Fest once a year, socializing with the elite members, and participating in murder mystery competitions." I sighed. "He checked in yesterday."

Sophia, unfazed by the gore, quipped, "And he checked out this morning."

Mike raised an eyebrow in her direction and turned back to me. "What else can you tell me about the group staying here?"

"MLI members are mostly titled Europeans and A-list Americans, all mega-rich. They're ultra-exclusive and have never had any reported incidents since the club was formed fifteen years ago."

"Well, they have now." He studied the corpse. "This is a major case, and the whole world is about to come down on our heads. I can't afford any mistakes."

Sophia shrugged. "Call in the FBI and make it their problem."

He sucked in a breath. "No way. This is *my* turf, and *I'll* handle it."

He nudged me. "Can you lock the study until the county medical examiner and crime scene unit arrive?"

"Yes, of course." I strode to my desk, pulled a key out of a drawer, and handed it to him.

He led us out the door and locked it.

"What do you want us to do?" Still shaken by the gruesome sight of the weapon buried in Edmund's bloody head, I rubbed the goose-bumps off my arms.

"Gather all your guests and staff in the great hall. And I'm sorry, but you two will have to be considered suspects. It's standard procedure."

Sophia grabbed his arm. "Have you forgotten that's the room with all the weapons on the wall?"

He sighed. "Oh, right, use the ballroom."

"The guests are already gathered in the dining room. I could have the housekeeping staff join them."

"Sounds good." He paused. "Serve everyone breakfast so they won't get antsy waiting to be interviewed, and I'll talk to the kitchen staff separately."

I frowned. "I had a feeling that hosting Mystery Fest might be a mistake, but I never dreamed it would result in a murder."

Mike scrutinized me and arched an eyebrow. "What is it about Valhalla Castle? Since you returned home from the Navy in January, I've lost track of the body count."

I had no answer. My eyes moistened as I stared at my feet.

He pulled me into his arms. "Sorry, babe, I didn't mean to upset you."

"I thought everything was back to normal, but now we have another murder here." I balled my fists. "I can't believe this happened again."

He hugged me and planted a kiss on my forehead. "We'll get through it."

My loud doorbell boomed Wagner's "Ride of the Valkyries" and interrupted our tender moment. Mike strode to the entrance.

Sophia put her hand on my shoulder. "Nothing in the past six months was your fault. You know that, right?"

"But stuff like this never happened when my parents were alive."

"We'll deal with this, and everything will be good again."

"I wish I could believe that." I thought about what her Mafioso son Marco had said about my castle being a murder magnet.

She patted my back. "Don't worry. I grew up around dead guys. I've got you."

We stepped aside as Mike led the medical examiner and crime scene unit to the study.

Sophia and I hurried to the rectangular dining room with twenty-foot-high walls covered in teal silk that matched the upholstered mahogany chairs. A hand-carved mahogany table seated forty-four and could be expanded for sixty. Painted portraits of Nordic ancestors lined the walls with a few paintings of Cherokee relatives added after my parents inherited the castle.

We found Edith Pickering standing in the doorway. An elegant socialite from Palm Beach with perfectly coiffed white hair, the president of Mystery Lovers International always wore the latest designer fashions.

I took her aside and informed her of Lord Helmsley's murder. "Do you think you should cancel the rest of the conference?"

"Oh, my, this is such a shock, but canceling is out of the question." Edith paused and tugged at the wrists of her delicate lace gloves, gathering her poise. "Jett, dear, finding Edmund like that must have been traumatic for you. Are you all right?"

"I've been better," I said, blowing out a sigh. "Thanks for asking."

"My friend from Scotland Yard is a guest speaker and will join us any minute. I suggest you have a brace of brandy while he sorts this out."

"Wait, who did you say is coming?"

FOUR

After the loud sirens and cops bustling about, dealing with the guests was easier than expected. They knew something big was up.

I overheard Amelia ask Fiona if she'd seen Edmund, but I kept quiet about him.

We waited until everyone was settled in the dining room, after which Sophia left to take care of my dogs.

While the kitchen staff served everyone, I said, "Enjoy your breakfasts. A police detective will join us soon. He has something to discuss with you." I held off telling them about the murder until a half-hour later when Mike arrived.

The foreign members were gathered around the nearest end of the table with the Americans seated close by. The maids were settled at the far end, looking uncomfortable.

I opened with, "Ladies and gentlemen, thank you for your patience. I apologize for disrupting the scheduled events, but there has been a tragedy." I paused while everyone turned to me. "Lord Edmund Helmsley was found murdered in the study this morning."

After the gasps and surprised murmurs died down, I continued, "I know Lord Helmsley was a friend, and I'm sincerely sorry for your loss." I glanced at Mike. "We want this terrible crime solved quickly and your safety ensured. This is Detective Mike Miller of the Banyan Isle Police. He's in charge, so please give him your full cooperation."

Mike pulled out his electronic tablet, and I began the introductions.

Prince Gaspar Borbón sat at the head of the table. Fit at sixty-five, the Spanish royal was a wealthy shipping magnate. His buff body-guard, Jorge Santos, paced behind him.

Gaspar twirled his handlebar mustache and spoke in perfect English with a Castilian accent, "Detective Miller, please tell me Lord Helmsley is alive, and this is merely a ruse for a murder mystery breakfast."

Mike frowned. "No, Prince Gaspar, this is an inquiry into a real murder. How well did you know the victim?"

He paused in mid-sip of his espresso. "Oh my, you are serious." He set the cup down, gathering his composure. "We were casual friends. Mostly saw each other at Mystery Fest every year."

Mike glanced at the short, flashy redhead seated on Gaspar's right. Stunning at sixty-six, Fiona Campbell wiped away tears.

After I introduced her, she dabbed a tissue at the corners of her green eyes and addressed him with a light Scottish brogue, "Forgive me, Detective Miller, but you seem a bit young to head such an important investigation. Have you any suspects?"

"It's too early for that, but someone in this castle is the murderer. Has to be."

Fiona crossed her arms. "Are you suggestin' *I'm* a suspect?"

He clenched his jaw. "Until we gather more information, everyone here is a suspect. That's standard procedure."

Fiona looked up at him. "Fine, but what's being done to ensure our safety?"

"Armed guards are patrolling the castle and grounds, and more will be added soon." He clutched his tablet. "Mrs. Campbell, were you aware of any enemies Lord Helmsley might have had among the conference guests?"

She sniffled. "No, Edmund was well-liked—a bit stiff, but he loosened up after a few whiskies."

Mike turned his attention to the man seated across from Fiona, Count Aldo Medici from Italy. Standing quietly behind him, Nico Bernardi was his fit, fortyish bodyguard.

Aldo greeted Mike and looked at Fiona. He spoke English with a slight Italian accent, "Fiona, dear, I believe you were arguing with Edmund in the airport limo yesterday."

She huffed. "It wasn't serious. Just our usual political disagreement about Scotland separatin' from England."

Gaspar nudged Aldo. "Have you forgotten your argument with Edmund about who should be our next club president?"

Aldo wiped his eyes. "A mild disagreement. Edmund was a dear friend." He sipped espresso as I continued the introductions.

Seated beside Aldo, Natalya Petrov was the only female billionaire oligarch in the world. Her haughty tone carried a light Russian accent. "As I recall, everyone in the limo joined in that argument, including you, my dear Fiona." Her moist eyes were filled with sadness.

Mike was losing control of the interviews as I introduced him to the German billionaire.

An international playboy, Baron Klaus von Helsig sat on Fiona's right. Oxford-educated, Klaus spoke English with a hint of a German accent. "Really, Natalya, it was a harmless discussion and hardly a motive for murder. We all loved Edmund."

She fixed her gray eyes on Klaus. "Obviously, none of us did it." Natalya gazed across the table. "What do you think, Lady Amelia?"

Seated on Klaus's right, Amelia appeared sad but eager to join the fray. The guest-of-honor's blue eyes revealed a sharp intellect as the seventy-year-old sniffled into a tissue and stroked the gold lion's head on her fancy cane.

"Yes, I'd like your opinion, Lady Amelia," Mike agreed.

Amelia stirred milk into her tea and spoke like the British aristocrat she was. "Although heart-wrenching, this is a unique opportunity for us to honor our friend and solve a real murder." Her dewy eyes shed tears as she said, "Losing Edmund is a terrible tragedy, but we may as well embrace the challenge and ensure justice is served."

Mike's tone turned harsh. "Wait a minute, I can't have you people interfering with a police investigation."

Aldo joined in, "Sorry, Detective, but I agree with Amelia. We should all forego the usual fictional murder competition and set about solving our friend Edmund's murder."

"Aye," Fiona agreed, "we owe that to dear Edmund."

Everyone at the table nodded, and Mike's face reddened.

Amelia gave Mike a brave smile. "Detective Miller, you are fortunate to have so many murder experts at your disposal. We know Edmund was killed in the study, so let's start with the basics—time of death, murder method, Edmund's attire, and whether the murder weapon has been recovered." She stiffened. "It wasn't the missing battle axe, was it?"

He thrust his hands on his hips. "At this point, you're all suspects, and as such, I'm not at liberty to share any information with you." He glared at the group. "I must insist you people stay out of my murder investigation."

Klaus's baritone boomed, "Don't be foolish, Detective. You need help solving this, and we'll find out what we want to know anyway. Why not save time and tell us now?"

A short, balding man in his mid-fifties wearing a tailored suit with a crisp white shirt and French cuffs strode in. He flashed his credentials. "Good morning, I'm Detective Chief Inspector Neville Wright from the Metropolitan Police, otherwise known as Scotland Yard, and I'm taking over Lord Edmund Helmsley's murder investigation."

Mike's jaw dropped. "Sir, I'm Banyan Isle Police Detective Mike Miller, and with all due respect, this crime is way outside your jurisdiction. This is *my* case."

"Oh, no, my dear fellow. This murder has international significance, especially for the UK. Lord Helmsley was an esteemed member of parliament and likely to be our next prime minister." He tugged at his cuffs. "There could be a terrorist plot afoot to undermine our government."

"FBI agents can look into that, but I'm handling this investigation," he said firmly.

Amelia ignored Mike's objections. "Thank God you're here, Neville. We're all eager to help find Edmund's killer. Have you been to the crime scene?"

"Oh, yes, after an officer guarding the study door informed me the victim was Edmund, I called London for authorization." He paused. "Ghastly scene—Viking battle axe buried in the back of his skull."

Amelia winced at the gory news and continued, "Time of death?"

"The medical examiner checked my credentials and said Helmsley died in the past two hours. Rigor mortis had begun to show on his face." He ran his eyes over the group. "Had to be someone inside the castle."

The Europeans sat back and smirked at Mike.

He crossed his arms. "DCI Wright, what are you doing here?"

Neville straightened his regimental tie. "Edith booked me to be a guest speaker at this event, a fortunate coincidence. Saved a lot of time for Scotland Yard to have a man on the scene so quickly."

"And does the Met normally share crime scene details with civilians?"

"They're not civilians to me; they're valuable resources. Lady Amelia has assisted me on several key cases, and I dare say the members of this group have years of experience solving complex fictional murders." He jutted out his chin. "I consider them assets."

Mike glared at him. "Well, I consider them suspects, and you have no authority here. I insist you stay out of my investigation."

"We'll see about that." Neville pulled out his cell phone. "Pardon me while I make some calls." He stepped away.

I nudged Mike. "Shall I continue with the introductions?"

He nodded.

"This is Dina Fenton from Texas." I noticed she was teary-eyed.

Mike asked relevant questions as we continued down the table.

I tried my best to remain almost invisible during his strained inter-actions with the guests. When I thought I might have a chance to slip away, Neville returned, and two men entered after him. I recognized them from a sticky situation that occurred here recently.

The tall man in his mid-thirties introduced himself as FBI Special

Agent Taylor. He nodded in the direction of the shorter, slightly older guy and said, "And this is FBI Special Agent Barnes. We're from the Miami Field Office, and we're taking over this murder investigation."

Mike knew them from a previous incident at my home. He stuck out his hand and said, "Good to see you again, gentlemen—Banyan Isle Police Detective Mike Miller. This is *my* case, but I'm happy to include the FBI."

"I don't think so, gents." Neville showed the Feds his credentials. "This is a matter for Scotland Yard. Our prime minister called your president to ensure I'm included in this investigation."

I glanced at Mike, who looked like he wanted to strangle the snobby detective. The Feds glared at the Brit, and I swear the room temperature dropped ten degrees during the icy silence.

Sophia breezed in, and like me, she disdained the two FBI agents who had been less than helpful the last time we had a big problem at Valhalla.

She looked up at them and said, "Not you two again. Doesn't the FBI have anyone who plays well with others?"

All the guests laughed, the Feds' faces turned red, and Neville smirked. Mike rolled his eyes and glanced at his watch.

My security expert walked in and kept a stone face as he read the room. Tim looked at me. "I doubled the guards inside and out. Anything else I can do?"

I leaned in and whispered in his ear, "Get me out of here, and we'd better take Sophia with us before she causes an international incident."

Tim cleared his throat. "I'm Tim Goldy, CEO of Trident Security, and I provide the guards here at Valhalla. Please excuse us. Miss Jorgensen and Mrs. DeLuca are urgently needed elsewhere in the castle." Without waiting for a response, Tim expertly guided us out of the room and down the hall.

The Feds seemed so relieved Sophia was leaving they didn't object.

I glanced at Sophia. "Where are the dogs?"

"In your bedroom. They've been fed and walked."

"Good, thanks." I turned to Tim. "Did anyone try to leave?"

"No, everyone remained inside the castle." He hesitated. "It looked like Mike was having jurisdictional issues with the Feds and the Brit."

"This case could be good for his career, but the FBI will take over now."

Tim nodded. "You might get a visit from MI6 under the guise of the UK's State Department, and our CIA might stick their noses in too."

I groaned. "Make sure the guards don't let in anyone from the news media."

I noticed Sophia was grinning. "What are you so happy about?"

"Did you see the way Aldo smiled at me?"

"Oh, geez." I rolled my eyes.

FIVE

Two hours later, Sophia and I sat at a round glass-top table on the tiled back terrace, which ran the length of the castle and overlooked the Atlantic Ocean. My in-house chef, Karin Kekoa, who was an exotic mix of Hawaiian and British, sat with us under the overhanging roof. Like me, she too had served in the U.S. Navy.

The Feds and the snotty little man from the Metropolitan Police sat across from us with the ocean at their backs. After receiving a call from the White House, the FBI director ordered his agents to welcome Neville onto their team, and they wisely included Mike as their local liaison officer. He sat beside me as a gentle breeze carrying the scent of the sea stirred my long hair.

DCI Neville Wright took charge. "Let's start with where each of you were today before you found the body. Miss Jorgensen?"

"I took my dogs for a quick run in the backyard right before a rainstorm hit at seven, and then I met with Sophia, and we discussed today's scheduled events."

Mike asked, "What happened next?"

"The schedule sheet instructed guests to meet in the dining room at eight for breakfast." I took a sip of iced tea. "We were headed there when we heard the dogs howling in the study."

FBI Agent Barnes asked Sophia, "And where were you before you met with Miss Jorgensen?"

"I left my room at seven, went downstairs, and Count Aldo Medici found me in the south wing hallway on the first floor. We had a brief chat before I joined Jett." She smiled. "He's a wine connoisseur and owns several vineyards in Italy."

Mike asked her, "Any chance he'd been in the study?"

She shrugged. "I suppose it's possible. I didn't really notice where he came from."

Neville chimed in, "That means the count could be the killer. Was his bodyguard with him?"

"No, he joined us in the hallway before they went to the dining room."

Agent Taylor said, "Did you discuss your Mafia history with the count?"

"No." Sophia sat back and glared at Agent Taylor.

He paused. "If Count Medici has ties to the Mob in Italy, and they had a beef with the victim—remind me where your father lived before he emigrated to the US."

Sophia stared him down. "You know my late father, *Don* Francesco Calabrese, was born in Sicily. We still have relatives there."

Barnes added, "And didn't your late husband, Vincent DeLuca, disappear under suspicious circumstances?"

Taylor smirked. "Rumor has it he's wearing concrete boots on the bottom of Long Island Sound."

"Vinnie went missing twenty years ago, and it has nothing to do with Lord Helmsley's murder." Sophia glared at the Feds. "This is harassment."

"Not if Lord Helmsley's murder was a Mob hit," Barnes said.

Neville asked, "Mrs. DeLuca, did Count Medici say how he felt about the UK leaving the European Union?"

She shrugged. "We didn't discuss politics or the Mafia. Aldo was interested in me."

Neville turned to Karin, my chef. "I understand your late mother was British. Where were you early this morning, and what are your feelings about the UK?"

Karin sighed. "Feeding everyone at this conference is a big responsibility. I was busy finalizing menus and organizing my temporary kitchen staff. Then I started the breakfast preparations." She focused on Neville. "I'm an American born citizen who has no interest in UK politics."

Mike broke in, "Did any of you notice someone hanging around the weapons displayed in the great hall before that battle axe went missing yesterday?"

We all shook our heads.

Agent Barnes said, "Miss Kekoa, you served on destroyers in the US Navy for eight years." He glanced at me. "And Miss Jorgensen served in Navy Intelligence for six years. You both have had combat training and must've had briefings on the UK."

I arched an eyebrow. "Briefings on the UK? Seriously? You've been watching too many spy movies."

Agent Taylor quipped, "Let's not forget Mrs. DeLuca's deadly accuracy with that Glock she totes around."

Sophia shook her head. "Lord Helmsley was killed with a Viking battle axe." She turned to me. "Honestly, Jett, can't you call somebody and get us better FBI agents?"

I looked directly at the Feds. "My close colleagues in Navy Intelligence, the CIA, the NSA, and the DIA keep in contact with the FBI Director. Perhaps I should give them a call and put a stop to this obvious harassment."

The Feds pushed back from the table.

Agent Taylor stood and said, "Remove the weapons in the great hall and lock them in a storage room. And don't leave home until further notice." He and Agent Barnes left in a huff.

Just as well, because two news helicopters began hovering overhead, and their thundering rotor blades made conversation impossible.

I pulled Mike close and said in his ear, "I'll do everything I can to help you solve this. I don't want the Feds or that snot from London getting credit."

Mike held me long enough to say, "Watch out for the Italian guy."

———

Karin, Sophia, and I ducked inside, escaping the noisy news helicopters, and headed for the spacious kitchen, which was a beehive of activity. Although there were less than thirty people to feed, counting the guests, residents, and visitors, the facility had served as many as five hundred people during charity balls.

The wall-mounted weapons in the great hall were heavy, so I called Tim and arranged for his men to move them into a storage room. After pocketing my phone, I turned to Karin.

She threw up her hands. "I planned on serving our guests lunch on the oceanfront terrace, but those loud helicopters will ruin everything."

My phone vibrated constantly. I checked the texts and read forty messages from various news outlets. "We'd better plan on serving all the meals in the dining room or ballroom until the media circus dies down."

Sophia nodded. "That'll work." She glanced at Karin. "They've all had breakfast in the dining room, right?"

Karin checked with her staff. "Yes, their plates have been cleared, and some of the guests are still enjoying coffee and tea."

Most of the kitchen staff were women, and their bustling activity suddenly ceased. I spun around and spotted my mother's younger brother filling the door frame with six-foot-three inches of masculine perfection. My uncle, Hunter Vann, had golden skin, thick black hair, and gold eyes like his late older sister.

An airline captain, Hunter returned from a four-day flight pattern and changed out of his uniform into snug jeans and a T-shirt that hugged every muscle. He looked at us and arched an eyebrow. "Seems like every time I leave my favorite women alone something drastic happens. What am I supposed to do with you?"

"I know what I'd like you to do." Sophia dived in for a hug.

He gave her a light kiss too. "Please tell me you didn't kill that English lord."

I reached out to him for a hug. "This is one time I can honestly say Sophia and I had nothing to do with what happened. Somebody killed Lord Helmsley in my study."

"Sorry about that, but I'm glad you two aren't involved." Hunter looked at Karin. "How are you holding up with the murder and all these guests to feed?"

She smiled. "Better, now that you're here. You missed seeing us grilled by the FBI, Mike, and a condescending jerk from Scotland Yard." She went up on tip toes and kissed him, then said to Sophia, "Better check on the guests in the dining room."

"See ya later, handsome." Sophia slapped his firm behind on her way past.

Hunter rolled his eyes and smiled at Karin. They'd been dating the past two months, but he'd always been a wild spirit, and I worried if things went south, I'd lose my fabulous new Hawaiian chef and friend.

He put his arm around me. "I was hoping you'd hang out with me today at my hangar."

"I'd love to, but the FBI won't let me leave home. They're treating everyone in the castle as murder suspects. Sorry, Unc."

"Is there anything I can do?"

I took his arm. "Would you mind meeting the guests from Europe and the UK, including the guy from Scotland Yard? They knew the victim better than anyone here at the conference, and I'd like your impression of them."

We headed for the dining room where all the guests were busy comparing notes on the murder victim. They tapped info into their iPads as we entered, and Sophia chatted with American guests and staff near the far end of the table.

Everyone turned toward us. The women stopped talking and stared at Hunter.

"Sorry to interrupt," I said. "I'd like you to meet my uncle, Hunter Vann. He's a pilot with Luxury International Airlines, and he also operates a flight school and maintenance shop near here in a pilot community called Aerodrome Estates."

Klaus's eyes lit up. "A pilot? Me too, but I only fly small private planes, and I love aerobatics. Do you have any stunt planes?"

"There are several at the field where I live, including a German biplane called a Bücker Jungmann. She's a fully-restored, 1939, red-and-blue beauty. Her owner keeps it in my hangar and lets me fly it."

"I am familiar with Jungmanns," Klaus said. "They are a joy to fly and very rare."

Hunter thumbed at me. "Jett's a pilot too."

Klaus arched his eyebrows. "An airline pilot?"

"No, I have a commercial pilot license and a flight instructor certificate, but I mainly fly general aviation planes and vintage aircraft."

"Let's plan to drive out there once the police release us," Klaus suggested.

I smiled. "I'd love to, but we'll have to coordinate with my uncle's schedule."

Hunter checked the calendar on his phone. "Let's see—today is Friday. Meet me at my place at four p.m. on Monday for some aerobatic flying in the Jungmann."

I smiled at Klaus. "I'll take you there. Meet me Monday in the foyer at three-thirty."

"Thank you." The German grinned. "I'll look forward to it."

Fiona distracted Hunter by offering her hand and saying, "So nice to meet you."

He kissed her hand.

She fluttered her false eyelashes. "I've never met anyone like you. Your eyes are such an unusual color."

"I'm a Cherokee, like Jett's mother."

"Really?" Natalya said. "I've never met a Native American."

Lady Amelia interjected, "I believe the politically correct term now is Indigenous People with Native Americans referring to those who were living in North America when the Mayflower landed."

"Call me Hunter. I'd like to offer everyone my condolences for the loss of your friend." He glanced around. "Any clues on who might've killed him?"

Amelia dabbed her eyes with a tissue. "We're working through our grief by comparing notes on what we know about Edmund and who might have had a motive."

Klaus added, "We're wondering if there was a reason he was murdered so soon after arriving here."

Natalya fixed her cold eyes on Hunter. "*Da,* the timing could be key."

Hunter glanced at the group. "Have you seen the forensic evidence?"

Aldo shook his head. "No, but if we had access to it, we might learn if the killer is a man or a woman."

Neville, who sat beside Edith, flashed his credentials. "I am a Detective Chief Inspector from the Met, and I'll soon have access to all the evidence and reports."

Hunter asked Neville, "Could a woman be the killer?"

Fiona interrupted. "Surely a woman couldn't wield a battle axe."

I joined in. "It's not too heavy. I tried swinging one around a few years ago."

"The angle of the injury could give a clue to the height of the murderer," Klaus said.

"*Sí,* and we were told the killer attacked him from behind," Gaspar said. "Someone must have hidden in the study and waited for him to enter."

Aldo added, "Someone might've called him and lured him there."

"The authorities will have a record of all the calls Edmund received." Edith glanced at me and then Neville. "I'm not sure which detective has Edmund's cell phone."

I shrugged. "I'll ask Mike."

"No worries," Neville said. "I'm on the case now and will solve this quickly."

"We're counting on you to share the forensic reports with us," Amelia said, smiling at him.

"This has nothing to do with the murder, Lady Amelia, but I noticed you had a guitar case when you checked in. Do you intend to play for us?"

"Oh, no, dear, I'm not a musician. I merely delivered the antique guitar as a favor to a friend in the States. She came and collected it shortly after I arrived yesterday."

"I see." I smiled at the group. "I hope you help the authorities solve this murder quickly for everyone's sake."

Hunter checked his watch. "It was a pleasure meeting everyone, but I must get back. Good luck with your investigation."

"Come back soon," Fiona cooed as all the women smiled and waved.

Hunter guided me down the hallway.

After we were out of earshot, I asked, "What's your impression?"

He glanced over his shoulder. "The men seem like a bunch of entitled playboys, and that detective is full of himself. The women, except Amelia, are like fierce divas accustomed to having their way." He looked into my eyes. "My gut tells me someone in that group is the killer, so watch your step."

"Right, and if one of them did it, it'll be an even bigger international incident." I sighed.

Hunter put his arm around my shoulder and walked beside me. "It might be best if Neville took the heat for solving this."

"I want Mike to get credit for closing the case, but I'd love to see that British snot harangued by international journalists."

Hunter stopped and looked into my eyes. "Jett, be careful. There's a murderer roaming free in your castle, and he or she might not be done killing."

SIX

B efore lunch, members of Mystery Lovers International held their annual meeting in the ballroom, situated at the north end of the castle, where polished oak flooring reflected crystal chandeliers in a room larger than a basketball court. Three sides had fifteen-foot-tall windows draped in red velvet and French doors that opened onto a wraparound Italian-tiled terrace.

Round tables seated ten, so everyone sat on the sides facing the stage at the tables nearest to it, and I observed from the mahogany bar built along the wall in the back of the room.

President Edith Pickering stood behind the podium and addressed the group. "It has been my honor to serve as president for the past year. Despite the loss of our dear friend Edmund, it's time to elect a new president and choose a country for next year's conference. Since we Americans have the majority, it's only fair to elect a European member every other year. Therefore, I nominate Count Aldo Medici. Are there any other nominations?"

Natalya Petrov raised her hand and said, "I nominate Fiona Campbell."

Edith scanned the members. "Anyone else?"

No one responded, so the voting slips were handed out.

"Write Aldo or Fiona on the paper along with your choice of country. A waiter will collect the votes, and I'll count them." Edith waited at the podium and filled out her vote.

Then she tallied the votes and announced the results. "Our new president, who will assume office at the end of this conference, is Fiona Campbell, and our next Mystery Fest will be in Belgium. Congratulations to Fiona."

Edith continued, "We'll have several months to ferret out the perfect setting for Belgium's conference in a castle, manor house, or an interesting hotel."

Everyone applauded and then gathered for lunch.

Edith waved me over to a table where she sat with several members. She took a sip of cabernet. "Everyone is determined to catch Edmund's killer, so we scheduled a séance tonight at midnight, Jett."

"We're hoping Edmund will tell us who killed him," Amelia said. "It's best to do this as soon as possible after the subject's death."

Fiona chimed in, "More than ten people overwhelm the spirits, so we decided on seating eight of us with Hunter and you at a round table."

"Why us?"

"You and your hunky uncle can use your Wolf Clan spiritual connections. Which room should we use?"

"The study was the scene of the crime. Would that be a good place if the authorities will allow it?" I asked.

Amelia nodded. "I'll ask Neville to arrange permission for us." She pulled out her map. "Where is the study?"

"It's on the first floor in the southeast corner of the castle."

Seated across from me, Prince Gaspar added, "Fiona found all the items we'll need at a local shop she discovered online, and the store will deliver them later today."

"What sort of items?" I asked.

Fiona responded, "Oh, you know, various colored candles and a crystal ball."

Dina, the Texan with the huge diamond ring, added, "I participated in a séance at an old castle north of London last month. It was a real hoot."

That surprised me. "Did you see any ghosts?"

"Saw one in the swirling smoke from the candles—looked like a woman in a flowing white gown." Dina chuckled. "Scared the bejesus out of everyone."

I glanced around at the guests. "And you're all certain you want to do this?"

Klaus, the German baron, put on his monocle and looked at me diagonally from across the massive table. "*Ja*, we are not frightened by departed spirits, and we want to solve Edmund's murder." He paused. "Ghosts can be helpful. One showed me where my late Uncle Heinrich hid this signet ring." He showed us his centuries-old ring with a royal crest on it.

I noticed Aldo and Gaspar also wore signet rings bearing royal crests from their ancestors. Both men sported perennial tans and suave, debonair mannerisms that oozed class and confidence.

Natalya joined in. "We conduct a séance almost every year at Mystery Fest. I like to be surprised, and I suspect your castle holds many secrets." Her deep voice held an ominous tone. "Perhaps Edmund will name his killer."

I regretted agreeing to the séance, but it was too late to change my mind. Maybe nothing unpleasant would come of it.

Natalya looked across at Baron von Helsig. "What have you been doing this past year, Klaus?"

He adjusted his monocle. "Lots of incognito traveling around Europe, seeing how the common people live, and scouting locations for a murder mystery."

That sparked Amelia's interest. "Tell me about your main character."

"I'm thinking a wealthy nobleman serial killer who masquerades as a pauper."

"Interesting." Amelia paused. "I'm fairly certain that hasn't been done."

"So, your travels are research for your book?" I asked Klaus.

"*Ja*, it helps spending time among people who could be potential victims in the story. Amelia could advise me." He turned to her. "After all, you're *the* best-selling mystery author."

She gave him a slight nod. "I'd be happy to help, Klaus." She looked at Natalya. "Anything new in your life?"

"I enjoy maintaining my membership in an ancient women's club."

"Sounds mysterious," Fiona said. "Should I join?"

"Sorry, darling. The club is only for women with my unique skill set."

Prince Gaspar arched a brow and changed the subject. "What about you, Lady Amelia? Still helping Scotland Yard bring all the miscreants to justice?"

"I enjoy the complicated murder cases. The work is challenging and sometimes provides ideas for my books. Besides, I can't bear killers getting away with murder." She smiled. "Is your horse charity doing well?"

"*Sí*, the charity provides homes for older horses in Spain that would otherwise be euthanized for dog food," Gaspar explained.

"What about you, Aldo?" Fiona asked Count Medici. "How are your wineries doing?"

"All is well. My vineyards in Tuscany support the surrounding communities and keep everyone happy."

"And what about you, Jett?" Dina asked. "I understand you founded a women's shelter in West Palm Beach."

I nodded. "I'm expanding it to provide college educations for women who want better-paying jobs. The proceeds from the beach polo match and this year's Mystery Fest will bring in enough to fund several full scholarships."

"Glad to hear something good will come from this year's event," Dina said.

SEVEN

I spent the rest of the afternoon helping rearrange the scheduled events and coordinating with law enforcement. I was surprised Neville came through with permission from the FBI for the séance in the study. The CSI team had finished gathering evidence, and a special cleaner for crime scenes had removed all traces of body fluids.

After taking the dogs for a late afternoon run in the backyard, I put them in my room and headed downstairs. As I reached the ground floor, two men waited for me in the foyer. I recognized one who'd been my CIA contact during my work in Navy Intelligence. He introduced me to the other man who had an English accent. Probably an MI6 agent.

The CIA guy said, "Jett, may we have a word in private?"

"Sure. We may as well chat in my study—the scene of the crime." I led them there.

Once we were seated, the guy from MI6 asked, "Miss Jorgensen, have you any inkling who might have killed Lord Helmsley?"

"My gut tells me it was someone in the tight-knit group from Europe and the UK. They're holding a séance here tonight at midnight in the hopes of unmasking the killer, and they've asked me to attend."

"That's an interesting twist," my CIA friend said. "Please keep us informed of any developments."

"I'm not looking forward to it. Some really bad people died in this castle, and I don't want to encounter any of them."

"Is the group hoping to hear from Lord Helmsley?" the MI6 agent asked.

"They're assuming he'll communicate with us since his death was so recent, and they're hoping he'll name his killer."

My CIA friend arched an eyebrow. "Any chance that's possible?"

"Anything is possible, but Edmund was attacked from behind, so he may not have seen his killer." I glanced at the men. "I'm not expecting spirits to talk to us, but I might pick up on guilty vibes from the killer if he or she is at the table."

"Jett, we're counting on you to keep us informed and keep the press out of it," my CIA friend said.

"No problem. I have no intention of allowing the press access, and I definitely don't want to talk to them on the phone." I hesitated. "I can't stop the guests from leaking info, but I'm betting they won't because they value their privacy. And no worries about my staff. They're always discreet."

"Thank you, Jett, and we'll keep you in the loop if we learn anything," the CIA man said.

I walked them out and hoped I'd have nothing weird to report about the séance.

Later, Prince Gaspar cornered me in the hallway and asked me to sit with him at dinner.

We entered the expansive ballroom and joined six of the British and European guests. That left two open seats. Neville and Edith sat with some Americans.

As Gaspar held the chair for me, Klaus hurried to grab the seat on the other side of mine. *Hmmn, Spanish royalty vying with German nobility, not that I'm interested.*

The older women weren't at all threatened by my youthful good looks because they noticed the obvious romantic vibes between Mike and me earlier. Not so with the men, who were oblivious.

Gaspar kissed my hand, playing the role of Don Juan. "I admired the portrait of your parents in the great hall and the painting in the foyer of your mother with the wolves." He smiled. "Were they pets?"

"Yes, Mother had a close connection with animals, especially wolves. As you know, she was Shaman of the Wolf Clan."

"Shaman?" Klaus broke in. "Does that mean she was a medicine woman?"

"A shaman is a spiritual leader and natural healer, but my mother also earned a medical degree from Harvard. She was wise and kind, and I miss her every day."

Natalya smiled smugly. "I read that the handsome detective you're dating is the one who helped you shoot your parents' killer here in the castle."

I glanced around the table. "Yes, he did."

The comments about Mike resulted in disappointed looks from the men.

Klaus said, "Forgive me for changing the subject, but I've been wondering if Edmund's ghost will haunt the castle and lead us to his killer. After all, he was a ghost enthusiast."

Amelia said, "I'd love for him to tell us who killed him, but if he was struck from behind, he might not know who did it."

Fiona shrugged. "We'll find out tonight at midnight."

Mike sauntered in. "Mind if I join you?"

Fiona patted the empty chair next to her. "Please do."

Aldo asked, "Any progress on the investigation?"

Mike nodded. "The housekeeping and kitchen staffs have been cleared." He hesitated. "There's a strong possibility one of the Mystery Fest guests is the killer."

Fiona asked, "Any idea which one?"

"We're looking into possible motives." He glanced around the table. "How important is it whether Scotland votes to separate from the UK?"

Fiona set down her wine glass. "I'm Scottish, and I'm working hard to get the votes for a free Scotland."

"What about the rest of you? Any opinions one way or the other?" Mike asked.

"I think it's fair to say those of us who aren't British prefer a free Scotland for business reasons." Natalya nodded at Klaus, Gaspar, and Aldo. "Right, gentlemen?"

The men agreed.

"And what was Lord Helmsley's position on Scotland?" Mike asked.

Amelia answered, "Like me, Edmund was for preserving the union at all costs."

"So, if he became prime minister, several of you might miss out on lucrative business deals." Mike paused. "Money is always a strong motive for murder."

"Not in our case." Klaus sat back. "We're already wealthy."

"That's never stopped anyone before." Mike tried a new topic. "Were any of you dating the same woman as Helmsley?"

The men snickered, and Fiona and Natalya looked smug.

Fiona said, "We're all single and enjoy each other's company."

"*Da*, we are not interested in monogamous relationships," Natalya agreed.

Mike lowered his voice and glanced from Gaspar to Aldo. "Any chance one of your bodyguards did it?"

Aldo shook his head. "Nico has been with me for two years. I trust him, and he'd have no reason to kill Edmund."

Mike turned to Gaspar. "What about yours?"

Gaspar hesitated. "Jorge has been with me about a year, and he passed rigorous background checks. I can't imagine he'd have a motive."

Mike sighed. "I'll look into him." He gazed across at me. "Jett, can I steal you?"

"Yes, of course." I slid back my chair and stood. "Please excuse us."

We strolled into the two-lane shooting range, which doubled as a panic room, and closed the soundproof door.

"Your first full day of the conference has been hectic, especially with the murder." Mike pulled me into his arms. "I miss having time alone with you."

"Any chance we can get together soon?" I leaned in for a kiss.

"I'll try." He kissed me with an intensity that took my breath away, then pulled back and said, "Be careful. One of your guests is a killer."

He left, and I rejoined several potential murderers.

————

My best friend and next-door neighbor, Gwen Pendragon, flashed her Palm Beach Police Detective badge and was allowed entrance to my home. Like me, Gwen was twenty-eight and an only child whose parents were murdered. Also like me, she was dating a police detective, but hers was with the Palm Beach Police.

Gwen found me in the ballroom where I had returned to my tablemates. She introduced herself and said, "Please accept my condolences for the loss of your friend."

The men seemed taken with her curvaceous good looks. She wore an emerald-green cocktail dress adorned with an unusual, centuries-old brooch from her late English aunt.

Aldo asked, "Are you investigating Lord Helmsley's murder?"

"No, but Jett's my best friend, and she's had a rough several months." Gwen smiled. "I wanted to see how she's doing after another murder here."

I asked her, "Can you believe the media circus outside my house and all the helicopters? I'm beginning to wonder if Valhalla Castle really is a murder magnet."

"I thought everything here had returned to normal, but now you have this to deal with. Sorry, Jett. Would it help to spend a little time over at my place?"

"I'd love to, but I have responsibilities here, and everyone staying in the castle is now a murder suspect, including me. I'm not allowed to leave home until the Feds release me."

"Call your lawyer. Offer to give the FBI your passport until your name is cleared." Gwen glanced at her watch. "I must dash. Clint is coming over."

Natalya interrupted, "Gwen, may I have a brief word in private?"

Surprised, she said, "Of course, walk with me."

———

Gwen led Natalya to the soundproof shooting range behind the ballroom and closed the door. "What's on your mind?"

Natalya looked pointedly at Gwen's ancient brooch made of gold and crystal with rubies and sapphires. "You are wearing Guinevere's Lance."

Gwen's eyes widened, and she placed her hand over her brooch as she took a step back. "But you're Russian—how could you know that?"

"Relax, your secret is safe with me." She held out her left hand and displayed an unusual ring. It was a black widow spider made of black onyx inlaid with an hourglass-shaped ruby in its abdomen. A tiny gold dagger ran diagonally behind the spider's body.

Gwen examined the ring. "I've never seen a ring like this. What does it signify?"

"Sisterhood of Black Widows," Natalya answered in her deep voice. "SBW is an ancient society of female assassins that goes back thousands of years—but unlike you, our members aren't descendants of the royal line of Queen Guinevere." She looked at Gwen's hands. "Do you have the matching ring that goes with the brooch?"

"The true purpose of Queen Guinevere's brooch and ring has been kept secret for centuries. How could you possibly know anything about it?"

"Twenty years ago, I crossed paths with the Duchess of Colchester, your late Aunt Elizabeth. Turned out we were stalking the same target, a horrid man who'd been murdering children for years and escaping justice. She got there first, and I arrived as she employed Guinevere's Lance and dispatched the killer. I saw the weapon that had been hidden inside the brooch, and I showed her my ring and told her the history of

SBW." She smiled. "We agreed to keep each other's secrets, and she asked me to share this story with her niece if we ever happened to meet after her passing."

"It's hard to believe you met my Aunt Liz, but how else could you know the secret?"

"Does Jett know about your brooch and ring?"

"Nobody knows. I'm trying to protect my aunt's legacy. I'd be mortified if Jett knew about Aunt Liz's clandestine activities."

"Tell me about the ring. Does it open like mine?" Natalya pressed the ruby, and the ring popped open, revealing a small compartment that could hold a powder or liquid.

"Yes, it carries a strong sedative that dissolves instantly in a liquid, rendering the target immobile so that a woman could easily deploy the weapon in the brooch." Gwen paused. "I agreed to keep the secret of Guinevere's Lance, but I never agreed to carry on executing extreme criminals who had escaped justice. I'm not an assassin."

Natalya smiled. "Of course not, dear. Neither am I." She winked. "But you must admit the centuries-old history of our jewelry is fascinating."

Gwen checked her watch. "Clint is waiting for me. I really must dash, but thank you for sharing," she hesitated, "and for keeping my secret."

———

I took the south staircase to the fourth floor and strode past the many oil paintings—ones on the east wall depicting Viking chieftains and scenes at sea and ones on the west wall depicting Cherokees with wolves and Native Americans on horseback. My large bedroom suite was on the south end and extended from the castle's east to west sides.

After I entered my bedroom, Pratt and Whitney, named after my favorite aircraft engine manufacturer, greeted me. I petted them and said, "Good dogs," proud that they'd found Edmund in my study. With the right training, they would grow up to be effective sleuthing assistants.

I led them downstairs and outside across the back terrace to the broad, tree-covered backyard. Sophia joined me and brought the frisbees. It was twilight, and the annoying helicopters were gone. I flung the frisbees, and the dogs chased after them.

Sophia tapped my shoulder. "I saw Gwen stop by, but I couldn't get away from needy guests before she left again."

"She wanted to check on us and offer her support."

"That was sweet."

The dogs bounded back and dropped their frisbees on my feet.

I tossed them toward the beach and watched the dogs catch up as the discs arced downward in the dim light. The pups leaped into the air and snatched them.

I pulled out my cell. "I'm calling my lawyer so he can arrange for the Feds to release their hold on us."

"Good idea." Sophia tossed the frisbees.

I spent a few minutes on the phone with my lawyer, and he assured me everything would be handled within the hour.

After the call, I said to Sophia, "He said we'll be good to go soon."

Next, I called my P.I. mentor, Darcy McKay. "Hey, I guess you heard on the news I'm tied up here with a high-profile murder."

"Sorry about that," she said, "but we planned on you being unavailable during that mystery conference anyway. Did they cancel it?"

"No, the FBI wants all the guests to remain here until the killer is caught—could be one of them—so they decided to continue with the events."

"That's understandable. They might be stuck there several days. May as well get what they paid for instead of sitting around sad and bored."

"Oh, I forgot to tell you that my dogs found the murder victim and alerted me. Pretty amazing for seven-month-olds, huh?"

"Jett, your dogs are naturals for detective work. I'll help you train them."

"Thanks, Darcy. I'll call after things are resolved here."

As Sophia and I headed back to the castle with the doggies in tow, I said, "Mike said one of the Mystery Fest guests is the killer, and it might be Aldo, so be careful."

"Aldo is a pussycat. No way he killed Lord Helmsley, but I'll keep my guard up."

FBI Agents Taylor and Barnes waited for us on the terrace.

Taylor said, "We're here to collect your passports. You'll be free to leave this property for brief outings, but we'd prefer you sleep here every night."

"That was fast. Our passports are in the study." As we followed the Feds down the hallway, I smiled about my lawyer being so effective. I didn't fire him after all the heartache his late son caused me, and now he never missed a chance to make it up to me.

It was a relief to see that Lord Helmsley's blood had been cleaned off the oak floor. I swung open a painting of my great-great-grandfather, dialed in the code to the safe, and pulled out passports for Sophia, Karin, and myself.

Agent Taylor handed me a receipt for the passports.

"All righty, you gentlemen have a nice evening." I waved goodbye to the Feds.

EIGHT

After our brief meeting with the FBI, Sophia met Aldo on the oceanside terrace at a table for two. They shared a vintage bottle of *Biondi Santi Brunello di Montalcino* from Tuscany.

Sophia looked into his ocean-blue eyes. *Haven't dated for twenty years. That handsome face and deep, masculine voice—so sexy.*

"It's nice to finally have a chat with you, my dear," Aldo said. "Tell me, from where did your family originate in Italy?"

"Sicily. My people go back to the eighteen hundreds. And you? Are you from Tuscany?" She sipped the smooth red wine.

"*Sí*, but my ancestors also came from Sicily. I have a villa there. The island is so beautiful, don't you think?" He swirled the wine in his glass.

"Oh, yes, in fact, I think Italy is the most beautiful country in the world." She smiled. "I love visiting *la famiglia*."

"*Molto bene*. My dear Sophia, you must come to Italy with me after Mystery Fest, and I will take you on a personal tour of my country. It is so lovely this time of year."

What a smooth operator. I just met him. "That's a generous offer, Aldo. Let me think about it." She took another sip of wine.

"I understand you're a widow. How long ago did he pass?" Aldo looked into her eyes like she was the only woman in the world.

"Twenty years ago, he betrayed me and my family." She lowered her voice. "*Il adultero* is wearing concrete boots on the bottom of Long Island Sound." She shrugged. "You know how it is."

"Ah, *sí*, one does not betray one's family. It is a *peccato mortale*, and the patriarch does not wait for divine justice." He took a sip. "Your father dealt with him, no?"

Sophia nodded. "My father, *Don* Francesco Calabrese, was *il capo* of the New York Mafia." She paused. "After I raised my sons, I moved to Florida, away from all that."

"My dear, you're a fascinating woman, and I look forward to knowing you better."

"I feel the same." She sipped her wine. "Tell me about your wife. Was her passing recent?"

"Cancer claimed *Contessa* Celia fifteen years ago. Her loss devastated me. I waited three years before I dated anyone, but I never met the right woman." He smiled. "Perhaps you'll change all that."

"I might." She tapped her glass against his and finished her wine. "Please excuse me. I need to check on preparations for the séance. I'll see you before midnight."

———

Sophia and I found Karin in the kitchen around eleven. She and her staff were busy making gourmet finger food for the next day.

Karin said, "Big news—the charity polo match on your beach is back on for tomorrow morning. The Feds took all the guests' passports and gave them permission to leave Valhalla for day trips. The event hosts will be here to install the VIP tent at zero dark thirty, and we're making the food for the match now."

"I believe Gaspar is scheduled to play," I said.

Karin nodded. "Even at sixty-five, I heard he's still quite good."

Mike sauntered in. "Still plan to hold a séance tonight?"

"Yes, and I'm dreading it." I snuggled against him.

He searched my eyes. "Sorry, Jett. Anything I can do?"

"Not unless you can make Edmund's ghost tell us who killed him." I nuzzled his neck. "What about you? Any new evidence?"

"I can't prove it yet, but I suspect Fiona did it. She invested loads of money promoting a free Scotland, which Edmund was against. A text message sent to him yesterday said: 'Meet me in the study at 7:00 a.m.—top secret.' It came from her cell phone."

"Isn't the text message enough to arrest her?" Sophia asked.

Mike shook his head. "Fiona claims anyone could've picked up her phone and sent the text—she leaves it lying around a lot." His eyes widened. "Jett, didn't you tell me a long time ago that you found a secret passage in your study?"

"Right, I forgot all about it—haven't used it in years."

"Where does it lead?" His eyes brightened.

"There's a hidden spiral staircase leading to the three bedrooms above it, with entrances through the back walls of the closets and my turret stairwell." I paused a moment, remembering the room assignments. "Aldo is in the bedroom on the second floor, Fiona is in the one on the third floor, and my bedroom is above hers."

Mike snapped his fingers. "That's it. Fiona could've used the secret passage to enter the study without being seen and escaped the same way." He hesitated. "Don't tell Neville or the FBI about it."

"I won't. Was there any forensic evidence in her room—something with Edmund's blood?"

"She's too smart for that. I need to trick her into using the secret passage again so I can prove she knows about it." He raised his eyebrows. "Any suggestions?"

"I'm too hungry to think about it. I was so occupied chatting at dinner, I barely ate anything." I glanced at my watch. "We don't have much time. The séance is in the study at midnight, which is supposedly the most spiritual hour."

"That's okay. I'll wait until tomorrow to search the secret passage," Mike said.

"How about a nice little ham, bacon, and Gruyère quiche?" Karin offered. "They're fresh out of the oven." She pointed at several quiches in round white stoneware dishes.

"Yes, I'd love one." I nudged Mike. "Hungry?"

"Thanks, I'm good." He glanced at Sophia. "Any ideas how we catch Fiona?"

She smirked. "Join Jett at the séance and ask the spirits for help."

Karin handed us food trays, and we carried them outside to the terrace.

Mike rolled his eyes at Sophia as he walked beside us. "I prefer hard evidence, but give my regards to Edmund's ghost if you see him."

———

Earlier, when I invited him, Hunter admitted his psychic senses might prove useful, so he agreed to join me, Dina, five Europeans, and two Brits. He arrived right after the staff moved a ballroom table and ten chairs into the study. Edith had wanted to attend, but the table only seated ten, and her friend Neville insisted on taking her place.

Hunter and I positioned the table near the bookcase that hid the secret passage, close to where Edmund had been murdered. Four large candles were evenly spaced on the table—a violet candle to enhance psychic powers, blue for improved communication, orange to attract good spirits and banish bad ones, and silver to enhance psychic powers and repel negative spirits. The candles would be the only source of light for the séance.

I added lemongrass incense to attract the good spirits and increase psychic powers, and I placed a framed photo of Edmund flat on the table. Hunter mounted a wide-angle video camera with audio high in a corner so it would capture everything in the room. He hit "record."

Even though Valhalla Castle was well over a hundred years old and numerous people had died here, I wasn't expecting anyone from the spirit world. I hoped the killer would be overcome by guilt and confess.

Fiona held a cantaloupe-sized crystal ball. "Perfect, ay? It's real crystal and is supposed to fill with light if a spirit is present." She placed the sparkling orb, secure on its holder, on the table's center.

The rest of the participants filed in and gathered around the table.

"Turn off your cell phones and put them away—no distractions," I warned. "We decided we don't need a Ouija board. Hunter's and my strong spiritual connections through the *Aniwaya* Clan should be sufficient."

Hunter lit the candles and incense as everyone took their seats. I closed and locked the door, then switched off the lights before joining them. Dina perched between Hunter and Aldo, and I settled between Klaus and Hunter. The bookcase was behind Neville, who was between Amelia and Natalya, with Gaspar and Fiona on either side of them. My seat was directly across from Neville.

Lucky me, facing his condescending scowl.

I kept a wary eye on Fiona as I nudged Hunter. "Ready?"

He reached over and gently squeezed my right hand. "Begin."

"Everyone, join hands and close your eyes for a moment." I waited as we linked hands. "We're here to summon the good spirits of Valhalla Castle. If you hear us, spirits, please give us a sign." I opened my eyes and glanced around the dark room.

At first, all was still.

Everyone jerked a little after a brilliant bolt of lightning flashed outside the corner windows, followed by a deafening thunderclap. The large chandelier hanging from the center of the high ceiling shook, causing its dangling crystals to clink together like tinkling bells, and a heavy downpour raged against the closed windows. Klaus squeezed my left hand so hard it hurt.

Several people gasped and stared wide-eyed at the chandelier.

I reassured everyone. "Just an isolated thunderstorm, and it'll be over soon. Don't break the chain."

Klaus loosened his grip on my hand, and a cold breeze came out of nowhere and swirled the incense smoke around us, blowing out the candles.

Goosebumps erupted on my arms as my long hair lifted around my shoulders. *What the heck? The door and windows are closed. Where's that breeze coming from?*

The room temperature plummeted, and darkness enveloped us, but only for a moment. The crystal ball slowly filled with a hazy blue light, dimly illuminating our shocked faces.

Natalya arched her brow and faced me. "You and Fiona rigged this, didn't you?"

"I've done nothing," I said. "I'm as surprised as everyone else. I swear."

Fiona protested, "The ball was delivered a short while ago. How could I rig it?"

"I can vouch for Jett," Amelia said. "She was busy until right before the séance. Let's continue and see what happens."

Everyone mumbled their assent.

I steeled myself and said, "Thank you for coming, good spirits. We beseech you to show us the murderer."

At first, nothing happened. It seemed like everyone was holding their breath, not sure what to expect.

Suddenly, books rattled in the bookcases, Edmund's photo spun around, and a strange yellowish glow illuminated the faces of the four Europeans, three Brits, and Dina.

I nudged Hunter and whispered, "Is my face glowing?"

"No," he whispered. "Is mine?"

"Nope, only the foreigners and Dina."

Dina elbowed Hunter. "Is my face lit up?"

He whispered, "Yep."

"This is ridiculous," Neville said. "All seven of you couldn't have done it. There was only one blow with one weapon."

"Your face is lit up too, Neville," Hunter pointed out.

"That's Detective Chief Inspector Wright to you, and this is obviously a sham."

"Don't accuse the spirits of lying," Natalya warned. "You'll make them angry."

"Humph. I'll say whatever I bloody well wish."

In rapid fire, four books flew off the bookcase and hit the back of Neville's head, landing on the floor behind him.

Everyone gasped.

"Ow!" Neville rubbed his head. "Who did that?" He glanced at his tablemates.

Natalya arched a brow. "No one at the table, *obviously*."

Amelia looked down at the books, which were glowing. "Oh, dear, I read these. They're all murder mysteries with multiple murders in the stories."

A chill raced down my spine, and my voice quavered. "Spirits, what are you telling us?"

"Are we all going to die?" Fiona asked, her voice cracking.

Lightning struck nearby, followed immediately by thunder so loud it seemed like a bomb exploded. The chandelier shook again, the crystal ball went dark, the candles reignited simultaneously, and the room temperature returned to normal.

Holy cow! I never expected all this, but I've never summoned spirits before.

"Nice going, Neville. You insulted the spirits, and now they're gone," Dina said.

She nudged Aldo. "Did you and your friends here murder Edmund, kind of like the passengers in *Murder on the Orient Express*?"

"No, Dina. Your face was illuminated too. The crystal ball must have malfunctioned. Right, Fiona?"

Fiona stared into space, her mouth agape. Natalya nudged her, jolting her out of her trance.

The violent storm outside ended as suddenly as it had begun—not unusual for Florida weather.

Fiona looked at me. "Jett, did you make all this happen?"

"No." I glanced from Aldo to Gaspar. "Any chance your bodyguards staged all the weird stuff?"

Aldo said, "No."

"I'm as bewildered as everyone else," Gaspar said. "And where did the cold wind come from? The windows and door were closed."

Neville slid his chair back and crossed his arms. "Well, don't expect me to believe spirits blew out the candles and reignited them. And that crystal ball—humph." He grunted and stood. "I knew this would be a waste of my time."

"Oh, yeah? Then why'd you insist on joining us?" Dina asked.

He tugged at his cuffs. "I wanted to observe how everyone reacted and spot the guilty party."

"And how'd that work for you?" I asked.

Neville shrugged. "Several people seemed guilty, but only one person could've murdered Edmund."

My hand trembled as I checked my watch. "It's late. Better turn in so everyone can be fresh for the big polo match tomorrow morning." I smiled at Gaspar. "We'll be rooting for you."

Everyone wished each other a good night and departed for their rooms, leaving Hunter and me to sort out what happened.

Sophia hurried inside after the guests left. "See any ghosts?"

"No, but I definitely felt something otherworldly." I nudged my uncle. "How about you?"

He nodded. "One or more spirits answered our call, but you asked the wrong question."

I tilted my head to the side. "What do you mean?"

"Instead of asking who killed Edmund, you asked the spirits to show us the murderer." He paused. "Apparently, all the people that were seated at the table with us are murderers, but only one killed Edmund."

Sophia clutched Hunter's arm. "That can't be right. I don't believe Aldo killed anyone." She searched our eyes. "I mean, we would've heard about it if they killed people, right?"

Hunter shook his head. "Not if none of them were ever caught."

"Let's review the video." I reached up and hit "stop" before retrieving the memory card and inserting it into my desktop computer.

We pulled up chairs and watched the monitor after I hit "play."

Sure enough, the camera caught images we didn't see during the séance. Glowing entities floated around the room and interfered with the candles and Edmund's photo. A blurry entity threw the books at

Neville, while another reignited the candles. The spirits vanished right after Neville broke the hand chain.

"Well, that was a shocker," I said, my hand trembling as I switched off the computer.

Sophia shrugged. "Wispy white entities are no big deal. I saw way scarier stuff back in Brooklyn. When I was a kid, we had bodies on display in open coffins in our living room before the funerals. Uncle Benny's ghost wandered around our house with blood oozing from bullet holes in his chest and forehead, and my cousin Vito's ghost looked grotesque with his throat slit so deep his head hung to one side."

"Eeew." I stood. "Um, after the polo match tomorrow, I think I'll do some deep background checks on our tablemates and see what comes up." I took their arms and led them down the hall. "Time for bed. Are you staying over, Hunter?"

"I have a flight in the morning, so no. You ladies be careful." He kissed my cheek, kissed Sophia's lips, waved goodbye, and sauntered out to his black McLaren sports car.

I glanced back down the hall toward the study, and an icy chill ran down my spine.

Are there really eight murderers in my home?

NINE

B right and early the next morning, a heavy roller machine packed the sand flat on the area marked for the polo match. Numerous horse trailers arrived and parked on the broad back lawn under the banyan trees. Temporary corrals were roped off in the shade and large tubs were filled with water for the polo ponies.

Scents of horses mixed with the salty sea air, and an occasional whinny overpowered the squawks of excited seagulls. A one-hundred-by-thirty-foot tent with open sides stood on the beach behind the polo pitch so the house guests, donors, and local dignitaries could watch the match seated in shady comfort. It was scheduled for 10:00 a.m. so the event wouldn't be too hot for the horses.

At 8:00 a.m., Gaspar sauntered into the dining room, looking impressive in his polo gear, his riding boots polished to perfection. He was on a team of celebrities and professional players pitted against a similar team for an exhibition fundraiser.

The delicious aroma of crisp bacon stirred my stomach juices as I spotted Fiona seated beside Klaus and wondered if she really was the killer. She was only five-two with fine bones, but that didn't mean she couldn't swing that battle axe. I had to find a way to lure her into using the secret passage, assuming she had already used it to kill Edmund.

Farther down the table, Aldo and Sophia enjoyed breakfast together, Natalya sat beside Amelia and Edith, and Neville sat across from them.

I joined Gaspar and breathed in the musky scent of his aftershave.

"Good morning, Jett. Ready to cheer me to victory?"

"You can count on me. I love watching polo." I dug into an omelet with ham, cheddar, and diced tomatoes.

After eating, I slipped away and called Tim. "Any suspicious activity observed by your guards?"

"Nope. All was quiet last night."

"Good. I hope it stays that way."

———

The polo match began on schedule at 10:00 a.m., heralded by the loud blast of an air horn. Unlike serious matches between professional polo teams, beach polo was meant to be a fun activity for both the spectators and the players. I scanned the crowd and noticed Fiona seated at the north end of the front row, sipping espresso while her friends enjoyed champagne.

"Good morning, everyone." I smiled at Fiona. "Want champagne or a mimosa?"

"I need my caffeine first. After this final espresso, I'll dive into the champagne." She lifted her cup and took another sip.

"All righty, let's cheer for Gaspar's team." I stepped aside, and the horses held my attention as they raced back and forth across the sand, chasing a soccer-sized ball. The players were aggressive, jockeying for position and whacking the ball with their mallets as the horses galloped past, the sand muting their thundering hooves.

The match progressed without incident for the next hour with spectators smiling and laughing, giddy from the free-flowing champagne.

Everyone stood and cheered after Gaspar scored a goal. Everyone except Fiona, whose face was planted on the tiny table in front of her. I wondered how she could pass out after drinking so much caffeine. Her cup was empty, and an overturned glass of champagne lay beside her head.

The upper class was known for keeping their cool. Klaus, Natalya, Amelia, Neville, and Edith were seated on Fiona's right. They calmly waved at me and nodded in her direction, no doubt assuming she had drunk too much. Farther down, Aldo and Sophia were focused on the match and seemed unaware of the situation.

Crouching beside Fiona's end seat, I checked her pulse and hoped the crowd wouldn't notice.

No pulse.

My gut churned.

I glanced at her friends and shook my head. Before I had a chance to stand and signal the paramedics parked near the polo field, a woman seated behind the first row screamed and pointed at Fiona.

I yelled to the EMTs, and they came running.

The only news agency allowed at the event rushed over and began filming and taking flash photos. My security guards closed in and pushed back the media people, but all the spectators crowded closer.

I leaned into one of the paramedics and whispered, "Preserve the scene while you work on her. It might be murder."

He nodded and checked Fiona. "How long since her heart stopped?" He laid her out and applied the portable paddles.

I checked my watch. "A few minutes. Can you save her?"

He frowned and shook his head as spectators crowded closer.

"Move back! Medical emergency!" I pulled out my cell and called Mike. "Get to the polo match fast—Fiona Campbell might be dead."

He shot back, "Any signs of foul play?"

"No, but the scene's chaotic. Paramedics are working on her, and everyone's trying to push in close and get a better view. The guards are doing their best, but we need help."

"I'll be right there. Protect the potential crime scene."

During the five minutes I waited for Mike, camera flashes from spectators exploded around me, and something glinted in the sand beside Fiona's table. I placed my feet close together on either side of it while I guarded the victim's coffee cup and champagne glass.

Neville blustered over, acting like he was in charge, but my feet blocked his view of the tiny item in the sand. If it was important evidence, I wanted Mike to find it.

"Step aside, dearie. Police business," Neville said.

Sirens blared as police cars and emergency vehicles roared up to the tent.

"Sorry, Neville, the detective in charge asked me to guard the death scene." I glanced around. "Here he comes now."

Several police officers arrived with Mike, and he told them, "Keep the crowd back, but don't allow anyone to leave." He glared at Neville. "Don't contaminate my scene."

Neville's face flushed as he took a step back. "Now see here, I've been cleared to work on this investigation."

"Wrong." Mike stood toe-to-toe with Neville. "You were cleared to work on the Helmsley murder. This is a new case that could be a natural death."

Neville jutted out his chin and looked up at Mike. "We have two dead British citizens who were in perfect health. The cases are obviously linked."

"We don't know that, but if they turn out to be related, I'll loop you in." Mike turned after a paramedic tapped his shoulder.

"She's dead. No chance of reviving her."

"Thanks. The M.E. will take it from here." Mike pulled on gloves and sealed Fiona's coffee cup and champagne glass inside evidence bags.

I whispered, "There might be something important between my feet."

He bent down and picked up a narrow glass vial about two inches long. "This could be what poisoned her if she was murdered."

I studied the container as he held it in his gloved hand. "It looks like a nicotine cartridge used in a vapor pen."

"Have you noticed any of your guests vaping?" Mike scanned the crowd.

"Oh, geez, Sophia's new squeeze uses one to help him quit smoking. I hope this doesn't belong to Aldo, but I haven't seen anyone else vaping."

Mike gazed across at Aldo and Sophia, standing several feet away from us. He looked at the vial again. "I'll check if the prints on it are Aldo's. Got any face powder?"

"No, but you can try powdered sugar off one of those pastries." I ran over, grabbed one, and carried it to him. "Here."

He dusted the print and took a photo with his phone. "I'll email this to the lab."

Meanwhile, the polo match continued unabated, the players intent on winning and oblivious to the drama in the spectator tent thirty feet from one side boundary.

Police officers moved the spectators away from a ten-foot-square area at the north end of the tent, and I helped Mike tape it off while we waited for the CSU team and the M.E.

"I hate to call them, but if I don't play nice with the Feds, they'll cut me out of the investigations." Mike pulled out his cell and called the two FBI agents in charge of Lord Helmsley's murder case.

The medical examiner arrived and examined the body. He glanced at Mike. "She exhibits signs of poisoning, but I won't know which poison until I run a tox screen."

Mike showed him the glass vial. "Could she have been poisoned with liquid nicotine in her espresso?"

The doctor examined the cartridge. "A full dose of this would definitely kill her, and she wouldn't have tasted it in the strong coffee."

"Everyone here will have to be interviewed." Mike leaned close to me. "Allow the organizers to continue the polo match while the Feds and I interview the spectators one by one."

"Good idea. That'll keep everyone occupied and minimize the chaos." I weaved through the crowd to the event coordinator and explained the plan.

As I re-joined Mike, his phone pinged.

He glanced at the text. "Got a match on those prints. They're Aldo's."

"Sophia isn't going to like this." I spotted her and Aldo standing by the polo pitch.

Mike sighed. "Keep them here while I search his room. I believe you said he's staying on the second floor, east side, at the south end."

"Yeah, his room is directly beneath Fiona's room." I gazed at Sophia and felt guilty. "You know, somebody could have worn gloves and stolen that vial."

He gently squeezed my shoulders. "Or Fiona wasn't poisoned with it. I promise I'll explore every possibility."

Tim pushed through the throng and joined us. "How can I help?"

Mike shook his hand. "Thanks for coming. Ask your security guards to help my men form a perimeter around the spectators and ensure no one leaves. The Feds and I will interview everyone as soon as possible."

Tim nodded. "On it." He pulled out his phone and made some calls.

———

Mike searched Aldo's room and found a vape pen and extra nicotine cartridges on the dresser in plain sight. He noted the liquid nicotine was the strongest dose sold. After checking everything in Aldo's room, Mike looked inside the large wall closet.

He checked behind Aldo's clothes and noted the paneled wall along the back appeared normal—no obvious control lever to open a secret door. Wolf-head hooks were mounted on the closet's side walls at both ends.

Mike tried the one on the right. It wouldn't budge. He moved to the other end of the closet and tried the left one. The snarling wolf head turned 180 degrees to the right, and a center panel on the back wall swung open into a dark spiral stairwell. Musty air breezed into the closet.

Mike pulled out his cell phone and activated the flashlight. Before entering, he shined his light on the dusty oak steps and found foot-prints. Someone had been careful to slide their feet and smudge the prints, making it impossible to discern the shoe size or if they were made by a man or a woman. The prints showed someone went down and up the steps.

He closed the outer closet door behind him and entered the secret passage. Inside the stairwell, he closed the hidden door and ascended the steep, curving stone steps, following the blurred dusty footprints. He found a similar wolf head mounted on the stone wall at the third-floor landing behind Fiona's closet.

He twisted it to the right, and a door in the back of her closet opened. After parting the hanging clothes, he entered her bedroom. All the rooms had been searched after Lord Helmsley's murder, but he conducted another search now. Fiona's room held nothing new, so he slipped back into the secret stairwell and noted the smudged footprints continued upward. He climbed the steps to Jett's suite on the fourth floor.

Why do the footprints lead up to Jett's room? Is the killer after her too?

He rotated the wolf head, and a door opened into a corner stairwell that led up to the turret room above Jett's bedroom. A normal door on the opposite side of the stairwell led into her suite. He peeked inside and was greeted with kisses from Pratt and Whitney.

"Hello, pups. Yes, I'm happy to see you." He petted them. "Be good now and Jett will come and get you soon." Mike closed the door and heard sniffing and soft whining on the other side.

Pointing his cell phone light downward, he descended the stairs all the way to where the smudged footprints ended on the ground floor, and he found another wolf head on the wall. He twisted it to the right, and a section of the study's oak bookcase swung open.

Mike hurried through the door and closed it. He examined the bookcase with the hidden door and searched for a way to open it. He stood six feet two inches tall and studied books on the shelf a few inches below his eye level. An old volume bound in black leather caught his eye—*The Murders at the Rue Morgue and Other Short Stories* by Edgar Allan Poe. He pulled out the book published in 1878.

It figures Jett's ancestors chose a book published before this castle was built in the early 1900s. He checked the empty space where the book had been shelved and spotted a round wolf head emblem embedded in the wood on the back panel of the bookcase. A firm push against it resulted in the stairwell door opening.

Hah, I found it. Did the killer use this to escape undetected?

He closed the bookcase and strode back out to the makeshift polo field on Jett's beach. FBI Agents Taylor and Barnes were already there, interviewing spectators. The Scotland Yard Inspector hovered nearby.

Mike wondered, *Is Aldo the killer? I'll see how he reacts to my questions.*

TEN

M ike strode over to where Aldo sat with Sophia under the tent. "Sorry to intrude, but I need a private word with Count Medici." He thumbed toward Jett's backyard.

Except for the distant sounds of horses and the polo announcer's voice on a loudspeaker, the area was quiet—no helicopters overhead. The news choppers had been restricted to five miles outside Jett's property, and the on-site reporters had been hustled off the property after taking a flurry of photos and shouting questions.

Mike guided Aldo to a bench under a sprawling banyan tree. "As you know, your friend, Fiona Campbell, died an hour ago." He studied him. "I'm sorry for your loss."

Aldo glanced at the tent. "What happened, Detective? Was this another murder?"

"It's possible. I have a few questions. Did you bring a vapor pen to the polo match?"

He arched an eyebrow. "What an odd question for a death investigation."

"Please indulge me." Mike kept a poker face.

"Yes, I carry one and keep a spare in my room. I'm trying to quit smoking." He pulled a vapor pen from his breast pocket. The nicotine cartridge was almost full.

"Did you bring an extra cartridge with you to the match?"

"No, a full one lasts a long time." He frowned. "What's this about, Detective?"

"An empty nicotine vial was found on the sand beside Fiona's body." Mike paused for emphasis. "Your fingerprints were on it."

"I discard my empties. Anyone could have fished it out of a waste bin."

"Is there a chance the empty cartridge fell out of your pocket in the tent?" Mike studied Aldo's eyes. If he was guilty, he was one cool customer.

"I drop the empty vials in my room's wastebasket. Besides, it would be very difficult to add poison to a vape cartridge, and Fiona only smokes fine cigars."

"Liquid nicotine *is* poison if the vial's contents are ingested in one dose."

Aldo's surprised reaction seemed genuine. "I had no idea. The label had the usual smoking warning."

Mike hesitated. "Were you jealous Fiona slept with Klaus and Gaspar?"

"I couldn't care less about that." He glanced toward the tent. "I'm saddened by her death, but my romantic interest lies solely with Sophia."

"Can you think of anyone who might've wanted Fiona dead?"

"I thought everyone liked her." He shook his head. "I certainly enjoyed her company at the yearly Mystery Fest events. We were charter members."

Mike sighed. "I thought the Scotland separatist movement was a motive, but Edmond was against it, and Fiona was for it."

Aldo shrugged. "Perhaps Fiona wasn't murdered."

"We'll know as soon as the M.E. completes the autopsy." Mike glanced toward the crowded polo tent. *If not Aldo, someone in there is a murderer.*

———

The polo exhibition ended at noon, but it was 3:00 p.m. before all the witness interviews were completed. As we hoped, Gaspar's team won the match, and he scored one of the goals.

Mike pulled me aside in the tent. "This investigation is frustrating. Nobody saw anything useful, and I can't narrow down a motive for either murder."

"I might be able to help. Last night's séance was scary and somewhat successful, but I asked the wrong question."

Mike blew out a sigh. "What happened?"

"I'll spare you the bizarre details. I asked the spirits to show us the murderer, and all the Europeans, Brits, and Dina were highlighted with glowing faces."

"How is that helpful?" Mike arched his brows. "Only one person killed Edmund."

"Yes, but it appears they might all be murderers. Neville insulted the spirits, and he got hit with four mystery novels that had multiple murders in each book."

Mike's jaw dropped. "What do you mean by 'got hit?' Are you saying a *ghost* hit him with the books?"

"Yep, they flew off the shelf and bonked him on the back of his head."

He stared at me for a beat. "Think the spirits were warning you the guests with the glowing faces will be murdered?"

I shrugged. "It's possible, considering one just died. I'll use my intelligence contacts for comprehensive background checks and see if I can discover whether each one murdered somebody. Might help you with motives."

Mike looked over my shoulder. "The Feds are headed this way. Keep this new info between us and let me know what you discover."

I hugged him. "You can count on me."

"Ahem," a voice from behind me said.

I turned around and faced the two FBI agents. "Hello. How may I help?"

"Your Mystery Fest has turned into a Murder Fest. What happened to all the extra security you promised?"

"We have plenty of security guards, but they can't be everywhere at once." I arched a brow. "Where were you guys?"

"We were hard at work in the Miami Field Office doing deep background checks on all your guests," Agent Taylor said indignantly.

"And what did you discover?"

"That's confidential." He glanced at Mike. "We need a word in private with Detective Miller."

"Right, I'll leave you to it." I headed back to the castle, hoping I could learn something useful for Mike.

Sophia intercepted me on the back terrace. "Are they charging Aldo with murder?"

"They don't have enough evidence to arrest him, and they can't afford to make a mistake with a rich and powerful Italian nobleman."

She smiled. "Good. I don't think Aldo killed anyone."

I squeezed her shoulder. "Not today, but he may have killed someone in his past—that is, if the spirits are to be believed."

"I'm counting on you to figure that out, Jett."

"I'll see what I can dig up on my computer."

As we headed inside, Aldo swooped in and whisked Sophia away.

I trotted upstairs to liberate my dogs. I needed some puppy kisses to cheer me up before diving into research.

Must find the killer before more people are murdered.

———

After taking the dogs for a run, I entered my study, closed the door, and called the CIA guy who had visited me earlier with the man from MI6. He owed me some favors, and I assumed I'd have to cash them in all at once. The dogs curled up at my feet, content, but the possibility of ghosts roaming around nearby made me uneasy.

"How'd that séance turn out?" my CIA friend asked.

"The spirits implied that the Europeans, Brits, and Dina Fenton are all murderers and that several people will be murdered at Valhalla Castle. Still no idea who killed Edmund or Fiona." I sighed. "What can you tell me about my Russian guest?"

"Natalya Petrov?" my spy buddy asked. "We've had our eyes on her for years, along with all the Russian oligarchs. She's KGB, Russia's 1976 Olympic gold medal fencing champion, a ruthless businesswoman, and we suspect she killed all four rich husbands."

"Her KGB training would've provided her with lots of ways to murder someone and not leave a trace. Any chance you know what motives she might've had to kill Lord Helmsley and Fiona Campbell?" I mindlessly gazed at the painting of my Danish great-great-grandfather.

"Can't help you there. She and Fiona had mutually beneficial business deals involving the distribution of Fiona's Scotch in Russia and Natalya's vodka in the UK, and Lord Helmsley helped facilitate their UK connection." He paused. "We suspect Natalya may have advised Fiona on the use of prussic acid spray to eliminate Fiona's abusive father and wealthy husband. Both died of respiratory arrest in their sleep, and by the time autopsies were performed, all traces of the poison had vanished. That left Fiona as the sole heir to her father's whisky empire and her husband's riches."

"Wow, talk about ruthless. How about the other players? Any dirt on them? Looks like I'll have to cash in all my chips." I leaned back in my cordovan desk chair and glanced up at the crystal chandelier.

"We're taking a lot of heat for Helmsley's murder and now the Scotch whisky heiress, so consider this a freebie. We want the killer caught even more than you do." He paused—probably checking his notes. "Here's the thing. Helmsley was a strong advocate for preserving the union, but Lady Amelia is the only one who agreed with him. All the others were for a free Scotland because it would benefit their businesses."

"But is that enough of a motive to kill him?"

"Helmsley cracked down on businesses with Mafia ties. He was chairman of the Commerce Committee and canceled Prince Gaspar

Borbón's lucrative shipping contracts and Count Aldo Medici's wine imports, pending investigations."

"Wait, you're saying Gaspar and Aldo are in the Mafia?"

"Not *in* but connected. The Borbón family's Mafia ties date back to the early 1800s when they controlled Naples, and the Medici family line also connects to the Mob in Sicily and Naples since the 1800s."

My mind raced, thinking of all the possibilities, and not wanting Sophia caught up in it. "What about Klaus von Helsig?"

"He's a wealthy international playboy with a dark side. He's on our radar because he disappears for a month after every Mystery Fest, but we haven't discovered his secret."

"And Lady Amelia? Anything juicy?"

"Sorry. She's clean—does some consulting with the Met and writes a ton of bestselling mysteries."

"Speaking of Scotland Yard, anything of note on DCI Neville Wright?"

"He shot a terror suspect a few years back, but it was ruled a clean kill."

"What about the American members of Mystery Lovers International?" I recited their names and waited while he typed them into his intel program.

"Hmmn, they're all clean except Texas oil tycoon Dina Fenton—her husband died under suspicious circumstances, but no charges were filed."

"Well, thanks for the intel. I'll call if I discover who the killer is." I pocketed my phone and fired up my computer.

After checking Klaus and Aldo, an Internet search for Gaspar revealed a news story from six months ago: "Wealthy playboy Prince Gaspar Borbón, fifth in line to the Spanish throne, reported his girl-friend lost at sea during a cruise in the Mediterranean. Borbón claimed she fell off his 200-foot yacht late at night. Her body was later found washed up on Mallorca. The coroner confirmed Lola Dupre, 25, a French citizen, was three months pregnant when she drowned."

Is Gaspar guilty of her murder? I can't imagine her falling off a huge yacht in the middle of the night. I bet she refused to have an abortion, and he got rid of her.

Sophia opened the door and strolled into the study. "Find anything?"

I filled her in on Gaspar and what my CIA contact had shared about him and the MLI members. "And I ran an Internet search on Klaus and found lots of society photos of him with voluptuous arm candy. He tends to frequent classy casinos in Europe."

"No surprises there. Anything else?"

"His hobby is flying aerobatic airplanes, and he placed third in a few amateur aerobatic contests in Europe. I couldn't find any criminal activity or news stories that implicated him in suspicious deaths. He must be good at covering his tracks."

"What about Aldo?" Sophia asked.

"His wife, Countess Celia, passed away fifteen years ago—breast cancer. He's had some high-profile romances over the years, but none that lasted. You know about his Mob ties—no biggie for you. If he ever murdered anyone, I couldn't find evidence of it, but he has a lot of dangerous friends."

Sophia smiled. "Aldo knows my sons run New York. Unless he has a death wish, he wouldn't dare harm me."

I sighed. "You're good at cutting to the chase. Who do you think the murderer is?"

"Never trust a Russian. My money's on Natalya—beautiful and lethal."

"She doesn't seem to have a motive, but that doesn't mean she didn't do it." I stood and stretched. "Natalya was KGB, so she'll know about your Mafia family. That might make her more likely to open up with you over drinks. Tell her about Vinnie and ask her advice about simpler ways to eliminate family problems."

"Good idea. And you can buddy up with her by offering some fencing practice."

"I was never a world champion like her, but I competed successfully in college, and I still have all my equipment." I imagined myself crossing swords with Natalya. "A little friendly sparring might be a good way to get to know her better."

"And in case I'm wrong about her, you and Hunter can pal around with Klaus at the private airport where Hunter lives." Sophia patted my back.

ELEVEN

The rest of the day was filled with Feds and cops everywhere.

Gwen called about Fiona's murder. I filled her in and asked, "Who do you think did it?"

"Natalya—that woman scares me. She has the eyes of a killer."

"Sophia and I think so too. Hey, I didn't get a chance to ask what Natalya wanted last night when she spoke with you in private."

"Oh, that. She noticed the antique brooch my aunt gave me. Turns out she's quite the ancient jewelry enthusiast and wanted to know all about it."

"She likes weird jewelry. Did you notice that creepy spider ring she wears?"

"Yeah, it's a black widow—seems to fit her personality. Call me if you learn anything new."

———

Neville gave a speech at dinner for the Mystery Fest guests. I wished he had stayed at Edith Pickering's estate on Palm Beach, but he insisted on a room at Valhalla Castle after Edmund's murder, so I was stuck with him. Fiona's death had made things far worse.

The mood at dinner was somber with all the guests feeling down-hearted after losing two longtime friends. And I was confused. I'd been fairly certain Fiona killed Edmund, right up to the moment she was poisoned. Now I suspected Natalya.

And what had happened to my beloved home? When I was a child growing up in the castle, it had been such a happy, warm place. Now it seemed cold and sinister with creepy spirits swirling around unseen. I hated feeling unsafe in my own house. My dogs were good at sensing danger, so I kept them close and planned to have them sleep on my bed that night.

I was jolted out of my thoughts when Mike called my cell. "Hey, babe, sorry I haven't had time for you. This second murder has me running ragged. I was almost certain Fiona killed Edmund, that is, until someone killed Fiona. It might be Aldo, or he could've been framed. Warn Sophia about Aldo. I know she likes him."

"She knows, but she doesn't believe Aldo is the killer. What if Fiona killed Edmund, and someone close to Edmund killed her for revenge?"

"The second killer would have to know Fiona killed Edmund, and it didn't seem like any of his friends had a clue who did it." He sighed. "This case is exasperating. I'll see you tomorrow."

I pocketed my phone and took the dogs for one more run in the backyard. Afterward, on our way to my bedroom, the fourth-floor hallway in the south wing was deserted, but my pups stopped ahead and turned to me. They raised their hackles as a slow, steady thump, thump sounded behind me. Was someone following me? I spun around, but no one was there. The thumping stopped. My pups had obviously sensed something sinister.

A chill ran down my spine as cold air washed over me. My dogs turned and looked toward my bedroom at the end of the hallway. The fur on the back of their necks had smoothed down, and they started walking slowly toward my door. I followed, wondering what had happened in the corridor.

We entered my bedroom suite, and the dogs trotted over to the turret-room door in the east corner where the secret passage led down to the study. They sniffed at the door and looked at me.

My Glock was in a thigh holster under my dress. I drew the pistol and inched the door open. The turret stairwell was empty. Steeling my nerve, I turned the wolf head and opened the door to the secret passage. Cold air washed over me again, and a faint thump-thump echoed down the spiral steps.

My dogs tried to nudge me away from the door with their noses, and my irrational mind screamed, *"Don't go down there!"*

My rational mind took over. *I'm armed, and I know how to defend myself. I should investigate that noise. The killer might be sneaking around, stalking another victim.*

I switched on my cell phone's flashlight and stepped into the stairwell. My dogs rushed down ahead of me. They'd been protecting me since the day I brought them home as small puppies. I worried someone might hurt them so I hurried after them.

Would Aldo hear us blunder past his closet? Or was he the one making the distant noise?

With every completed turn down the spiral staircase, the thumping became louder, and my heart beat faster. I paused, trying to slow my rapid breaths, but I had to keep going to catch up to my pups. I raced downward.

Pratt, my honey-colored dog, was in the lead. I knew that because Whitney was mostly black with a tan chest, and I spotted her black tail ahead of me as I rounded a turn and passed the wolf head that was even with the third floor behind Fiona's closet. Her door was closed.

Aldo's room was on the second floor. I slowed as I reached the wolf head control. His door was closed, and I couldn't hear anything on the other side. The thumping was farther down the stairs. Was I being led to the study?

Whitney's tail vanished, so I hurried to catch up. I found the dogs waiting for me at the foot of the stairs in the small area behind the hidden door. The thumping sound was now in the study.

I took a deep breath and inched open the door. The thumping stopped. Was someone in there? I froze and listened.

Nothing.

A blast of ice-cold air hit my face as I stepped inside. I gasped, and my breath came in short spurts, as my light cast dark shadows around the room. I didn't want to risk exposing the secret passage to a guest, so I closed the stairwell door, switched on a nearby desk lamp, and scanned the room, unsure what or who might be lurking nearby.

The study entry door was closed and guarded on either side by life-size statues of Thor and Odin. It occurred to me that either statue was big enough to hide behind. Edmund's killer could've hidden there, waiting for him to enter the room.

Someone could be hiding there now.

The dogs sniffed the floor where Edmund had died, circled the room, and returned to me. They would know if someone was hiding in the study.

I didn't want to believe spirits had led me here, but the unexplained cold air came from somewhere. Glancing around the dark room, I asked, "Why am I here?"

Something dropped onto the floor behind me. Startled, I jumped and turned.

A book lay on the floor. I shined my light on the cover. The title was *A Strange Case of Nine Murders* by Chinese author Wu Jianren. I checked the copyright page. It was published in 1906 and translated into this English version in 1998. My relatives on my father's side had always been big mystery fans.

I placed the book on my desk near the lamp and opened it to read the inside book jacket.

The book slammed shut, and my heart skipped a beat.

Every time I opened it, it closed again, all by itself.

It finally dawned on me that I wasn't meant to read the novel. The significant part was the title, *A Strange Case of Nine Murders.*

So far, there had been two murders during Mystery Fest. Was a spirit warning me there would be seven more?

TWELVE

After an early morning run with my dogs, I settled into a chair on the back terrace while it was too early for the noisy news helicopters to begin their annoying vigil overhead.

I stared out at the restless sea, wondering if my late-night experience had been a harbinger of more murders. Sophia joined me, and I told her about it, ending with, "The thing is, it doesn't help me to know there will be more murders. I want to prevent them, but how can I if I don't know who the killer is?"

"Makes me wonder how helpful the spirits really are. I mean, if they know about future murders, chances are they also know who the killer is. Why didn't they tell you his or her name?" She reached down and petted the dogs.

"If the ghost is someone I killed, he won't help me. Think he's seeking revenge?"

Sophia shrugged. "Maybe, or if the ghosts are bored, several murders would be entertaining for them, and they'd get some new buddies to hang out with."

"Geez, I hope that's not what's happening. I'd like to think they're trying to help me. I only called the good spirits."

"It's possible their world has rules—they can warn us, but they can't do anything that could change what happens here. That's up to us."

"Huh, that sort of makes sense." I stood. "Ready to face everyone at breakfast?"

"Aldo will be there." She smoothed her auburn mane. "How does my hair look?"

"Good. The humidity is low this morning—no frizzing."

Mike sauntered onto the terrace. He was so handsome, he looked like he stepped off an action movie set. He glanced from Sophia to me. "Good morning, ladies. You look lovely today." He lowered his voice. "I hope you discovered something new about the case. I'm counting on you both to help me catch the killer."

I filled him in on my spirit encounter.

"Nine murders?" He ran his hand through his thick brown hair. "We already have an international disaster on our hands. I don't even want to think about how the public would react to so many deaths. We need to catch the killer fast. Let's come up with a plan."

"Jett and I already have one." Sophia looked around to make sure no one was within earshot. "We think it might be Natalya. Jett's going to buddy up to her with a fencing session, and I'm going to get her drunk and see what tales she tells."

Mike rolled his eyes. "Remember, whoever's doing this is very clever. If she's the killer, you're both in danger, so be careful."

Sophia checked her watch. "I'm meeting her for drinks tonight after dinner. She was KGB, so she may know which players killed someone in the past. I'll use my Mob stories to lower her guard and get the dirt on everyone."

Mike turned to me. "Explain the swordplay."

"Natalya is an Olympic fencing champion, so I asked her to spar with me and give me some tips. We'll cross swords tomorrow morning."

Mike shook his head. "Oh good. She can *accidentally* stab you through the heart and call it a day."

"Not with a blunt-tipped foil. Besides, if she's the killer, she's too smart for anything so overt."

"Foils have been known to break near the tip during a powerful thrust. Then the sharp blade spears the opponent's chest, and it's game over—forever."

"You worry too much." I gave him a lingering kiss, and that ended his thoughts about Natalya.

She wouldn't kill me, would she?

———

During a busy day of mystery workshops and panels for the guests, Sophia and I snooped in the guest rooms to no avail.

That night after dinner, Sophia and Natalya shared an iced bottle of the Russian's favorite vodka at an isolated table on the back terrace. Security guards patrolled at a discreet distance under a bright moon.

A gentle ocean breeze carried the scent of the sea as Sophia nodded in a guard's direction. "They keep a close watch on me because I come from a powerful Mafia family—probably think I'm the killer—idiots!" She took a sip of ice-cold Zyr vodka.

Natalya laughed. "They don't trust Russians either."

The women sipped vodka and talked about their families and their upbringing.

Sophia admired Natalya's spider. "I love your black widow ring—so unusual."

"Thank you. It's my favorite piece of jewelry, and it's centuries old." She glanced at Sophia's left hand. "Tell me about your ring."

She held out her hand and displayed an antique ruby ring meant for a man. She wore it on her middle finger, but her hand was so small she needed a sizer wrapped around the back side to make it fit. "This is a Cosa Nostra ring from the eighteen hundreds. It's been in my family for many generations."

"Have you noticed the antique brooch Gwen wears?" Natalya asked.

"Yeah, her late aunt gave it to her before she died. Said it's a family heirloom, but it's a bit too gaudy for my taste."

Natalya grinned. "I like you, and I find your honesty refreshing—no pretense."

"Hey, I am who I am—no big deal, and I like you too, Natalya."

After several sips, Sophia said, "*Men*—I like a little romance now and then, but I'll never get married again." She lowered her voice. "My late husband, Vinnie, is wearing concrete overshoes on the bottom of Long Island Sound—bastard cheated on me with a woman from a rival family."

Natalya leaned forward. "Prussic acid sprayed into his nostrils while he's sleeping is a lot easier, and it leaves no trace if you wait a few hours before noticing he's dead." She chuckled.

Sophia smiled broadly. "Much better than concrete boots. Wish I'd known you twenty years ago. Could've saved my father a lot of trouble."

Natalya whispered, "I gave Fiona the same advice when she suffered from an abusive father and husband. We women need to stick together." She sighed. "She was a dear friend. Wish I knew who killed her."

"I'm betting one of the men did it, but don't count on the FBI to catch him." Sophia poured her glass into a nearby planter while Natalya wasn't looking and asked, "Do you suspect Aldo, Gaspar, or Klaus?"

"Aldo would never get his hands dirty. Besides, he's a pussycat." She glanced around. "It could be Gaspar or Klaus."

Sophia leaned forward. "Why do you suspect them?"

"I'm fairly certain Gaspar drowned his pregnant girlfriend, and Klaus might be a serial killer." Natalya took another sip of Zyr.

"Whoa, Gaspar drowned a girl, and Klaus is a serial killer?"

"Gaspar didn't want to marry the girl or deal with a child, so I suspect he eliminated the problem in a way that can't be proved. As for Klaus, I've noticed a pattern with him over the past fifteen years since Mystery Fest began." She paused and looked around, checking no one was close enough to overhear her. "Every year after the conference, he disappears for a month or so. Soon after, I read about murder victims whose deaths mimic the cases we studied that year."

"Why hasn't he been caught?"

"Could be he uses clever disguises and false identities so no one can prove where he was at the times of the murders." Natalya narrowed her eyes. "Edmund and Fiona probably suspected him, so he killed them."

"Any idea how to make him confess?" Sophia asked.

"*Nyet*, but we'll think of something."

"Right. We'll nail the bastard." Sophia high-fived her.

———

As I crossed the back terrace after taking the dogs out, I ran into Mike. He looked tired but happy to see me. I glanced at my watch—10 p.m. "I hope you aren't bringing more bad news."

He pulled me into his arms and gave me a passionate kiss. My heart rate skyrocketed as he said, "I've really missed spending time with you." He glanced down at the dogs. "Any chance we can steal a little quality alone time?"

Sophia strolled over and asked, "Want me to take the dogs?"

I smiled. "It's like you read our minds."

"It doesn't take a genius to decipher your thoughts after *that* kiss." She grinned. "I'll see you tomorrow morning." Sophia petted the dogs. "Come with me, my angels."

We watched them disappear inside, and Mike nuzzled my neck. "Your room?"

I grabbed his hand, and we headed inside. "We'll take the elevator —wouldn't want to waste your energy on the stairs."

As soon as the elevator doors closed, he hit 4 and drew me into his arms. Another intense kiss lasted until we reached the top floor. We covered the distance to my room at the end of the hall in record time.

I closed and locked my door.

Mike pinned me against the wall and gave me a kiss that took my breath away. He lifted my dress over my head and unclasped my bra. I yanked his polo shirt over his head and ran my hands over his hard, muscular chest and broad shoulders.

He was all hot steel and sex appeal as he scooped me into his arms and carried me to my king-sized, four-poster bed. We writhed around, entwined in passionate, intense lovemaking that ended with us passing out in a state of total ecstasy.

Early in the morning, he slipped away to resume his police detective duties.

THIRTEEN

Natalya sat beside me at breakfast. She lowered her voice and leaned close. "I saw the kiss your hot boyfriend gave you on the terrace last night. Judging by that smile on your face, I assume he followed up with a steamy night."

I grinned. "I really needed that."

"Needed what?" Klaus asked as he took a seat across from us.

"A satisfying session with her hunky boyfriend." Natalya smiled.

Without missing a beat, Klaus said, "Jett, if you'd ever like to enjoy a tumble with a far more experienced lover, I'd be happy to oblige."

Gaspar joined us in time to hear Klaus's offer. "If you're open to new lovers, my lovemaking skills are legendary and guaranteed to satisfy a vibrant young woman like yourself, Jett."

I rolled my eyes. "Thank you, gentlemen, but this isn't a competition. I'm quite happy with my man."

Natalya laughed. "Now that you're relaxed, let's spar with foils after breakfast."

"I'd love that. It's been ages since I fenced."

She glanced at the mahogany grandfather clock. "I have a little over an hour before the first mystery session today. Where shall we meet?"

"The ballroom in fifteen minutes." I drained my coffee and headed up to drag all the fencing gear out of my bedroom closet.

As I walked away, I heard Klaus say, "Better go easy on her, Natalya. I won't be happy if you make that lovely young woman bleed."

———

I brought two sets of white fencing gear that had one black and one white head cover with mask. Natalya and I were approximately the same height and size, so everything fit her.

She chose the black mask. Did that mean she identified with the dark side? As she examined her foil, I handed her red chalk to coat the blunt tip so we could easily keep track of points without an electronic scoring system.

I chalked my foil and paced off the 46-foot-long and 6.6-foot-wide fencing piste. Using white chalk, I marked the boundaries, the start lines near the mid-point, and the warning lines near each end.

We stood at the start points, saluted each other with our foils, pulled down our headgear, and assumed the proper stance.

Natalya said, "*En garde.*"

I answered, "*Allez,*" meaning "go," and advanced.

Although Natalya was sixty-seven, she was fit with quick reflexes. She lunged, and I parried her attack.

Wow, she's really good!

She kept me on the defensive as she backed me over my warning line and left a red mark on the center of my chest.

"*Touché moi,*" I said, touching my chest and acknowledging the hit. "I'd expect nothing less from an Olympic Fencing Champion." We re-centered, and I tried an immediate beat attack, but she easily parried and scored with a stop thrust.

"*Arrêt,*" she commanded, and we stopped. She removed her mask. "Would you like some tips?"

I pulled off my mask. "Yes, please."

"Be more aggressive and keep me on the defensive. Don't let up, even for a second." She sauntered back to her start line and donned her mask, as I did the same on my end.

After the usual "*En garde*," I charged her with a high-energy *flèche* attack.

My right forearm stung from the strain of swinging the sword. Each clash against her weapon sent pain shooting through my arm as the ballroom filled with the sharp clangs of metal hitting metal.

How is she so strong at sixty-seven?

Natalya parried, but I kept up the attack so she couldn't put me on the defensive. Soon, she backed over the warning line at her end, and I managed a jab on her lower chest.

"*Touché moi*," she said, and pulled off her mask. "Well done. You learn fast."

Removing my faceguard, I checked my watch. "We have time for one last point. Care to take a quick breather and go again?"

"*Da.*" She smiled and stepped up to the line. "*En garde.*"

I hurried back to my mark, and we began our final match.

Metal clashed and rasped as we lunged and parried forward and back, neither one easing up. At twenty-eight, my stamina outlasted hers, and, after much effort, I won the last point, ending our match in a tie. She was such a skilled swordswoman that I wondered if she allowed me the final point.

"*Arrêt*," I said, yanking off my mask. "You're one tough opponent."

She uncovered her face and bowed. "It was my pleasure."

We stripped down to our skin-tight yoga pants and tops, sat beside each other at a ballroom table, and filled our glasses with ice water from a pitcher.

She turned to me, and I looked at her ring. "Is that a black widow?"

"*Da*, is very old, but is my favorite ring."

The deadly spider fit her personality perfectly. I took a long drink of cold water.

She continued, "I like antique jewelry, especially pieces with historic significance, like your friend Gwen's heirloom brooch. Surely, you've seen it?"

"Yes, her aunt gave it to her. She told me she wears it sometimes for good luck."

"Do you have any jewelry like that?"

"I have an old wolf head amulet carved in amber that was handed down through my mother's Cherokee ancestors. It's pretty, and it's supposed to hold some ancient power, but I'm not familiar with the ritual necessary to activate it. Might only be a legend."

"You always surprise me, Jett, and I enjoyed our sparring."

"Thanks for a lively session. You're an excellent instructor."

"We women must stick together." She took a swig. "You never know if these skills might come in handy, especially with a murderer lurking about."

I dabbed my face with a towel. "Any idea who the killer might be?"

She glanced around and lowered her voice. "It might be Klaus."

"Does he have a motive?"

"Could be he likes risky targets." She drained her glass. "Serial killers usually escalate over time and seek greater challenges, like killing crime experts at an international mystery conference and not getting caught."

"You think Klaus is a serial killer?" I played along not wanting her to know Sophia had told me about their conversation.

Natalya repeated what she'd told Sophia.

I acted surprised. "Chilling, but if you're right, why kill his friends, and who will be next?"

She shrugged. "Like I said, we're crime experts. The spirits at the séance indicated all the séance guests, except you and Hunter, may be at risk."

Uneasy, I looked around. "I'd better advise my security guards to keep a close watch on him. Aldo and Gaspar have bodyguards, so he might target you, Dina, or Amelia next."

Seeming unconcerned for her own safety, she said, "Amelia is the most vulnerable. She is seventy, walks with a cane, and has no self-defense skills." Natalya checked her cell for the time. "I'll warn her at the crime-solving workshop this morning."

We parted ways, and I wondered if she was right about the German nobleman or if she implicated him to take suspicion off herself.

After showering and dressing in jeans and a polo shirt, I took the secret stairs down to my study, descending slowly and listening for intruders.

Except for my breathing and footsteps, amplified by the narrow passage, the spiral staircase was silent. I reached the bottom and twisted the snarling wolf head to the right, waiting as a portion of the bookcase swung open.

After entering the study, I closed the hidden door. Ever since the séance, the room seemed to emit a strange energy that unnerved me. I glanced around, ensuring I was alone.

Seated at my desk, I pulled out my cell and called Mike. "Hey there, I'm still on a high from last night."

His deep voice resonated in my phone. "We should do that more often." He paused. "Did you spar with the Russian yet?"

I filled him in on our fencing match and who she thought might be the killer.

"Warn Lady Amelia and alert the security guards," Mike said. "But like you said, Natalya might be pointing suspicion at Klaus so she can kill Amelia and plant evidence to frame him."

"Why don't we send them all home today and end this?"

"Not possible—the FBI won't allow potential suspects to leave the country while they have an open investigation into two murders."

"Right. Heaven forbid we prevent more deaths," I huffed.

"I have to go, Jett. Call me if you learn anything."

FOURTEEN

S ophia managed to join Aldo for lunch and dinner, while I ate with my prime suspects and tried to glean more information.

No luck with that.

Between meals, I read up on serial killers.

That night, I took my doggies for a run in the backyard and sat in a chair on the terrace afterward, the dogs lounging at my feet. A sea breeze washed over me, lifting my hair, and cooling my skin. I leaned my head back and gazed up at the stars, wondering if the FBI knew something we didn't know. I hoped somebody would nail the killer soon.

Klaus sauntered over and interrupted my musings. "Good evening, Jett. May I join you?"

"Of course. Tell me all about your day." I patted a chair beside me.

He adjusted his monocle. "I enjoyed today's mystery quest, but I'm more interested in catching whoever killed Edmund and Fiona. Has your detective boyfriend made any progress on the case?"

"Not that I've heard, but we haven't talked much today. I've been studying serial killers in case I might find a lead that would help." I leaned down and petted my dogs.

"Serial killers? I'd love to hear about that," he said, his tone eager.

A member of the service staff stopped by. "Would you like a drink?"

"I'd love a glass of Opus One. How about you, Klaus?"

"Single malt whisky, straight up." He smiled. "Your Scotch is excellent."

I filled him in on my research, hoping he'd make a comment that would implicate him. No luck. Then our drinks arrived.

"I love a smooth red blend." I savored a sip.

He swirled his whisky. "Are you still taking me flying tomorrow afternoon after the last workshop?"

"Yes, my uncle is expecting us. Would you like to do aerobatics with him?" I took another sip.

"*Ja*, I would love that." He sipped his Scotch. "I entered a few amateur contests in Europe—never finished higher than third."

"That's way better than not placing at all. My uncle is an expert aerobatic instructor, and he can help you improve."

"*Wunderbar*. I'll look forward to it."

My dogs jumped up, wagging their tails, as Mike sauntered over. He reached down and ruffled their fur. "Jett, can I steal you?"

Klaus stood. "Good to see you, Detective Miller." He nodded at me. "I'll see you at breakfast." He picked up his drink and strode away.

My man pulled me up into his arms and gave me a searing kiss that implied another hot night might be in the offing.

I caught my breath. "My bedroom?"

"You read my mind." He took my hand and led me inside to the elevator.

After we reached my room, we took our time as the dogs fell asleep on the carpet. My challenge was to keep from making sounds that would wake them.

Mike made that impossible.

———

The next afternoon, I went over our plan again on the phone with Hunter. "Right, I'll drop Klaus off at your hangar, and you two can do some male bonding. He might be the killer, so get him talking, and hopefully he'll let something slip. Grab some dinner afterward, talk some more, and bring him back here." I pocketed my cell.

Klaus strode up, all smiles, wearing jeans, a polo shirt, sneakers, and a windbreaker. "I'm ready. Sorry the last workshop ran a little long."

"No worries, there's still time to fly with Hunter. You're going up in a vintage German biplane called a Bücker Jungmann."

"*Ja*, I remember, it has an open cockpit with tandem seats, and it's fully aerobatic—one of the best handling airplanes ever built." He grinned. "I flew one in Germany—absolute perfection."

As we climbed into my SUV, I said, "It's a thirty-minute drive to Aerodrome Estates, so we'd better get going if you want at least an hour of flying before sunset."

"I forget, does your uncle own the airplane?" He put on sunglasses.

"No, it belongs to a friend who keeps it in Hunter's hangar."

––––––

I waited while Klaus strapped into the front seat of the blue and red biplane, and Hunter settled behind him. As per FAA regulations for aerobatics, they both wore parachutes—not the backpack kind, but the type that filled deep-bucket seats. Their plan was to fly in the designated practice area southwest of Lake Okeechobee.

I pointed at thick smoke on the horizon due south of the lake and asked Hunter, "Will that be a problem?"

"They're burning the sugarcane fields today, but the wind is out of the northeast, so it'll blow the smoke away from us."

Klaus turned to me. "Why do they burn them?"

"It eliminates the leafy tops and makes the lower stalks easier and cheaper to harvest." I checked my watch. "Have fun, guys, and I'll see you back at the castle."

Hunter cranked up the new 180-hp Lycoming engine and taxied out. I watched as he performed the usual pre-takeoff checks before zooming down the runway and up into the late afternoon sky.

As I walked back to my car, I noted the windsock had turned, indicating a breeze out of the east. *I hope the wind doesn't shift again.*

———

Hunter climbed the airplane to 3,000 feet and skirted the shore of Lake Okeechobee, the second-largest lake fully within U.S. borders. Cool air washed over his face and tousled his thick black hair as the slowly sinking sun glinted off his aviator sunglasses.

He and Klaus wore headsets with voice-activated microphones attached to a battery-operated intercom system so they could easily talk to each other over the air noise from the open cockpit. The Bücker Jungmann, originally built in 1939, was newly restored and intended for good visibility, daytime flying only. It had no radios for communication or navigation.

After twenty minutes, Hunter wiggled the control stick. "Okay, we're in the practice zone, and you have the airplane. Try a roll first and get the feel of her."

"I've got the airplane." Klaus performed a barrel roll and stopped it after they returned to the right side up. His next maneuver was a snap roll, which rotated much faster, like a one-turn horizontal spin.

"Well done. Now fly straight and level inverted," Hunter suggested.

The German struggled to hold the airplane at 3,000 feet. "I don't like hanging upside down with gravity tugging on me. Feels like I'll fall out." He rolled upright.

"Want to do a loop?"

"*Ja,* I'll dive to 2,000 feet and pull up for the maneuver."

Hunter scanned the area. "Better hurry. Looks like the wind shifted, and that massive smoke cloud is headed our way. This will be our last stunt."

Klaus misjudged the descent and shot down to 1,500 feet before pulling up. The instant he added power, the engine exploded, cracking the front windshield, and engulfing the plane's nose in flames.

The engine failure was so violent, Hunter thought it seemed like a bomb detonated inside the powerplant.

After the deafening boom and the metal and oil shower, the biplane fell silent. The slipstream breezing past them softly whistled.

Searing flames lashed at the cracked front windscreen, which was splattered with oil, obscuring Klaus's view. Heat from the fire singed his eyebrows, and thick black smoke choked him.

"I've got the airplane," Hunter declared from the rear seat as his gut tightened. He used their momentum to shoot up to 2,000 feet, eased the stick forward for the best glide speed, and searched for a place to land.

He struggled to see past the engine fire and had to look to his left. "We're near the southwestern section of Lake Okeechobee," Hunter said, coughing from the noxious smoke streaming out of the burning engine. "No roads or empty fields within reach except the ones on fire. I'll have to put it down fast in that marshy section near the shoreline." He choked out the words, "If the fire reaches the fuel tank, we're dead."

Hunter aimed at the marsh as he put the airplane in a forward slip to lose altitude fast while not increasing airspeed. Thick smoke from the burning sugarcane fields rolled in below them, obscuring the ground. The altimeter read six hundred feet.

"This will be a blind landing. Would you rather take your chances bailing out? We're almost too low for a parachute jump."

"*Nein*, I think we're safer strapped into the plane."

Hunter yanked his five-point harness as tight as he could. "Snug up your belts and brace for impact. I'll try to touch down in a stall, but the fixed landing gear might flip us upside down in the water." He coughed. "If we end up inverted, remember to push on a side rail and take your weight off your seatbelt to unfasten it. And unbuckle your parachute or you won't be able to crawl out."

Engulfed in the engine's acrid smoke, Klaus choked out an unintelligible reply.

In seconds, they descended into a dense, dark netherworld. Hunter couldn't see the altimeter, making it impossible to judge their distance to the marsh. Mentally calculating their rate of descent, he counted down the seconds in his head, pulled back on the stick, and hoped for the best.

The Jungmann dropped the final ten feet, and the forward momentum flipped them inverted after the main wheels dug into the shallows. Now upside down, the flaming engine was mostly buried in murky water and mud, extinguishing the fire.

Disoriented from the sudden stop and hanging upside down in heavy smoke, Hunter released himself from his seat harness and parachute. He wriggled out from under the seat, landing face-first in the muck, and spit out putrid slime. "Klaus! Are you okay?" he yelled as dense smoke triggered a coughing fit.

No response.

The forward section of the fabric-covered steel-tube fuselage had buckled, trapping Klaus in the cockpit. The wings helped keep his mouth and nose inches above water as Hunter stood in weeds and deep mud and struggled to free him.

"Wake up, buddy." He squeezed his shoulder. "I need your help getting you out. Can you move your legs?"

Klaus coughed. "*Ja*, but the plane's frame is bent. Not enough room to get out either side, and my head is bleeding. I might have a concussion."

"Keep your harness fastened so you don't drop headfirst into the water. We'll have to wait for Fire Rescue." He pulled out his wet phone. "Crap! My cell shorted out. Is yours working?"

Klaus searched a moment. "Can't find it—must've slipped into the water." Talking triggered another coughing fit.

"Pull your shirt over your nose and mouth to filter the smoke." Hunter did the same. "There's a small baggage compartment behind the rear cockpit. I hope Ben put something useful in there." He waded to the rear of the wreck and wrenched open the baggage door.

"Aha!" He felt inside and found a first-aid kit mounted to the bulkhead and a waterproof flashlight that worked. "There's no emergency phone or radio, and no flares."

Klaus remained silent.

The sun had set, and darkness descended like inky sackcloth.

The crash scene was dead silent—not even the buzz of an insect or the splash of a nearby fish. Not a sound, except Hunter's occasional coughing.

Primeval alarm bells sent a shiver down his spine as he climbed up onto the plane's inverted belly, his feet dangling in the water. Sensing he was being stalked, he shined the flashlight around the wreck, scanning for predators.

Several sets of glowing yellow eyes fixed on him through the smoky fog.

Alligators.

Big ones.

Dozens lurking in the shadows, watching, and waiting.

FIFTEEN

I t was nine in the evening, and I couldn't reach my uncle or Klaus on their cells. I called Ben Foster, the biplane's owner.

"Jett, thank God. Have you heard from Hunter? He and that German guy borrowed my airplane and never returned."

The tension in his voice roiled my gut. "No, I was hoping you knew their whereabouts." I sucked in a breath. "Have you checked Okeechobee Airport and North County?"

"When they didn't make it back here, I called every airport in its fuel range. Nobody saw them."

My heart skipped a beat. *Can't bear to lose my uncle.*

"We've gotta look for them. They went to practice aerobatics southwest of the lake." I struggled to keep my voice steady. "Do you know anyone with a high-winged plane, like a Cessna 172, so it'll be easier to see the ground?"

"Jett, my buddies and I flew everywhere except the areas socked in with heavy smoke from those friggin' sugarcane fires. It's so thick we can't even use ground vehicles, and we don't have any boats or airboats equipped for zero visibility."

"There must be something we can do." I took a deep breath and tried not to worry.

"I notified the FAA, Fire Rescue, the Coast Guard, and the Civil Air Patrol. We've got to wait for the air to clear, which isn't forecast until sometime tomorrow." He softened his tone. "Sorry, I know how much Hunter means to you."

I croaked out, "Call me if you hear anything, and I'll do the same." Collapsing on a leather sofa in the great hall, I felt like all the air had been squeezed out of me.

My dogs sensed my anguish and comforted me with kisses. Sophia and Karin walked in and read my face.

Sophia looked into my watery eyes. "What's wrong?"

"Hunter...he—" I bit my lip and brushed away a tear.

She called Mike. "Get over here fast. Jett needs you. Something terrible has happened." She pocketed her phone and wrapped her arms around me.

Karin pulled out her cell and dialed my best friend, Gwen, next door. "Please come right away. Jett's really upset."

Minutes later, Gwen and Mike arrived at the same time and rushed to my side.

Mike scooped me into his arms and held me on his lap. "Tell me what's wrong so I can fix it."

Gwen sat beside me and grasped my hand. "I'm here for you. What can I do?"

Sophia crowded in with the dogs. "Whatever it is, we can help."

I took a deep breath and blurted out everything about the missing men. "And...and the smoke is so thick, they're saying we have to postpone the search until tomorrow, but they might not survive the night." I bit my lip. "We *must* find them. I can't lose my uncle."

Karin and Sophia exchanged glances, swallowed hard, and fought back tears. They both loved Hunter in different ways.

I was so upset, I didn't notice Natalya, Aldo, Gaspar, and Amelia standing behind the sofa. They must've heard the ruckus and rushed over.

Natalya said, "Jett, isn't it true all your security guards are retired SEALs?"

I looked at her and instantly got her meaning. "Right! Thank you." I jumped off Mike's lap and called Tim on my cell.

Confused, Sophia asked, "What's your point, Natalya?"

"SEALs have the means and abilities to do things civilians can't."

———

I rushed upstairs to prepare, and thirty minutes later, a helicopter with amphibious floats landed in my backyard. Tim Goldy and Kelly Mahone exited, decked out in combat attire with night vision and infrared gear mounted on their helmets.

Tim squeezed my hand. "Tell me about the plane they're in."

His obvious confidence and determination gave me hope.

"It's a vintage, open-cockpit biplane with a fabric-covered, steel-tube fuselage. If they crashed, it's possible they flipped upside down and the tubing buckled. You'll need a cordless Sawzall, and lights, blankets, and medical stuff." I thought a moment. "And lots of fire-power. That area has bears, panthers, water moccasins, hundreds of gators, pythons, and anacondas the length of a school bus."

Sophia said, "Yeah, thanks to irresponsible exotic pet owners, South Florida is rapidly becoming the new Amazon." She turned to the SEALs. "Any chance you guys have a flame thrower on board?"

"Too heavy. We've got everything we need, except blankets." Tim nodded at Sophia. "Bring us six, and we're good to go."

Sophia rushed off, and Karin grabbed Tim's arm. "How will you find them if you can't see anything?"

"Our helicopter is equipped with FLIR, weather radar with ground mapping mode, GPS, and all the instruments for flying in low visibility." Tim pointed at the chopper. "The amphibious floats enable us to land on water."

"What's FLIR?" Gwen asked.

"That's forward-looking infrared radar," Kelly replied. "Military helicopters use it to locate hostiles on the ground. It picks up their body heat."

Amelia said, "Oh dear, that means snakes and alligators won't register because they're cold-blooded."

Sophia hurried back with the blankets and had a pistol strapped to her thigh. "I'm coming too."

I was geared up. My special belt held several full magazines for my Glock, which was holstered on my right hip. The belt also held a sheathed combat knife and a pouch with a waterproof magnesium light. Night-vision binoculars hung on a strap around my neck, and knee-high boots covered my lower legs over my jeans.

"Let's go." I paused to kiss Mike goodbye.

He grasped my hands. "Don't go. It's too dangerous."

"Hunter's the only family I have left," I said in a firm tone. "I'm going!"

"Then I'm coming with you."

"Sorry, we can only take one person so we can carry the two men," Kelly explained.

I pulled free of Mike and squeezed Sophia's arm. "My *Aniwaya* intuition might help find him."

She slumped her shoulders, and Mike frowned.

"Okay, Jett, but be careful. You mean a lot to everyone." Sophia hugged me.

––––––

Hunter reached behind him and drew the Glock 26 from its holster in the small of his back. He carried this smaller pistol while he was sport flying. The magazine held six rounds, plus he kept one in the chamber. Seven shots wouldn't last long against a horde of hungry predators.

Klaus coughed and choked out, "Hunter? You still here?"

"Hang in there, buddy. I'm right behind you." He slid closer to the forward cockpit along the inverted fuselage and lifted his feet out of the water. "We've got company—gators—lots of them, but don't worry. I'll shoot the big ones, and the rest will eat them instead of us."

"Don't let a small one reach in and rip off my face."

"I won't—" Hunter sensed danger and spun around in time to spot a huge alligator lunging at him. He put a round between its beady eyes, and the loud gunshot echoed across the water and made his ears ring. The shot triggered a flurry of splashes from cold-blooded onlookers as the dead reptile floated a few feet away.

Too close.

It wasn't long before two large alligators became embroiled in a tug-of-war over the bloody corpse floating near the wreck. They dug in their teeth and jerked their heads side to side, splashing water everywhere.

Hunter's heart hammered his chest as he looked down, and a much smaller gator darted in at Klaus from the opposite side.

There was no time.

He fired into its head, the sharp report scattering the crowd and making his ears ring even more. That left Hunter with five shots and more alligators than he could count. He shined the flashlight on a huge head twenty feet out. The yellow eyes gave him an aiming point, and he took his time squeezing the trigger.

Another bullseye.

His regular target practice had paid off, and the violent result scattered the crowd and lured them farther out to the fresh kill. Soon, another feeding frenzy erupted, sending loud splashes through the eerie smoke.

A temporary reprieve.

He shook his head. *Never thought I'd end up like this.*

A scream from Klaus brought him back from his brief reverie.

"Help! It's biting my hand!"

Hunter holstered his weapon and drew his knife. After stabbing the three-foot gator in the head several times, he pried open its mouth, freed Klaus's hand, and tossed the dead reptile away from them.

"Your hand's bleeding. I'll get the first aid kit." He slid along the fuselage to the baggage compartment and pulled out the plastic box. After wrapping Klaus's hand in gauze, he said, "Next time, try to hold the bugger's mouth shut."

The shock and trauma from the crash, combined with the vicious attack and hanging upside down, took its toll on Klaus. He coughed.

"Should've known my bad deeds would come back to punish me." More coughing. "Damned karma!"

"Bad deeds?" Hunter leaned over the side and tried to read his face, but his eyes were closed. "What bad deeds, buddy?"

No response.

He reached down and felt for a pulse.

Barely alive.

Straddling the fuselage, he hung his legs on either side of Klaus's head. He'd know if a small gator sneaked in for a bite. Scanning the water with his flashlight, he noted the number of eyes focused on him had multiplied.

We won't last much longer.

As the predators closed in, a twenty-foot python slithered up behind him.

SIXTEEN

Seated in the center back seat of the Bell 429 Global Ranger, I held one of their Sig Sauer Cross Sniper/Hunter Rifles with a night scope on my lap while Tim and Kelly concentrated on the flight instruments, GPS, and both radars. We wore headsets with voice-activated microphones connected to the cabin's intercom system.

No one spoke as we raced toward the unknown and zero visibility. The retired SEALs were risking their lives to save Klaus and my uncle. I wasn't qualified to fly helicopters, but as an airplane pilot, I understood that the flight conditions were extremely dangerous.

We cut across the lake to avoid ground obstacles and remained in clear air until the last few miles over the southwestern portion. Tim descended to fifty feet above the water to get better details on the infrared screen, which was risky, but chances were there wouldn't be any obstructions in that remote, shallow area.

After we entered the thick smoke, visibility went to zero. Tim throttled back to a slower speed and flew a search grid back and forth, nearing the shoreline.

On our tenth turn to the south, I felt a strong sensation that my uncle was nearby to the west and called out, "Turn right."

Tim banked right and said, "Two warm bodies—looks like they're about a hundred yards out."

We headed straight for the images on the FLIR screen. I peeked at the display and noted one body was upside down and stationary, while the other appeared to be making stabbing motions.

Kelly flipped on the floodlights, but they couldn't penetrate the dense smoke. Tim concentrated on the ground mapping radar and FLIR as he began a gradual descent.

Kelly glanced back at me from the copilot seat. "Pull your belts tight."

About fifty yards out, the ground mapping radar painted a horizontal protrusion ahead, but it was only a few feet above the waterline as we descended through twenty feet. The ground-mapping mode couldn't pick up thin obstacles, which is why we never saw the forty-foot mast on the derelict sailboat driven into the shallows during the last hurricane.

There was no warning when the helicopter impacted the mast between the left float and the cabin, shearing off the pontoon and snapping my head forward. I tasted blood from biting my tongue, but my five-point harness held me firmly in place on the center back seat.

The abrupt collision, combined with our forward speed, thrust us into a nosedive. So close to the water, there was no time to fully recover, and the rotor blades impacted the lake and broke apart. Metal shards knifed through the marsh like deadly machetes, some pieces skipping across the surface.

The windshield cracked and muck splattered over it as our ride whipped around on the right float, violently spinning through a forward trajectory. The pontoon dug into the mud ten feet from the biplane and brought us to a sudden stop, sending water cascading over the muddy windshield, cleaning it. The buried float acted like a brace that held the cabin above the shallow waterline.

The men weren't moving. I released my seat harness and crawled forward. Tim's head bled from where it had slammed against the right-side window. Kelly's head was in the same condition after impacting the left side. Too bad the five-point harnesses couldn't hold their heads in place.

I squeezed their shoulders and yelled, "Wake up, guys!"

No response.

I checked their pulses, which were strong, then looked past them through the windshield. The force of the crash had temporarily opened the smoke curtain. Somehow, the chopper's floodlights survived and illuminated my uncle in the swirling smoke battling a giant snake that had wrapped around him.

Time was critical, but first I had to deal with dozens of alligators crowded around the accident site. There were so many, they didn't have time to escape after our helicopter skidded onto the scene.

Past Navy combat experience kicked in, switching my persona into fierce warrior mode.

I flung open the side door and shot the six biggest gators between me and my uncle. I peppered the smaller ones with rounds from the rifle before leaving it on the back seat and closing the door to keep the men inside safe.

The water was knee-deep where I jumped in and slogged toward my worst fear—a huge snake. I hoped I'd never have to face another giant reptile after the king cobra at Valhalla Castle a few months ago.

Forget it. Must save Hunter!

Moving as fast as possible in the muck and weeds and shooting reptiles on the way, I barely discerned the inverted biplane in the dense smoke. The noxious air triggered a coughing fit, so I pulled my shirt up over my nose and mouth.

After I reached Hunter, I holstered my pistol and drew my knife. The snake attacking him was enormous, and I momentarily froze.

Barely able to breathe, he choked out, "Cut off its head."

Terrified, I grabbed the snake's neck. *He can't hurt me while he's busy killing my uncle.*

The snake's fangs were buried in Hunter's left shoulder, and its body was wrapped around him, squeezing the life out of him. Desperate, I sawed on its thick neck, eventually cutting off its head. It was as if the snake's muscles had a mind of their own, maintaining their powerful grip a little longer. I wasn't sure where to cut next when the entire carcass suddenly released and slid into the marsh.

My uncle collapsed, gasping.

"I'll check if your ribs are broken," I said, sheathing my knife and sliding my hands over his wet body. "I can't find any breaks, but some bones might be cracked."

He wheezed and struggled to fill his lungs with air as he squeezed my arm and croaked, "Klaus—trapped upside down."

"I'll need help. Tim and Kelly got knocked out during the crash, but their pulses are strong, and I'm hoping they can help us after they wake up."

"Did you call in our location to Search and Rescue?" He wheezed again.

"There wasn't time. The snake was killing you." I pressed my finger against his carotid. His pulse was weak, and his skin was clammy—shock. "Your shoulder is bleeding. Are you strong enough to wade with me to the chopper? I'll tend your wound, wrap you in a blanket, and keep you warm."

"Behind you!" he gasped.

I turned, drew my Glock, and blasted a huge gator. It was on the same side where the snake parts had dropped into the water. Seconds later, a feeding frenzy began.

"Good. All the dead stuff will keep them occupied." I put my arm around him. "Let's get you inside the chopper so I can work on saving Klaus. We have cell phones, a SAT phone, comm radios, and an Emergency Locator Beacon on board. I'll make sure the rescue squad and Tim's men know where to find us."

It was only ten feet to the wrecked helicopter and another few paces around it to the passenger door. I held the pistol in my right hand and used my left arm to support Hunter. As we struggled through the shallows, the floodlights reflected off dozens of glowing yellow eyes staring at us through the swirling smoke.

———

One of the retired SEALs guarding Valhalla Castle took Mike aside. "We have a situation."

Mike glanced back at the group waiting for word on the rescue. "What happened?"

"We lost radio contact with the chopper, and nobody is answering their phones."

Mike steeled himself. "Do you guys have a backup plan?"

The guard nodded. "This will be a coordinated, all-hands-on-deck mission, and we'll need your help."

"Anything—name it." Mike tried not to think that Jett might be injured or worse.

"We can't leave the people here unprotected, so I'm asking you to assign two cops to patrol the grounds while you and another officer keep watch over everyone inside."

Mike jutted out his chin. "I'll assign men to protect the house and grounds, but I'm coming with you. That's *my* woman out there."

"How long will it take to get your men in position here?"

"Thirty minutes, tops, but how will you locate the crash sites?"

"Our company has a large airboat ready to go, and we know exactly where they are. All our vehicles and people are fitted with GPS locators."

Mike's cell rang, and caller ID indicated it was Jett calling. "Jett, thank God! Are you okay?" He tapped "speaker" so the man next to him could hear, and everyone crowded around them.

"I'm good, but our helicopter hit a sailboat's mast and crashed close to the biplane wreck." She explained that Tim, Kelly, and Hunter were injured but safe inside the chopper's cabin, and that Klaus was in extreme peril, trapped upside down in the forward cockpit with dozens of hungry gators closing in.

The guard said, "Tell us about Klaus. What needs to be done to get him out?"

"The steel-tube fuselage buckled around him. His seat harness is holding him a couple inches above water, and the seat is bolted to the floor tubing. The fastest way to keep him from drowning is to take him out through the side. Cut off the fabric and saw through the side brace, unbuckle his seat harness and parachute, and pull him out quick." She paused. "We have the necessary tools in the chopper, but I need strong guys for this, and time is critical. He's in shock and won't last much longer."

Mike said, "We have your GPS location, and we're coming for you in an airboat. Are you in the helicopter with the men?"

"No, I'm straddling the biplane's fuselage, guarding Klaus. I'm worried gators will attack him." Her tone rose two octaves. "Hurry. They're closing in."

Sophia tapped Mike's shoulder. "Gwen, Karin, and I are armed. We'll protect the people here while you go and rescue them. Save the men and bring our girl back safe."

The guard smiled and checked his watch. "Wheels up from Jett's backyard in ten."

"I'll be ready in five. My house is a block away." Mike rushed out the door.

———

The instant the skids touched the pavement in the marina's parking lot, Mike leaped out of the helicopter with four combat-hardened veterans, and they jogged to the long pier. A thirty-foot airboat equipped with GPS navigation, radar, FLIR, and electronic depth sensors idled at the end with several men on board looking combat-ready.

A grizzled man with a scruffy gray beard fished from a lawn chair on the pier. He shouted to the departing men, "You boys best watch out fer Nessie—a green anaconda longer than yer boat—seen her swim-min' serpent-like in the lake."

Mike nodded. "*Right.*"

The guy next to him said, "Huge green anacondas have been spotted in this area and farther south."

Mike shook his head. "Great, just what we need along with hundreds of gators."

The other guy laughed and checked his combat knife as their boat approached a thick wall of smoke blanketing the southwestern portion of the lake.

Someone handed Mike a smoke mask. "Thanks," he said, fitting it to his face.

He watched as the airboat pilot spotted the derelict sailboat on his ground radar and forward depth finder, slowed, and navigated around it. On the other side, the FLIR screen painted five warm bodies—three inside the chopper's cabin and two farther away. The pilot maneuvered the boat between the wrecked helicopter and the inverted biplane.

The powerful fan engine on the airboat cleared the smoke enough for Mike to spot Jett holding a rifle while seated atop the plane's belly with Klaus hanging beneath her. She recognized him and waved, her mouth and nose covered with her wet shirt.

Someone on the boat pointed a floodlight at her, and an enormous anaconda rose up behind her.

"Jett, behind you!" Mike yelled.

SEVENTEEN

I turned with my rifle pointed upward, and a monstrous snake tried to bite my head. The barrel went into its gaping mouth, and its curved fangs caught on the scope as I pulled the trigger again and again. Face to face with the biggest snake I'd ever seen, I gasped for breath with my mouth and nose under my wet shirt. My heart jackhammered my chest as I emptied the magazine into the serpent's head.

It felt like the monster was trying to jerk the weapon out of my hands and retreat, which had to be impossible after all the holes I'd blown through the back of its skull.

Mike wrapped his arms around me. "Let go of the weapon, Jett."

I released my grip, and the bloody head and almost forty-foot body were dragged backward, pulled by several gators who'd chomped onto sections of its vast length. They engaged in a tug-of-war to see who would claim the prize.

I choked, "Get us out of this smoky netherworld."

Lifting me into his arms, Mike said, "The team will free Klaus now." He slid off the fuselage and carried me onto the airboat where he wrapped me in a blanket.

Peering at the wrecked chopper, I said, "We have to help the guys in there."

"Paramedics are already checking them. Once von Helsig is freed, we'll motor back to where two helicopters will fly the injured to a trauma hospital."

Using a Sawzall, the men cut away the fabric and steel tubing and extricated Klaus in under a minute. Meanwhile, paramedics shuttled Hunter, Tim, and Kelly onto the airboat. The two former SEALs were awake but had bloody head wounds—all because they volunteered to help me save my uncle, who was barely conscious.

Klaus was carried on board, and someone yelled, "He's not breathing."

They laid him flat on the deck, and paramedics began CPR. They applied the portable cardiac paddles to his bare chest and yelled, "Clear!"

I watched anxiously as his torso heaved upward with each jolt.

After a few tries, one of the medics said, "I've got a pulse. Start the IV."

The boat captain nudged me. "Do we have all the crash victims?"

"We're good," I said, coughing. "Time to leave this horror show."

Those were my last words for a while because someone strapped an oxygen mask to my face. We raced across the lake through the darkness and smoke, waves slapping the hull and spraying my face with lake water. Halfway to the marina, we broke through the smoke curtain and continued in clear air. Grateful, I gazed up at the star-filled sky and prayed silently for the injured men.

After we docked, Mike said, "I want you to go in one of the choppers and get checked out. I'll drive back and meet you in the ER."

It was obvious from his tone that objecting would be pointless, and I wanted to stick close to my uncle, so I hopped into the open front seat on the bird carrying Hunter and Klaus. The pilot punched 64FD into the GPS, which guided us to St. Mary's Hospital Heliport, the location of the nearest trauma unit.

Fear knotted my gut during the landing as I worried about whether it took too long to rescue everyone. Would my uncle and friends survive? In seconds, both men were strapped onto stretchers and wheeled inside. A nurse stuck me in a wheelchair and followed close behind them. Inside, we were separated so the men could undergo various tests and treatments.

Tim and Kelly were brought in on the other helicopter and whisked away to check for concussions and brain bleeds. If I hadn't agreed to host Mystery Fest at Valhalla, none of this would've happened. I prayed again for everyone's recovery.

An ER doctor pronounced me healthy and kindly let me take a hot shower and change into clean surgical scrubs in the doctors' locker room.

I dried my hair and called Sophia, who brought me clothes and shoes. She, Gwen, and Karin arranged for Banyan Isle Police Officers to protect the castle guests so they could wait with me. Mike was miles away in a Hummer, and it would take him an hour to join us.

Pacing in the waiting room, I explained in a tense tone, "ER docs are running tests on them."

"But they're going to be okay, right?" Karin asked, fear showing in her eyes.

"I sure hope so." I blinked away a tear. "When I saw my uncle with that huge snake wrapped around him—"

"That must've been terrifying," Sophia said, trying to hide her anxiety. "I know how you feel about snakes."

I shuddered. "I had to put aside my fear and focus on saving Hunter."

Time seemed to stand still as we made small talk. Then a middle-aged man in scrubs breezed through the waiting-room door. We stood.

The doctor glanced at his clipboard and said, "Who's here for Hunter Vann, Klaus von Helsig, Tim Goldy, and Kelly Mahone?"

We crowded around him, and I said, "We are."

"Family?"

"Yes. How are they?" Gwen asked, bending the truth about family.

"Mr. Vann has bruised ribs, deep puncture wounds, and inflamed lungs, but he'll be released tomorrow and should heal in a couple weeks." He checked the clipboard. "Von Helsig has a concussion, trauma from the crash, lung inflammation, bite wounds in his hand, and cardiac issues. We'll keep him under observation another day or two." Another glance at the info in his hand. "The other men have mild concussions and minor head wounds, and they'll go home midday tomorrow."

"May we see them now?" Sophia asked.

"You can visit Vann, Goldy, and Mahone up on four, but von Helsig is in the ICU. He'll be moved to a private room later."

We thanked him and rushed up to the fourth floor where we found Hunter in room 402 and smothered him with kisses. He smiled through the oxygen mask and reached for us.

I stroked his cheek. "Are you hurting?"

He pulled the mask aside. "No pain. They put something in my IV."

"I was terrified I'd lose you—especially after I saw that huge python." I hugged him gently. "Don't ever scare me like that again."

"If you hadn't come when you did, I'd be snake food now. Thanks, Jett." He took a breath of O2. "The others?"

Sophia and Karin fluffed his pillow and gave him ice water while I answered, "Klaus was the worst. His heart stopped briefly, but paramedics got it going again." I gave him the full report on all three men.

He removed his oxygen again. "Klaus might be the killer. He talked about karma and said his bad deeds had come back to punish him."

"Did he confess to killing Edmund and Fiona?" Sophia asked.

"No, I tried to find out what he meant, but he blacked out."

"We'll ask him tomorrow," Sophia said. "I can't have the Feds falsely accusing Aldo."

I glanced at Hunter's electronic screen. His heartbeats looked steady, and his pulse and blood pressure readings were normal. "Don't count on Klaus confessing. Now that he knows he's not dying, he'll deny saying anything about his karma."

My uncle nodded. "I missed the opportunity for a confession. Sorry."

I patted his hand. "No worries. We'll keep a close watch on him after he returns to the castle." I stepped back so Gwen could move closer.

"He might not be the killer." Hunter reached for Gwen and grasped her hand. "There's something else." He paused and took another hit of oxygen. "Someone might've planted a bomb in the engine compartment with a timer that started with the engine. Ask Palm Beach County's Bomb Squad to search for it."

I shook my head. "The FAA will seal off the crash site and take jurisdiction."

"Screw the FAA," he said. "That crash could have been the result of attempted murder."

Gwen's persona as a Palm Beach Homicide Detective kicked in. "Wait a minute. Are you saying now that Klaus isn't the killer, and someone tried to blow him up?"

Another O2 hit. "It's possible. All the conference guests heard me say which plane we'd fly, where it was kept, and what day and time we were going."

I nodded. "If it was a guest at the castle, they had a few days to plan the sabotage and hire an expert to do it."

Sophia sat beside him. "So, either Klaus is the killer, or the real murderer decided to take him out?" Her eyes lit up. "Or Klaus killed one victim, and whoever killed the other one decided to kill him too."

"But why do you think there was a bomb?" Gwen asked Hunter.

"After Klaus added power at the beginning of a loop, the explosion seemed too extreme for a normal engine failure," he explained. "The device was timed for when we'd be in the designated practice zone, which is over an isolated area."

"Oh, geez, I never called Ben." I pulled out my cell. "I was so worried about you, I forgot to tell him we found you."

"Who's Ben?" Sophia asked.

"He's the guy who owns the wrecked biplane." I bit my lip. "I hate giving him bad news."

"I'll tell him," Hunter offered.

"No, you should get back on oxygen. I'll put my cell on speaker so you can hear our conversation." I called Ben.

"Jett, any word on Hunter?" He sounded anxious.

I filled him in on everything that happened. "I'm sorry about your airplane. It's possible an explosive device was planted to kill the German guy who flew with Hunter."

"That seems a bit farfetched. The engine probably swallowed a valve."

"After the smoke clears, the Sheriff's Office will check for bomb residue."

"I guess the important thing is nobody was seriously injured." He was silent a moment. "My insurance might not cover damage caused by sabotage. I need to know if they find any evidence of tampering."

"As soon as I hear anything, I'll text you." I pocketed my phone.

Gwen stepped away to call the Palm Beach County Sheriff's Office. When she returned, she said, "The double-crash site will be crowded tomorrow with FAA and NTSB investigators and the PBSO Bomb Squad. And since Klaus is a foreign national and foul play is suspected, FBI agents will want in, especially if the accident might be connected to the murders at the castle."

"The more eyes on it the better." I checked my watch. "I'll look in on Tim and Kelly before we head home." As I walked down the hall, I wondered if one of the Mystery Fest guests had tried to kill Klaus and my uncle.

EIGHTEEN

Hunter, Tim, and Kelly were scheduled for discharge at noon, so I swung by my uncle's place and packed some clothes and toiletries for him to use at my house. I drove to the hospital and parked at 11:15 a.m. so I'd have time to visit Klaus. He'd been moved to a private room earlier.

I rapped on his door and walked in.

He pulled his oxygen mask aside and coughed. "Jett, good to see you."

I sat beside his bed and took his good hand. "How are you feeling?"

"Better—my lungs are irritated from the smoke, but the oxygen and drugs are helping." He held up his bandaged left hand. "A small gator bit me, and I still have a lump from hitting my head on the front panel." He coughed again and took a hit of O2.

"Do you remember what caused the crash?"

"*Ja,* the engine exploded after I added power for a loop." He put the mask on.

"Any chance there could've been a bomb in the engine?"

His eyes widened and he pulled aside the oxygen mask. "A bomb! You think someone tried to kill me?" He coughed and replaced the O2.

"It's one possibility. I'll know more after the bomb squad searches the wreckage."

He pressed a button to raise his back higher, and he lifted his mask. "I don't feel safe here. I'd rather be at the castle with my friends and your guards looking out for me."

"I'll come and get you as soon as it's medically safe for you to leave the hospital. In the meantime, focus on your treatments so you can recover quickly." I patted his hand and left him my cell number.

I hurried down to my car and pulled up as a nurse brought Hunter curbside in a wheelchair. I hopped out and opened the passenger door of my SUV. "You're coming home with me so my roommates and I can look after you while you recuperate."

He crossed his arms. "Thanks, but I can take care of myself."

"Karin will be disappointed. She was counting on you staying in her room while she catered to your every need."

That got his attention. "I suppose I could stay a few days." He slid onto the front passenger seat.

Tim and Kelly were wheeled out the front door and immediately hopped out of the wheelchairs. Their heads were bandaged on opposite sides.

I waved. "Hey, guys, would you like to spend a few days at my house? We'll take excellent care of you."

"Thanks, Jett, but we're good to go." Tim gestured behind me. "Our ride is here."

"Okay, but don't forget to give me a list of expenses for the wrecked helicopter, the manpower and equipment used for the rescue, and your medical bills. I can't thank you enough for helping save my uncle, and I'm really sorry you were injured."

"Just doing our job." Tim gave me a brief hug and nodded at Hunter.

Kelly smiled. "We were happy to help, and don't worry. We're fine now." He waved at my uncle and joined his boss in their company's black Hummer.

We made small talk on the drive home. Then I parked in front of the castle, and we entered the foyer. Karin and Sophia hugged Hunter, and the dogs greeted him.

He paused and looked up at the ten-foot Valkyrie statues guarding the twin staircases. "They look like they're about to whisk me away to the real Valhalla."

"Not on my watch. I need you." Though I grew up around the awesome winged women, I still found them a bit intimidating.

Karin kissed him. "They almost took you last night in that marsh, but you're way too young for Warrior Heaven."

Sophia quipped, "They wouldn't take him anyway." She rolled her eyes. "I didn't mean he's not worthy, but he's all Cherokee, not half Viking like Jett."

"Relax, ladies. The Great Hunting Ground in the sky can wait too." He squeezed Karin's waist. "What's for lunch? I'm starved—hospital food makes me nauseous."

"Anything you want, darling," Karin said. "Your wish is my command."

He grinned. "I like the sound of that. How about a juicy burger and some chips?"

"I'll take his bag up to Karin's room and meet you guys on the terrace." I grabbed the handle on his roller case and headed for the elevator behind the north staircase. Karin's quarters were in the north wing on the top floor.

By the time I made it downstairs and outside, Hunter was drinking beer at a round, glass-topped table that overlooked the ocean, and Karin, Sophia, and Mike were with him. My dogs reclined at Sophia's feet. An overhanging roof provided shade from the hot, midday sun, and a warm sea breeze flowed over the terrace.

Mike patted an empty chair beside him. "I saved you a seat."

I gave him a quick kiss and slid onto the chair. Chilled pitchers of beer and iced tea flanked a huge bowl of potato chips. I poured myself a glass of iced tea and grabbed a chip.

Mike put his arm around me. "How are your lungs?"

"A little cough every now and then. Hunter and Klaus were in the smoke much longer." Before I had a chance to say more, the kitchen staff served our burgers on toasted buns with all the fixings.

Sophia scanned the sky. "Good—those noisy news helicopters have stopped their daily vigil here and moved to the crash site. It's good to have peace and quiet again."

"Yeah, let's hope it stays that way—no more murders." Mike bit into his hamburger.

After enjoying a few bites, Hunter said, "I guess we'll find out later today if the plane was rigged with an explosive device. The bomb squad is searching the site now."

Mike stiffened and turned to me. "Nobody said anything about a bomb."

"Sorry, but by the time you arrived at the hospital, I was too tired to go into it." I told him what we suspected and why.

"Well, crap. I thought the murders had stopped."

"It's only a suspicion until PBSO completes their search." I sipped my cold drink.

My phone dinged with a text from Gwen: *Coming to see you.*

Fifteen minutes later, Gwen strode onto the terrace, and she wasn't smiling. She sat between Sophia and me. "An investigator at the crash site called. They found remnants of a bomb and detonator, and they're trying to nail down where the components were purchased."

Mike pulled out his cell and called Tim. He put the phone on speaker. "How are you today?"

"I'm good. What's up?"

Mike told him about the bomb. "Your guards are keeping records of anyone who leaves the castle—the dates and times they go out and return, right?"

"We keep a detailed record, as requested. What do you need?"

"Did any of the guests go out during the four days before today?"

"Hang on a sec." After a brief pause, Tim said, "Aldo's bodyguard, Nico Bernardi, left two days ago at two-fifteen p.m. and was gone four hours. That same day, Gaspar's bodyguard, Jorge Santos, departed at two-thirty for four and a half hours. No one else went anywhere until yesterday when Jett drove Klaus to Hunter's place."

"What about movements within the castle at night?"

"Let's see, four nights ago, Gaspar was in Natalya's room, Klaus was with Fiona, and several American women tried to get into Aldo's room at various hours. His bodyguard intercepted them." He paused a moment. "Same thing three nights ago, then the night before last Natalya slept with Klaus, Dina Fenton tried without success to enter Gaspar's room, and, uh, Aldo slept in Sophia's room. Basically, we're talking a lot of bed hopping every night. Shall I continue?"

"I get the picture. Thanks for the info, Tim, and make sure the guards continue to keep track of all the comings and goings." Mike pocketed his phone.

Sophia slinked down in her seat when we all looked at her. "What? I waited twenty years, but I couldn't let those women get their hooks into my Aldo. We're all adults. Get over it."

Mike suppressed a chuckle. "I did background checks on everyone at the castle after the first murder." Mike checked his electronic tablet. "Nico Bernardi served in Italy's Special Forces, COMSUBIN, which stands for *Comando Subacquei ed Incursori*. It's their version of Navy SEALs. He put in twenty years, retired, and took the job with Aldo."

"That means he had experience with explosives." Gwen glanced at Sophia. "Sorry."

"What about Gaspar's bodyguard?" I asked.

Mike checked his notes. "Jorge Santos served in Spain's FGNE, *Fuerza de Guerra Naval Especial*, which is their SEALs. He also put in twenty years before retiring and taking the job with Gaspar."

"Aha!" Sophia said. "That proves Jorge knew how to blow stuff up."

Finished with his meal, Hunter joined in. "Did one of those men act alone, or did he do it for his employer? Either the bomber had a motive, or his employer did."

Karin patted her lips with a napkin. "Or neither man did it, and we need to check if someone else could've hired an explosives expert."

"True," I agreed. "Just because Nico and Jorge have experience with explosives doesn't mean they're guilty of anything. And it's quite a leap from Special Forces soldier to hired killer."

"Don't forget Natalya," Sophia said. "She'd know how to hire the right person to sabotage the plane. She could have contacts in the Russian Mob, and they have a large network in Florida."

"Yeah, but Aldo and Gaspar could have connections with the Italian/American Mob here," Mike said. "My research indicated both their families go way back with the Mafia in Sicily and Naples."

Gwen sat back and looked at my uncle. "You're all so focused on the murders here you're assuming the bomb was meant for Klaus. What if it had nothing to do with the conference guests, and it was meant for Hunter?"

"*Me?*" Hunter's forehead wrinkled. "Why would anyone want to kill me?"

"You tell us," Gwen said. "Do you have any enemies? Perhaps a vengeful woman or a jealous man?"

"Nope, nothing like that, and I get along well with everyone at work."

"What about neighbors at Aerodrome Estates?" Mike asked. "Any conflicts there?"

He hesitated. "A married couple bought the house across the street from me six months ago. The husband is a retired Marine Colonel who owns a construction company. He's at least twenty years older than his trophy wife, and she's constantly flirting with me." He glanced at Karin. "I'm polite, but I never encourage her. The husband blames me anyway."

"Sugar buns, women are attracted to you like flies to honey," Sophia said. "That's not your fault."

"Tell that to Tracy Kincaid's husband, Ken. He glares hatred every time he sees me."

"A guy who owns a construction company would have access to explosives, but unless you slept with his wife, he doesn't have a strong enough motive to kill you," I said.

Hunter ran his hand through his thick black hair. "Trust me, she's not my type, and besides, I never mess with another man's woman."

"Well, *somebody* planted that bomb, and the spirits at the séance indicated all the foreign guests are murderers," Sophia said.

"Right, but the spirits also implied nine guests would be murdered like the title of that Chinese novel, *A Strange Case of Nine Murders*." I nudged Mike. "Have the Feds dug up anything useful?"

"If they did, they didn't tell me." Mike frowned. "Last night, I notified them about the crash, but working with them is mostly a one-way street that ends at the FBI's field office in Miami."

"I don't suppose that little snot from London has uncovered anything helpful." The words had no sooner left my mouth when Neville burst onto the terrace.

Edith, Amelia, Gaspar, Natalya, and Aldo trailed him.

"Ah, there you are." Neville strode to our table. "Any news on Baron von Helsig's condition?"

Mike answered, "I checked with his doctor an hour ago. Klaus is doing well and will be back here by midday tomorrow. His lungs are irritated from the smoke, he had a minor head injury and concussion from the accident, and he needed antibiotics and a few stitches for a gator bite on his hand. His heart attack was caused by prolonged shock, but it's beating normally now. The doc said he's strong, in good spirits, and eager to return here."

The group crowded around Hunter, and Natalya asked, "Why did you crash?"

He shot a glance at Mike and said, "The engine quit, and I had to descend through heavy smoke into zero visibility. After we landed, the biplane flipped upside down in a marsh." He took a drink. "Klaus was trapped in the forward cockpit, and dozens of alligators closed in."

"Yeah, and a giant python attacked Hunter, but Jett saved him." Sophia smiled sweetly at Aldo.

"Sounds like they had quite an adventure," Aldo said. "I'm glad everyone survived."

My *Aniwaya* intuition tingled as I tried to read their faces and discern if one of them looked disappointed no one died.

NINETEEN

T he two FBI agents showed up next. They singled out Aldo, his bodyguard, Nico, Gaspar, his bodyguard, Jorge, and Natalya for interrogations. Mike insisted on sitting in. So did Neville. That meant they'd be busy for a few hours.

I took Karin and Sophia aside. "I'm counting on both of you to protect Hunter and take care of him while I'm gone."

A deep male voice behind me said, "Going somewhere, Jett?"

I turned and faced Tim. "Hunter's hangar to ask if anyone spotted someone messing with the Bücker."

He stared at me for a beat. "I'm coming with you."

"Why? You think I need protecting?"

"Always." He smiled. "We'll take my Hummer. It's bulletproof."

I raised an eyebrow. "I'm never sure if you're joking."

Another smile. "Let's go."

His civilian tank was parked out front beside Odin's fountain. The fifteen-foot bronze statue stood with his sword held high, surrounded by four fanged wolves, their open mouths spewing water toward the cardinal points of a compass. I climbed aboard the black behemoth.

As he drove down the long driveway, he glanced at me. "What are you hoping to find?"

I brought him up to speed on the suspects. "I'm hoping somebody out there will recognize one of them."

We pulled up to the entry gate thirty minutes later. The guard looked inside the Hummer and spotted me. "Hi, Miss Jorgensen. Visiting Mr. Vann today?"

"This is my friend and security expert, Tim Goldy. We're stopping by the hangar to search for evidence on who sabotaged Ben Foster's biplane. It crashed last night."

"Oh no, is Ben okay?"

"Hunter was flying it with a friend." I gave him a few details. "Do you have a record of who passed through here the past few days?"

"Sorry, we don't keep written records."

The guard waved us through. My uncle's hangar home faced the main runway at Aerodrome Estates. A full-time mechanic named Bill Hill worked in the shop at the back of Hunter's flight school and aircraft maintenance facility.

"Let's go ask his mechanic if he saw someone in the hangar the other day." I led Tim to the repair shop.

Bill was bent over a workbench and stood after we walked in. "Hey, Jett, I heard about the accident. How's Hunter doing?"

I filled him in. "Did you see any strangers here in the past couple of days?"

He rubbed his chin. "Day before yesterday, Hunter was away working an airline flight, and I was busy rebuilding an engine in the shop. We don't lock the doors if one of us is here. As I walked through the hangar at the end of my workday, I spotted a guy with dark hair leaving. I called to him, but he didn't stop. I rushed after him, but by the time I reached the door, he was gone." He shrugged. "I checked the hangar—everything looked normal."

Tim brought up a photo of Nico on his phone and showed Bill. "Did he look like this? He's about five-ten."

He studied the picture. "Could be him—same height and hair color, but I didn't see his face."

"What about this guy? Also five-ten." Tim showed him a photo of Jorge.

"Huh, could be either one. Like I said, I only saw him from behind at a distance. Sorry I can't be more help."

"You might've been more help than you know. We'll check with the neighbors in case one of them saw him too." I thanked him, and we walked away.

No one was home next door, and the hurricane shutters were closed, implying the occupants might be away for the summer. A house across the street from Hunter's place had an open hangar, and a sign over the door: KINCAID'S HANGAR BAR.

"Uh oh, the guy who lives there hates Hunter—thinks he's messing with his wife, but he isn't."

Tim whispered, "Don't mention your uncle. Instead, tell him Ben Foster's biplane was sabotaged and ask if he saw anyone near it."

Kincaid had a gray crewcut and stood about an inch taller than me —looked fit for a guy in his early sixties. He didn't know I was Hunter's niece when I introduced us, explained why we were there, and asked if he saw anyone suspicious near the Jungmann.

He scratched the back of his head and frowned. "Yeah, yesterday that horny Indian who lives above there pulled the plane out, and an hour later he flew it with some guy."

"What about earlier? Any strangers in that hangar yesterday or the day before?" Tim asked.

Ken hesitated. "I saw a guy the day before yesterday, late afternoon. He was my height and had dark hair. Only saw his profile from a distance. He drove away in a black pickup."

Tim showed him photos of Nico and Jorge. "Was it one of these guys?"

He studied the men. "It's possible. Same hair and build."

"I don't suppose you got the license number?" I asked.

"No, but it was a Florida plate."

Tim handed him a business card. "Thanks for your help. If you spot him again, give me a call."

We tried a few other nearby homes, but no one had seen anything useful.

"Mike might be finished with the interrogations. Let's go back and ask if he learned something about the killer." I pulled open the passenger door on the big Hummer and hopped in.

Tim dropped me off thirty minutes later, and the Mystery Fest attendees were waiting for me in the great hall.

Edith spoke for the group. "Jett, people are anxious about their safety after two murders and an attempted one. The FBI refuses to allow anyone to go home. What can we do?"

"You could double up in the rooms at night if that will make you feel safer."

Dina Fenton rolled her eyes. "Most of us are kinda doing that already."

I did my best not to smile. "You need something to take your minds off the murders. We're holding a dinner dance in the ballroom tonight, and the band is excellent. Have some fun." I gave them a reassuring smile. "Meanwhile, local law enforcement, the FBI, and Scotland Yard are hard at work solving the case, and Trident Security has guards watching over you."

A woman stepped forward. "What's the attire for this evening?"

"Semi-formal, but the dinner-dance cruise on the final night will be formal, like the previous conferences." Edith checked her watch. "We have one more panel here in the great hall, and afterward, an hour and a half break before the festivities in the ballroom."

I slipped away and looked for Mike. He was in the hallway near the study and hurried toward me.

"We need to talk." He took my hand.

We went outside, took the walkway toward the ocean, and headed for the shaded lawn under huge banyan trees. A briny breeze washed over us as we passed oleander bushes covered with bright pink flowers. A side path took us to a shaded bench beside a bubbling birdbath.

Bursting with curiosity, I asked, "Anything new on the case?"

He slid beside me. "Aldo's bodyguard, Nico, claims he went to Tiffany's on Worth Avenue in Palm Beach to pick up a diamond tennis bracelet Aldo bought for Sophia. Said he plans to give it to her tonight at the dance. Nico also bought fine cigars for him from a guy he knows who sells Cubans."

"But Aldo quit smoking. He uses vape pens."

"It's not really smoking if all he does is puff on them. Nico said his boss never inhales the cigar smoke."

"Okay, but it doesn't take four hours to pick up a bracelet and buy some cigars."

"He also spent time with a call girl in Palm Beach. The Feds asked a PB detective to verify his alibi. Apparently, they know the woman, and she admitted Nico spent a little over two hours with her—a gift from Aldo."

"What about Gaspar's bodyguard?"

"Jorge was sent to a polo club in Wellington to deliver a case of high-end Scotch to the club owner as a thank you for loaning Gaspar the polo ponies for the exhibition match on your beach."

"That wouldn't take more than an hour and a half, assuming he chatted with the owner. What was he doing the other three hours?"

"He said he was bored at the castle and took the opportunity to drive around and enjoy being out on his own."

"So, no alibi. He could have acquired the components and planted the bomb."

"Good luck proving it. And Natalya laughed in our faces. She gave us nothing."

"Did you talk to Aldo and Gaspar?"

"Of course. Both denied any Mafia connections and insisted Klaus is a good friend. We have no hard evidence to the contrary, so we've got zilch."

I checked my watch. "The dinner dance starts in two hours. I hope you'll be there. No telling what might happen, and I don't want to be stuck dancing with the aging playboys."

Mike leaned in and gave me a lingering kiss. "I'll protect you tonight—all night."

I got his meaning and smiled. "I'll look forward to it."

My cell rang. It was Karin.

"Jett, Sophia is missing!"

My call to Sophia's cell went straight to voicemail. Mike and I hurried to the kitchen and found Karin. The scents of several chateaubriands roasting in the ovens wafted over me, stirring my stomach juices. My dogs were curled up in their beds in a corner, but the instant I walked in, they woke and ran over to greet me.

"Karin, are you sure Sophia is missing?" I held off my dogs while I waited for her response.

"My staff can't find her anywhere in the castle, she doesn't answer her cell, and she isn't with Aldo. He's attending a workshop in the great hall. If she were out on the grounds, she would've taken the pups with her."

The thought of her being hurt or worse made me feel sick inside. I grabbed her windbreaker off a wall peg and held it under my dogs' noses. "Find Sophia."

Noses to the floor, they led us through the castle to the front door.

"Where's Sophia? Outside?" I asked them.

Both dogs barked and nudged the door handle with their noses. Mike opened the door, and they rushed outside. The scent trail led us to my ten-car garage, so we looked inside. Her sedan was missing. The pups sat beside her empty parking space and peered up at me.

Mike pulled out his cell and called the front gate. "Did Sophia DeLuca drive out recently?" He listened. "Was anyone with her?" Another pause. "Okay, thank you." He pocketed his phone. "The guard said she drove out alone about an hour ago."

"That's not like her to leave without telling anyone. Maybe Aldo knows where she went." I glanced at my watch. "His afternoon workshop is almost finished."

We returned to the castle and waited outside the great hall until the Crime Solving Workshop wrapped up. The group filed out, chatting excitedly, and headed toward the twin staircases and elevator.

We intercepted Aldo, and I asked, "Have you seen Sophia?"

"Not since lunch, why?"

I held my phone. "She's not answering her cell."

He glanced from Mike to me. "Think something happened to her?"

"We're not sure." I pocketed my phone.

We walked into the foyer, and Sophia breezed through the entrance door with a dress bag over her arm.

She held it up. "I found this beauty at The Little Black Dress Boutique over on Main Street." She smiled at Aldo. "I'll meet you in the ballroom later for some dining and dancing, sugar buns."

"My dear, you didn't answer your phone. We were worried."

"The battery's dead because a certain someone distracted me last night, and I forgot to charge it."

"You almost gave me a heart attack, disappearing like that." I hugged her.

"Sorry, but you're too young for a coronary, and I wanted the right dress for tonight." She grinned. "Now if you'll excuse me, I need to get ready." She zipped upstairs to her room on the second floor.

Mike squeezed my waist. "I think I felt a few hairs turning gray at my temples. See any?"

"No, but I may have acquired some wrinkles." I tilted my head back. "Any there?"

He grinned. "Nope, looks like we made it through this little crisis unscathed."

"Time to dress for the dinner dance. I'll meet you in the ballroom in an hour."

He pulled me in for a lingering kiss, then sauntered out the front door.

TWENTY

I strolled into the ballroom wearing a low-cut, red silk cocktail dress and spotted Kelly sporting a tuxedo. "Hey, you're looking hot. What brings you here?"

"I'm surprised you have to ask, considering a body was dropped in the pool the last time you held a dance." He guided me to one side. "Any news on the bomber?"

"Plenty of potential suspects, but no hard evidence." I glanced around. "Are you expecting another murder attempt tonight?"

"At *your* house? Anything and everything's possible. Tim and I are circulating among the guests. We'll dance with single women while scanning the crowd."

"You'd better gird your loins. *All* the women here are single except Edith." I laughed. "These wealthy cougars are aggressive sharks ready to devour handsome young men. It'll be a feeding frenzy."

"*Really*, Jett?" He arched an eyebrow. "We're experienced Special Operators. We can handle randy older women."

"Have you forgotten what happened during the bachelor auction at my charity ball?"

"Oh…right. No matter. We'll deal with it."

"Here comes one now." I grinned. "Good luck."

Natalya sashayed over. "Hello, Jett, your security men are looking debonair this evening. Kelly, isn't it?"

He nodded. "You look ravishing in black silk, Natalya."

"Thank you, darling. Let's dance." She took his arm and pulled him onto the floor.

Sophia strolled in on Aldo's arm, looking like royalty in a black silk sheath. He radiated Old World elegance in his traditional tux as they settled at a table bordering the dance area and sipped glasses of Cristalle Champagne.

Gaspar intercepted me on my way to them. "Ah, Jett, you look delightfully devilish in that sultry red dress. May I have the pleasure of this dance?" He offered me his hand.

Just my luck, the band began playing a tango. Oh boy. He swept me away with a flourish and led me through every sensual move with practiced perfection. Yipes. I felt like a Stradivarius being played by a world-class violinist. This guy had moves developed from years of practice. International playboy prince indeed.

Mike sauntered in all suave and sexy in a custom-made tuxedo. He spotted me and headed over, arriving as the tango ended.

Gaspar bowed and said to him, "Thank you for allowing me to drive your Ferrari."

He grinned, pulled me into his arms, and said, "My pleasure."

The band played a romantic ballad, and we danced nice and slow with our bodies glued together. I glanced at the giant grandfather clock in the corner. The chateaubriand Béarnaise would be served in a half hour. This was shaping up to be a fun night.

That changed fast.

Someone opened a French door to the wraparound terrace on the east side, and a woman screamed as a ten-foot crocodile clambered inside with my dogs in hot pursuit. Karin rushed in behind them.

Chairs overturned and drinks spilled as guests darted away from the charging reptile. Its thrashing tail knocked over a table and sent glassware and wine bottles crashing to the floor. My dogs trampled through a pool of spilled red wine, leaving red paw prints in their wake. Guests scrambled to evade the deadly reptile.

"Ahhhhh!" A woman yelped as her chair was overturned by its sweeping tail. She sprawled on her back, and Tim helped her up and pulled her to safety.

"Pratt, Whitney, come!" I yelled.

They didn't seem to hear me over their loud barking.

The croc scurried into a corner beside the stage, and the band stopped playing. It turned and snapped its long, toothy jaws at my precious fur babies.

Tim yelled to the crowd, "Get back," as he, Kelly, and Mike moved the guests away from the beast and drew their weapons.

I didn't want my pups caught in the crossfire, so I grabbed the lead-based microphone stand off the stage, pushed past the armed men, and bonked the croc on the head with the heavy base. My first swing made a glancing blow, and it lunged at me. I side-stepped and swung again. The next hit stunned it a little, and my dogs dived in for quick bites that had no effect on its hard hide.

"Jett, move aside so we can shoot it," Mike shouted over the barking dogs.

I ignored him and yelled, "Pratt and Whitney, come!" They backed away, and the croc lunged. I jumped aside and landed another hard blow to its head. Determined to protect my dogs, I hit it again and again.

Meanwhile, my pups were hell-bent on protecting their turf. They kept barking, snarling, and snapping at the reptile.

Apparently, I got a bit carried away with the bonking. Mike snatched the stand from my hands. "That's enough, Jett. You got him."

The dogs snapped at its snout. "No!" I grabbed their collars and pulled them back. "Good doggies."

Behind us, my guests had quickly recovered from the melee and jockeyed for position to snap photos with their cell phones.

Karin was still a bit out of breath. "Jett, sorry about this. I was taking them for a run when they encountered that monster in your backyard. I didn't know we had crocs on the island or that they could move so fast. The dogs chased after it, and somebody opened the door at the wrong moment—"

Breathless, I said, "We don't have crocs on Banyan Isle."

Two uniformed cops entered the open door and stopped when they spotted Mike standing beside the inert intruder.

I quieted Pratt and Whitney so I could hear what they said.

"Sorry, Detective Miller, but remember that weird rock musician who recently bought the mansion two doors down?" an officer asked.

"Yeah, but what's he got to do with this?" Mike thumbed at the reptile.

"Well, he called us and reported that his pet crocodile, Tick-Tock, escaped. He asked us to find it before it attacked one of the neighbors' pets."

"Tell him we *found* it, and it endangered a room full of people and will have to be put down. If he gives you any grief, threaten to charge him with reckless endangerment." He toed the croc. "And haul this reptile out of here."

"Uh, how do we do that?" the other cop asked.

Mike holstered his pistol. "Both of you, grab his tail and drag him outside. Then call Fish and Wildlife to take him away."

With much effort, the cops dragged the heavy crocodile out the door and onto the grass bordering the terrace. As one of the security guys started to close the door, loud yells erupted outdoors followed by gunfire.

Mike squeezed my arm. "Stay here." He drew his Glock 40 and ran outside.

Everyone rushed to the windows. Turned out, the croc wasn't dead. It woke and tried to bite the officers. They yelled and opened fire, peppering the beast with bullets.

Mike took charge and calmed things down. He verified the croc was dead and made a call on his cell.

So much for a fun, romantic evening. At least the creature hadn't made too much of a mess—some overturned furniture, spilled drinks, and a trail of blood and wine. A server wiped blood off the microphone stand's base and set it on the stage, while a maid mopped the wet floor.

I turned to Karin. "Where's Hunter?"

"I convinced him to stay in my room and watch a movie on television." She glanced around. "If he came in here, the women would mob him, and he's supposed to be resting. I'll take Pratt and Whitney up there now." She clutched their collars and left.

Meanwhile, my VIP guests were laughing and comparing photos of the intruder. I guess it took a lot more than a rogue crocodile to upset a room full of murder experts.

I spoke into the microphone on stage, "Sorry for the intrusion. Shall we carry on with the evening?"

Everyone cheered. No jangled nerves remained among these people. I signaled the band to resume playing.

Dina Fenton met me as I stepped down. "Jett, this is so fun! I've never attended such an exciting dinner before. You really nailed that croc." She hurried off to her friends.

Klaus entered pulling an oxygen tank. "Sorry I'm late, Jett. Did I miss anything?"

He stood beside a portable oxygen tank on wheels. "I had to get out of that hospital, but I hired a private nursing service to check on me regularly. I would've been discharged in twelve hours anyway." He put on his monocle and glanced around. "Looks like everyone's having a good time. Where's Detective Miller?"

"He's handling the aftermath of something that happened before you arrived."

Natalya joined us. "Hey, Klaus, you missed all the excitement. We had a crocodile in the ballroom."

He coughed. "Is that a metaphor for something?"

"*Nyet.*" She laughed. "It was real. Jett's dogs chased it." She told him everything.

"It was a few thrilling minutes," I said. "Mike and two police officers killed it."

Amelia and Gaspar joined us and greeted Klaus.

"Glad to see you back." Amelia grasped his good hand. "How are you feeling?"

He held out his bandaged left hand. "It's a little sore where a gator bit me, I have a lump on my head, and my lungs are irritated from breathing so much smoke. That's why I'm on oxygen." He took a hit of

O2. "The meds they gave me help ease the coughing and make me sleep like the dead."

"Come and tell us all about the crash and your rescue." Gaspar led us to their table.

After describing the engine explosion and his ordeal in the marsh, Klaus finished with, "And the FBI agents think whoever is killing our friends hired a pro to plant that bomb."

I added, "They're trying to track down where the components were purchased."

"Why is someone doing this?" Amelia asked. "What motive could they have to kill any of us?"

Natalya glanced around the room. "Could it be something as simple as jealousy and a woman scorned? Edmund refused Dina Fenton's advances at the previous conference, and Fiona slept with Klaus the night Dina tried to hook up with him here."

Gaspar swirled his whisky. "She's quite wealthy—oil wells all over Texas."

"Oil companies use explosives on drill sites," Amelia said.

We all peered at Dina, who was dancing with Kelly.

Natalya elbowed Gaspar. "If she tries to get in your bed tonight, you'd better welcome her if you don't want to be next on her hit list."

Everyone chuckled, and their widened eyes peered at the Texan.

On cue, Dina, seventy and slender with bleached blond hair, left her dance partner and strolled to our table. "Good evening." She stood beside Klaus's chair. "Nice to see you back. Care to dance?"

He coughed and took a hit of oxygen. "It would be my honor, but alas, I am unable due to my injuries from the plane crash. I hope I'll be well enough for a turn with you at the dinner cruise later in the week."

"Feel better soon." She offered her hand to the Spanish prince. "Looks like it's you and me, Gaspar. Shall we?"

He stood and took her hand. "It will be my pleasure." He gave us a nervous glance and led Dina onto the dance floor.

I studied her face as they glided around the room. "She doesn't look like a killer, but a woman like that is used to getting her way and probably doesn't handle rejection well."

"Rumor has it her husband died under suspicious circumstances." Natalya sipped her vodka. "She has powerful political connections, and the D.A. in Houston decided the circumstantial evidence wasn't enough to charge her."

"If she committed murder and got away with it, she might do it again." I filled my glass from a bottle of *Châteauneuf-du-Pape* and took a long drink.

"*Da*, she may think she's untouchable." Natalya narrowed her eyes. "If she killed Edmund, she planned it before she arrived."

The tables were set for dinner, and salads and hot rolls were added as Edith and Neville joined us.

Neville asked Klaus, "Any idea who planted the bomb in the engine compartment?"

As one, we all turned our heads and gazed at Dina, dancing with Gaspar.

Neville followed our gazes. "You think Prince Gaspar did it?"

Natalya rolled her eyes. "*Nyet*, we think it might've been Dina." She filled him in on our speculations.

"Interesting." Neville focused on Klaus. "Best lock your bedroom door tonight."

Amelia nodded. "Right. She may try to finish what she started."

Chateaubriand Béarnaise was served with asparagus and red potatoes. As everyone savored the meal, I peeked at Dina, seated at a nearby table, and wondered if she truly was a black widow, like the spider on Natalya's ring.

TWENTY-ONE

It was 2:20 a.m., and Klaus slept deeply as moonlight filtered into his room through the open curtains by the balcony French doors. He snored softly in a steady rhythm.

Something creaked.

A shadowy figure crept toward the bed, pausing every few seconds. The man in the bed remained asleep as the stealthy intruder inched across the polished oak floor and then stood beside him, studying his face.

Klaus's snoring beneath the oxygen mask provided the only sound.

A gloved hand gently pulled back the covers, raised a dagger high above the German billionaire's chest, and plunged it into his heart.

The victim's eyes popped open in a wide-eyed expression of shock and terror that instantly froze into a still-life portrait of his demise.

The gloved hand turned off the oxygen tank and retrieved the slender blade after wiping the excess blood on a sheet.

Pausing a moment to study the corpse, the killer stared into lifeless blue eyes and departed in silence, leaving no trace.

———

Warm hands caressed me as I woke and looked into my boyfriend's sexy brown eyes. He pulled me close for a tender kiss.

"Sorry we didn't dance as much as you wanted last night. I couldn't believe your new neighbor threatened to sue you and the police for killing that monster he called a pet." He gently brushed my waist-length hair aside.

"What did you do about it?" I rolled onto my side and propped my head against my right hand and arm.

"I arrested him for reckless endangerment and harboring an exotic animal without a permit." He smiled. "That will blow holes in any wrongful death lawsuit over his beloved Tick-Tock."

"That idiot is lucky the croc didn't kill him." I was about to pull him in for another kiss when someone pounded on my bedroom door at the same instant both our cells rang.

"This can't be good." Mike answered his phone as he swung his legs over the side of the bed. He said, "Yeah, I'm with Jett. What's the problem?" A moment later, he said, "Crap!" and pulled on his boxers and pants.

I grabbed my phone and answered it.

"Jett, we're outside your door," Hunter said.

"Give me a sec." I donned a robe and opened my door.

Karin, Hunter, a woman in a nurse uniform, and my pups stood in the hall. Nobody looked happy except the dogs, their tails wagging.

"Bad news," Hunter said. "This nurse came to check on Klaus at eight this morning."

Mike eased up behind me, pulling on his shirt. "What happened?"

"I went to his room and knocked," the nurse said. "There was no answer, but the door was unlocked, so I went in and found him in bed, dead."

He sucked in a deep breath. "Any signs of foul play?"

She wiped away a tear with a shaky hand. "He has what appears to be a deep puncture wound in his chest—probably stabbed in the heart."

"What about evidence of a struggle?"

"None, but he was heavily medicated so his irritated lungs

wouldn't keep him awake all night." She sighed. "Chances are he was sound asleep when he was killed."

Karin broke in, "She dialed 9-1-1 and rushed downstairs where she bumped into us. I can't believe there's been another murder."

Mike said to the nurse, "I hope you closed his bedroom door."

"Y-yes." She brushed away another tear.

"Did you touch anything?"

"I've never seen a murder victim before, but I've seen dead people. The glassy eyes and pallor are unmistakable, so I didn't check his pulse, just called for police."

"I need to get to the crime scene right away. Where's his room, Jett?" He finished buttoning his shirt.

"It's at the other end of the castle on the third floor, directly beneath my parents' suite on the west side." As he dashed off, I said to Hunter and Karin, "Take her downstairs, and I'll deal with the guests." I let the dogs into my room, closed the door, and dressed in a rush.

When I reached Klaus's room, Mike stood beside the bed. "A medical examiner and CSU are on the way. Remain outside the door, Jett. I have to protect the crime scene."

I gazed past him to where Klaus lay under blood-soaked bedding. "How did he die?"

"Looks like he was stabbed in the heart." Mike thrust his hands on his hips. "He was supposed to lock his door last night like all the guests." He checked the French doors.

"Are they locked?"

"No." He opened the doors, eased onto the balcony, and looked up and down.

"Is it okay if I notify the guests? They'll be having breakfast."

"Yeah. Study their reactions and tell them to remain there."

The CSU team arrived with the M.E. right behind them. I stepped aside and let them survey the scene while I headed downstairs. My guests would be wondering why Klaus wasn't eating with them.

When I entered the dining room a few minutes later, everyone paused from their meals and looked at me. I gazed at Amelia, Gaspar, and Natalya. Their faces showed they feared the worst.

One snag—Aldo and Sophia were missing. I decided not to wait.

"I'm sorry to be the bearer of sad news. Baron Klaus von Helsig was murdered in his bed last night. The authorities are in his room, investigating. I'll know more later. In the meantime, you're to remain here until the detective interviews you."

Everyone spoke at once until Dina stood. "I demand to know how this happened. You said we were safe with extra guards patrolling."

I hesitated. "We're not sure. Klaus should have locked his door, but the nurse found it unlocked this morning."

"No, that's wrong," Dina said. "My room is next to his, and before I entered mine, I heard him lock it." She settled in her chair.

"That's true," Gaspar agreed. "I'm directly across the hall from Klaus, and I heard a loud click right after he closed his door."

Amelia appeared to be deep in thought. "Were the balcony doors locked?"

"No, but they're three stories above the ground, and there was a full moon last night. If anyone climbed up or dropped down from the roof or fourth floor, the outside sentries would've spotted him. They've been on high alert since this nightmare started."

"What will you do to keep us safe?" an American woman asked. "I'm scared."

"I'll meet with my head of security—add more guards and install video cameras."

Dina jumped up. "Absolutely no cameras indoors. Our conference contract forbids it."

"Why not?" I asked. "They could help us catch the killer."

Natalya's deep voice answered, "Because we are high-profile VIPs who do not want recorded evidence of our night-time activities ending up on the Internet."

"My security provider is very discreet. You can trust them."

"Sorry, but we're not willing to risk it," Dina said. "This is non-negotiable."

Several other guests voiced their agreement.

"All right." I gave in. "More guards, but no security cameras inside."

Edith and Neville walked in looking anxious.

Neville poked me. "See here, what's with all the police and emergency vehicles?"

I sighed heavily. "Klaus was murdered."

His face blossomed crimson. "I demand to be included in the investigation immediately!"

Mike would be angry, but I was too upset to deal with the Scotland Yard prig, so I said, "Third floor, north end, west side—Detective Miller is in charge."

"What about those FBI agents? Are they here as well?" he asked.

"Not yet. Von Helsig's body was discovered only a short while ago." I pulled out my cell. "Excuse me. I need to make some calls." I walked away and dialed Tim.

"Good morning, Jett. What can I do for you?"

"Klaus was murdered. Can you meet me here right away?"

"I'll be there in fifteen minutes."

I called Gwen. "We had another murder—Klaus von Helsig." I gave her the details.

"It sounds like the spirits were right. Didn't you tell me they predicted nine guests would end up dead, like the title of that book, *A Strange Case of Nine Murders*?"

"That might be what they tried to tell me, but I could be wrong."

"Any idea who the killer is?"

"Possibly a rich Texan named Dina Fenton. Mike will check her alibi."

"Is there anything I can do?"

"No, but let me know if you hear anything from the FBI or on the police wire."

"Nothing so far." She paused. "Sorry, I must get to work. Call if you need me."

I headed up to Sophia's room, hoping she and Aldo were safe. When I reached her door, a loud groan made me fear the worst. I used my pass key and burst through the door.

Sophia yanked up the covers. "Jett, what the hell?"

I've never been so embarrassed in my life. I turned away and blurted, "Klaus was murdered last night, you didn't come to breakfast, and I feared—"

"We're fine. We'll see you downstairs in a little while."

Nodding, I rushed out and closed the door. My face blazed bright red in a hall mirror as I strode past. I descended the stairs in record time and reached the ground floor as Tim entered the foyer through the front door.

He focused on my face. "What—?"

"Don't ask. Let's have a chat." I led him down the hall to the study.

After closing the door, he settled across from me in a cordovan leather chair. "I ordered my men to seal the property—nobody can leave, even for a brief errand, unless Mike allows it."

"Good." I glanced at the antique clock on my desk. "It seems unlikely the murderer will strike during the day. What if you assign extra guards to watch the hallways on the upper floors in both wings all night? Will that work?"

He nodded. "I'll have a man assigned to each area. They can place a chair against a wall halfway down the hall so every door can be seen."

"That should make everyone feel safer and hopefully put a stop to the murders."

Tim rubbed his chin. "Video cameras all over the castle interior would be better, especially on the bedroom levels."

"My guests already shot that down. They seem more concerned about their privacy than their safety." I shrugged. "I have to respect their wishes. It's in their contract."

"Understood." He checked his watch. "I'll schedule the extra guards for tonight."

TWENTY-TWO

After interviewing every guest, Mike joined me on the terrace where I sat at a round table with Hunter and Sophia. Karin was in the kitchen preparing the lunch that would be served to the Mystery Fest attendees in the ballroom.

Mike leaned over and kissed me before he took a seat next to me. "This case isn't getting any easier—too many guests without alibis." He hesitated. "I don't suspect anybody at this table, but I have to ask your whereabouts last night, all night, except Jett, who was with me."

"Karin and I are staying together while I recuperate," Hunter said. "And we kept the dogs with us last night in her suite." He smiled at me. "You're welcome."

Sophia wore a silly grin. "I guess you know Aldo spent the night with me." Her diamond tennis bracelet sparkled in the morning sun.

"Yes, and I'm not accusing him of anything, but I need to know if there was ever a time he could've slipped out for fifteen minutes. Possible?"

"Men that age have prostate issues and get up in the middle of the night to pee. I stirred when he went to the bathroom, but I fell back asleep and didn't wake when he returned. So, yeah, it's possible but unlikely." Sophia arched a brow. "Satisfied?"

Mike nodded. "Thank you."

I asked him, "Who didn't have alibis?"

"Dina, whose room is next door to Klaus, Gaspar, whose room is one door down and across the hall, Amelia, whose room is directly above his, Natalya, whose room is directly beneath, both bodyguards, and several other guests," Mike said. "Apparently, everyone was so spooked by the bomb in the airplane Klaus and Hunter flew that they decided to sleep alone with their doors locked."

"But Klaus's door wasn't locked," I said.

"According to witnesses, he locked his door. I'm assuming someone picked the lock, which can't be that difficult with those antique doors." Mike looked past me. "Oh, great, here come the Feds."

My least favorite FBI agents strode to our table. They nodded a curt greeting, and Agent Taylor said, "Detective Miller, we need to consult with you in the study."

"Of course." Mike stood. "Please excuse me." He followed the agents inside.

Hunter frowned. "This case—why would someone murder Edmund, Fiona, and Klaus?"

"Last night we speculated it might be Dina, a powerful woman scorned by both men and upstaged by Fiona." I shrugged. "Dina's wealthy husband died under suspicious circumstances too. We think she might be a black widow."

"Big whoop," Sophia said. "All four of Natalya's rich husbands died. She probably killed them and made it look like natural causes." She shrugged. "She hinted as much when we got drunk together."

"Fine," Hunter said. "But what's her motive for these murders?"

Sophia raised her hands, palms up. "No clue, but I bet the victims all had dark secrets, like the spirits tried to warn us when they lit up their faces."

———

The luncheon in the ballroom went off without a hitch. Everyone applauded Neville's speech about Scotland Yard and some of their most unusual cases. He was in his glory.

Edith joined him at the podium. "I'd like to thank DCI Neville Wright for his interesting talk and remind everyone you have an hour to freshen up before the poison workshop in the great hall at two."

I stood to one side as guests chatted in small groups and eventually filed out of the ballroom. So far, so good. My main concern was keeping my charges safe overnight. I didn't expect anything bad to happen during the day—too many possible witnesses.

It would've been nice to do some research with the powerful computer in my study, but the Feds were still holding court in there, and Neville joined them.

Instead, I dropped in on Karin in the kitchen. "Hey, how's it going? I loved the crispy chicken parmesan you served for lunch—so tasty."

"Thanks. We're serving Steak Diane for dinner tonight." Karin wiped her hands on a towel.

"Have you heard anything from your staff about suspicious activity?" I took in the busy scene with servers carrying in trays full of dirty dishes.

"Nothing that would point to the murderer—sorry."

"I have a gut feeling these murders aren't random, but well-planned executions. If I could figure out the motive, I could nail the killer."

"Well, you've got twenty-one experts on murder staying in the castle."

"Eighteen, as of this morning. And that's not counting Edith, who doesn't stay overnight, but who was present for Edmund's and Fiona's demise."

Karin said, "You're an apprentice private investigator—so solve this already." She chuckled. "Nothing like starting big."

"I already started big with the Body Drop Killer." I looked out the window. "What's Hunter up to today?"

"He's fishing off your pier. Sophia talked him into using her Italian sausage as bait."

"I hope he catches a big fish like we did."

I stood beside the door to the great hall as participants arrived for the poison workshop. They looked relaxed after a delicious lunch and a brief trip to their rooms to freshen up. So far, I counted fourteen people.

Aldo arrived. "Jett, any progress on solving the murders?"

"Nothing yet." I looked over his shoulder. "Where's Nico?"

"Mike gave my bodyguard permission to go out for more Cuban cigars in case I get stuck here after the conference ends. Those FBI agents won't let us leave until they catch the killer."

"Have you seen Gaspar and Jorge?"

"After lunch, Gaspar gave Jorge the afternoon off." He lowered his voice. "I think he wanted to use the same call-girl service Nico used earlier, and Mike let him go."

A blood-curdling scream drew our attention to the north staircase. I ran over and bolted up the stairs with several guests trailing behind.

Dina stood riveted to the second-floor landing beside Gaspar's tangled body. Blood streaked from his nostrils, and his bluish-purple skin appeared severely bruised.

I took her hand and pulled her away from the body. "Dina, calm down and tell me what happened."

"I…I didn't want to wait for the elevator, so I took the stairs. Gaspar must've tripped and fallen all the way down here from the third floor. But why does his skin look so strange?"

"I don't know." I squeezed her shoulders. "Did you see him fall?"

"No, he was like this when I came down the stairs."

Several guards, Mike, the Feds, and Neville arrived and pushed back the onlookers.

Agent Barnes said in a loud voice, "This is a crime scene, people. Everyone into the great hall, now."

I called Tim. "Looks like another murder, this time on the north staircase. Keep the property sealed but let Nico and Jorge back in later today."

"Understood. I'll notify my guards and be there in fifteen minutes."

———

That evening, Mike strode into the dining room where I was in the process of finishing a sumptuous Steak Diane with Peruvian mashed potatoes and snow peas, paired with a smooth red Château Lafite Rothschild. The sixteen remaining conference guests, plus Edith and Neville, dined with Sophia, Hunter, and me. The meal was delicious, but the mood was somber.

Mike addressed the group. "Anyone here take blood thinners?"

Aldo raised his hand. "I'm on Xarelto, 20mg pills, one a day."

"Where do you keep the bottle?" Mike asked.

"I leave it on the nightstand, but I forgot to take one last night," he smiled at Sophia, "and I didn't remember it today because I always take it before bed."

"So, the bottle is still on your nightstand?"

Aldo nodded. "Should be."

Mike waved him forward. "Show me, please." He thumbed at me. "Jett, come with us."

Sophia and Hunter stood.

"Sorry, Sophia, I need unbiased witnesses." Mike waved her back. "Stay here, but Hunter can come."

We hurried to Aldo's room at the south end of the second floor, one of the rooms connected to the secret passage from the study. He snatched the bottle off the nightstand and handed it to Mike.

Mike opened it and emptied the pills onto the dresser. "There are ten pills. How many were there yesterday?"

Aldo's eyes widened. "That's impossible. I brought a ninety-day supply with me, and I've only used eight pills since it was filled."

"That means you're missing seventy-two 20mg pills." Mike frowned. "The M.E. said Gaspar died from massive internal bleeding caused by the fall combined with a huge overdose of blood thinners."

"Someone must've stolen my pills yesterday and slipped them into his food or drink last night at dinner or at breakfast today." Aldo seemed genuinely stunned.

I peered at the pills. "These are tiny tablets, so the killer must've ground them into a powder so they'd dissolve in a beverage."

Hunter examined the pill bottle without touching it. "Might've dosed the victim yesterday to give the drug time to work."

"The killer shoved Gaspar down the stairs today, knowing he'd bleed to death, especially if he hit his head during the fall." Mike peered at Aldo. "Weren't you the last to arrive before Dina found Gaspar on the stairs?"

"Yes, but I had no reason to kill my dear friend. Dina is the obvious suspect. He spurned her advances last night at the dance. I overheard her suggest they spend the night together, and he put her off with an excuse that he wasn't feeling well."

I nodded. "Maybe he was already reacting to the drug overdose. Several of us discussed her as a probable suspect last night. She could've drugged his drink last evening, pushed Gaspar this afternoon, waited until he died, joined him on the landing, and screamed like she just found him."

"That's plausible, but I have to warn you, Aldo, the FBI will suspect you because the pills were yours, and you arrived at the great hall shortly before Gaspar was found."

I nudged Aldo. "Hire a good lawyer."

Hunter nodded. "Looks like someone is trying to frame you for murder."

TWENTY-THREE

Mike pulled me aside after Aldo returned to his seat in the dining room. "I'll sleep with you again in case anything happens tonight."

I nuzzled his neck. "Fine with me, but I don't know how much sleep you'll get."

After pulling out a chair for me, Mike stood at the head of the long table. "Ladies and gentlemen, I apologize for the inconvenience, but we have police officers searching all your rooms in case anyone lied about having blood thinner meds. We are determined to catch the murderer and ensure your safety. In the meantime, please lock your doors, especially when you're in your rooms, and be vigilant around your food and beverages." He left to supervise the searches.

My seat was between Amelia and Natalya. "So sorry for the loss of your friends, ladies." My gut churned. "Anything I can do for you?"

"No, but I might take my mind off things by working on an outline for my next mystery novel," Amelia said sadly, her voice hoarse.

"Can't help but get a few ideas from this bizarre conference." I took a drink from my wine glass, half-wondering if it was safe since I'd left it unguarded. "What about you, Natalya? Want something to distract you, like drinks and cards on the terrace?"

"I feel emotionally drained after losing four dear friends." She covered her yawn, her eyes moist. "I think I'll retire early tonight and recover my energy with a good, long sleep." She turned to Hunter. "Unless you'd like to join me?"

"Thanks, but I'm dating Jett's chef." He grinned. "Wouldn't want to make her angry."

I stood. "Stay safe, ladies, and I hope we'll have some answers tomorrow."

———

Unaware that a sedative had been added to her wine, Natalya took a sleeping pill and fell into a deep sleep, secure in the knowledge her door was locked and a chair was wedged under the door handle.

Three hours later, a dark figure entered the moonlit room and crept silently toward the bed. The intruder studied the sleeping woman as a grandfather clock in the corner struck midnight.

The prowler paused and stared at the bed's occupant, but the clock's chimes had no effect on the sleeping woman.

A gloved hand held a small spray canister disguised as a lipstick tube and positioned the nozzle close to Natalya's nostrils before dispensing a lethal dose of prussic acid. The aerosol form of cyanide triggered respiratory paralysis.

The spray tube slipped from the intruder's hand, hit the carpet, and rolled under the bed. After a brief hesitation, the killer crossed the room, pulled the chair away from the door, and unlocked it.

Before leaving, a final check of the victim satisfied the murderer that Natalya Petrov had shared the same fate as her four husbands. A gloved hand removed her spider ring and pocketed it.

———

Mike worked out his frustrations through intense lovemaking with me. Afterward, we both fell into deep sleep.

The next morning, I tried to slip away without waking him.

He grabbed my hand. "Hey, beautiful, where're you going?"

I leaned over and kissed him. "Pratt and Whitney need to go out."

"At least no one's pounding on your door, and our phones aren't ringing. It seems we made it through the night without another murder."

I slipped on shorts and a T-shirt. "Hope springs eternal. Meet me on the terrace for breakfast."

The dogs and I hurried down the hall and descended the south staircase. We didn't encounter any guests, but it was only seven in the morning. The fresh salt air washed over me as we traversed the damp, grassy expanse between the castle and the ocean. Gulls squawked and dived, the sun rose steadily over an azure sea, and all seemed right with the world.

The dogs and I finished our morning jaunt, and Mike met me at a terrace table. Hunter joined us, and a server brought us steaming hot coffee, ham and cheddar omelets, and whole-grain toast with an assortment of jams and butter.

Mike smiled. "I could get used to this."

"And I could get used to having you with me every night." I swallowed a forkful of omelet.

We reveled in the quiet meal and inhaled the sea air. After eating, we drank another coffee.

"Any revelations from the interviews after Gaspar's murder?" Hunter asked.

"Yeah, two of the guests lied about not taking blood thinners. Dina Fenton and Amelia Ainsworth claimed they didn't want to air their medical issues publicly. But they were on Warfarin, and the drug Gaspar overdosed on was Xarelto."

I checked the time—8:15. My cell rang. Sophia was calling.

"Jett, I'm in the dining room with Aldo and the guests, but Natalya isn't here. Should we let her sleep in, or should I send someone to check on her?"

"Hunter is with us. We'll check her room and let you know." I pocketed the phone as Mike stood and pulled out my chair.

"What now?" he asked.

I told the men.

"Let's go. I knew this morning was too good to be true." Mike led us inside, and the dogs followed us up the stairs.

Natalya's room was in the north wing at the end of the second floor on the west side, directly beneath Klaus's room.

Mike tried her door handle, and it turned.

Unlocked.

Not a good sign.

He said, "You two wait out here, and keep the dogs with you."

I stood in front of my pups, pointed down, and said, "Stay." They sat, and I peered past Mike through the open door and spotted Natalya lying on her back in bed.

Hunter peered over my shoulder. "Is she dead?"

Mike checked for a pulse, carefully pulled back the covers, and glanced back at us. "Dead—no signs of a struggle."

I felt sick. The magnificent Russian woman who sparred with me in a fencing match, and who allowed me to end it with a tie, was dead. Had she been murdered?

Twenty feet away, I squatted for a long-distance view under the bed. Something small lay about three feet from the edge.

"Mike, look under the bed. I see something there."

He crouched and peeked underneath the huge, antique four-poster. "I see it. Looks like a lipstick tube, but I'll wait for the crime scene team to retrieve it."

He stood and pulled out his cell. After calling for the M.E., CSU, and FBI, he looked back at us. "Call Tim and have him double-check that your estate is still sealed. Then join the guests in the dining room, inform them of Natalya's death, and see to it they stay there until they're interviewed."

———

The five murders were so close together that I felt like a broken record in the dining room, replaying the same instructions again and again. Hunter tried to soothe the upset women.

I explained there were no signs of foul play, and Sophia's eyes widened.

"A word in private, please." She led us into the hall.

The three of us walked out of earshot.

She lowered her voice. "Natalya and I got drunk together, and she told me how a person could spray prussic acid at the nostrils of a sleeping target, and the poison would stop their breathing and dissipate in a few hours so that it wouldn't be found in an autopsy. The victim would appear to have suffered a heart attack."

"Are you saying someone used it to kill Natalya?" Hunter asked.

"It's possible. They might find trace amounts in her nostrils."

I hesitated. "I spotted something under her bed that looked like a lipstick tube."

"Maybe the killer dropped it—could be a tiny spray canister," Sophia said. "It doesn't take much to kill someone."

I hated to ask, but I had to know. "Were you with Aldo last night?"

"Yes, except…"

"Except what?" Hunter arched an eyebrow.

"He left briefly around midnight because he forgot to take his Xarelto pill." She frowned. "He was gone half an hour—claimed he brushed his teeth, shaved, and used the toilet for a sit-down session."

"His room is at the end of the south hall on your floor, so about a five-minute walk one-way if he walked slowly," I said. "That leaves twenty minutes unaccounted for, unless he really did shave and stuff."

"His face was smooth, and I could smell fresh aftershave, not to mention his minty breath from brushing his teeth. I think he told the truth."

Mike strode down the hall to us. "The item under the bed was a tiny spray canister disguised to look like a lipstick." He hesitated and looked at Sophia. "Sorry, but Aldo's fingerprints were on it."

Sophia's face paled. "It can't be him. He's too smart to leave a murder weapon behind with his prints on it." She narrowed her eyes. "This has to be a frame job."

"That's possible," Mike admitted. "I need to ask him how his prints got there."

"I'd like to hear his answer too," Hunter said.

"Wait here while I get him." He paused. "Aldo might not want to talk in front of you three."

"He won't object if he has nothing to hide," Sophia said.

It wasn't long before Mike returned from the dining room with Aldo. "Do you mind answering a few questions in front of them or would you prefer a private interview?"

"This is fine. What would you like to know?"

Mike showed him a photo on his phone. "We found this under Natalya's bed. How did your fingerprints get on it?"

Aldo's face went blank for a moment. "Why would my prints be on a lipstick?"

"It's not what it looks like." Mike explained about the spray canister.

Sophia nudged Aldo. "Think, my darling. There must be an explanation for this."

He rubbed his chin. "Oh, wait, I remember. One of the women spilled her purse, and I helped pick up the contents, several things, including a lipstick."

"Which woman?" Mike asked.

Aldo frowned. "I can't remember. It was during the first day in the great hall."

TWENTY-FOUR

"**D**o you remember who you were sitting with?" Hunter asked Aldo.

"All of us were waiting in the great hall after check-in." He paused. "I was with several friends. I remember Dina dived right in and helped us pick up everything and drop it into the open handbag."

I frowned. "It must be Dina."

"Not necessarily," Mike said. "A man could've planted it with the dropped items and retrieved it later when the handbag's owner was distracted. Remember there were twenty attendees and two bodyguards when this event started."

"Seems like these murders were carefully planned long before Mystery Fest began." I smiled at Aldo. "I don't think you're the killer."

"Neither do I, sugar buns." Sophia gave Aldo a kiss on the cheek.

Aldo looked at Mike. "Are you going to arrest me?"

"No, but I'm sure the FBI will be very interested in talking to you." Mike arched a brow. "I hope you have a top-notch attorney."

"I'll hire one right now." Aldo pulled out his phone and stepped away.

I blew out a sigh. "The thing is, I don't see a motive for killing all those people. It's not like the victims had a lot in common other than they were wealthy and enjoyed Mystery Fest."

"That's not true," Sophia said. "The spirits at the séance indicated all of them were murderers. That's what they had in common."

Mike rolled his eyes. "Try telling that to a judge at a murder trial."

Sophia grabbed Hunter's arm. "Wait a minute. You saw objects moved around during the séance. What if Valhalla's spirits are killing guests that they think are murderers?"

"Lethal ghosts roaming around my castle?" I shook my head. "Nothing like that has ever happened in the more than one hundred years since it was built."

Sophia shrugged. "Hey, they've had a long time to get bored and vindictive."

"Don't ever think that," I said. "This isn't *The Shining*. Valhalla has nice ghosts."

"You both sound silly," Mike said. "No more crazy talk about killer spirits or ghosts of any kind here."

———

It was mid-morning, the place was crawling with Feds, cops, and CSI techs, and the M.E. had already taken Natalya in for an autopsy. Noisy helicopters were circling the grounds again, and my phone erupted every few seconds with calls and texts from media sources. I ignored their calls, but they kept calling anyway.

The music room's sound-proofed walls gave me respite from the chaos. I sat on a velvet-covered loveseat, staring out a window, seeing nothing, my mind drifting in a sea of clues. The dogs, sleeping at my feet, suddenly stirred at the same moment a hand tapped my shoulder.

I jerked and looked behind me. It was Tim and one of his security guards.

"Jett, sorry to disturb you. We owe you an apology." He paused. "This is Gabe. He's one of my best men, and he was guarding the hallway near Natalya's room last night."

"I promise you I was awake and alert my entire shift, and I'm sure she locked her door." Gabe frowned. "I don't know how the killer got past me. I should've seen him."

"I believe you." I squeezed Gabe's shoulder. "He or she must've entered through the balcony doors."

"That's no excuse," Tim said. "My company will refund your security contract and vacate the premises as soon as we find you a suitable replacement."

"Absolutely not!" I clutched his hand. "Tim, you and your brave men have saved me more times than I can count. I trust you and need you now more than ever. If retired SEALs can't spot the killer, no one can. I'm sticking with you guys, and that's that."

"Okay, if you're sure."

"I'm positive. I know you guys are doing everything you can. It's not your fault the guests won't allow security cameras inside the castle."

"One more thing: there's a guy at the gate named Ben Foster—claims he needs to speak to you and Hunter about an urgent matter concerning his Jungmann. You know him?"

"Yes, let him in. He owns the biplane my uncle and Klaus crashed in."

Tim rested a hand on my shoulder. "Relax. I'll bring him and Hunter here."

Feeling restless, I paced in front of the grand piano while my dogs sat and watched me, wondering what the heck was wrong now.

Pratt and Whitney rushed to greet Hunter as he sauntered in with Tim and Ben. He scratched their ears and laughed. "It's like they don't remember they saw me an hour ago."

I gave Ben a hug. "Sorry about your beautiful Bücker."

"Actually, I owe everyone involved an apology. Turns out my soon-to-be ex hired a hitman to plant that bomb. If I died before the divorce, she'd get everything, whereas the airtight prenup would've netted her very little in comparison."

Hunter's jaw dropped. "How'd they catch her?"

"The FBI traced the bomb's components back to purchases the hitman made. He wasn't a pro, just an out-of-work alcoholic mechanic who needed money. He agreed to turn State's evidence against my wife." Ben smiled. "The case is solid. I'll soon be single, and she's going away for fifteen to twenty years in a federal prison."

"Wow, and all this time we thought someone attending Mystery Fest hired the bomber. I can't believe Agents Barnes and Taylor nabbed them."

"They didn't. Explosives experts from the FBI's Miami Field Office caught the hitman and my wife." He gave us two thumbs up. "Sweet."

Tim had been listening. "Hunter and Klaus did you a favor borrowing your airplane. That could've been you, upside down in the marsh, surrounded by hungry gators and giant snakes."

"Darn straight." Ben held out his hand to Hunter. "Thanks, buddy. Sorry about Klaus. His murder was reported on television."

"Yeah, the murders here are a total mystery—no obvious motive," Hunter said. "At least now we know the plane crash was unrelated to what's happening at Valhalla."

"Have you considered the possibility there's more than one murderer?" Tim asked.

"You mean two killers working as a team?" I asked.

"Or a different killer for each victim—one motive and one murderer per crime," Tim said. "After the first murder, others could've seized the opportunity to take out enemies and hope the cops would think the first murderer killed all of them."

"I guess anything's possible." I pulled out my cell. "I'd better bring Mike up to date on the bombing. The Feds haven't shared much info with him."

Mike's normally relaxed voice was tight with tension. "What's up, Jett? Not another murder, I hope."

"No, but did the Feds tell you the bomb in the biplane was planted by a hitman hired by Ben's wife? They're engulfed in a bitter divorce."

"Those FBI agents never tell me anything—say it's their case. Thanks for the update."

"There's more. Tim has a theory there's a different killer and motive for each murder—all piggybacking off the first crime and hoping the Feds will assume one killer is responsible for all of them."

Mike paused. "You know, that's not a bad theory—treat each murder as a separate crime with a different killer. I'll look into it. Thanks, Jett. I'll see you tonight."

———

While the Mystery Fest participants spent their afternoon attending various workshops and panels, I locked myself in the study with my doggies and used the powerful desktop computer to research Amelia and some others.

My first quest was to discover who had been Amelia's fiancé so long ago. Internet search engines were a modern wonder. In minutes, I found her old engagement photo.

Holy cow! I couldn't believe it. The caption read: Amelia Ainsworth, daughter of Lord Robert and Lady Elizabeth Ainsworth, and sister of Roberta Ainsworth, will wed Edmund Helmsley, son of Lord Arthur and Lady Camille Helmsley, June 20, in a private ceremony at Cirencester Castle, the Ainsworth's ancestral home.

Amelia was a beautiful young woman of twenty in the engagement photo, and Edmund was a dashing young man of the same age. I studied the picture. Neither looked like murderers, despite the spirits' accusations at the séance. I searched but couldn't find any indication either of them had ever been charged with or accused of any crime.

A week after the wedding announcement, an obituary for Amelia's younger sister, Roberta, appeared in the same newspaper—a hit-and-run death. The canceled wedding wasn't formally announced, but the newspaper ran a brief article about it because the families were nobility. I wondered if Amelia still loved Edmund, despite her calling off the wedding, weighed down by the grief of losing her sister.

After their broken engagement, I was surprised Edmund and Amelia remained close friends. Perhaps he hoped he would eventually win her back. They seemed to be in close agreement on political issues, like Scotland remaining part of the UK.

After another search, I found an old wedding announcement about Edmund's nuptials to a wealthy Danish socialite. He must've decided waiting fifteen years for Amelia to change her mind was long enough. I knew from his recent bio for the conference that his wife died from cancer a year ago.

Although Amelia was known as a stoic, stiff-upper-lip Brit, Edmund's murder must have devastated her, not that she would ever show it publicly. A hopeless romantic, I wondered if they would have rekindled their romance at Mystery Fest had he not been murdered on the second day.

What a sad story of unrequited love.

TWENTY-FIVE

I t was late afternoon when I descended the staircase and encountered Sophia in the foyer, standing with Nico and Jorge, the only bodyguards at Mystery Fest.

She waved me over. "Jett, would it be okay if Jorge borrows your fishing gear? He's feeling kinda down since Gaspar passed, but he loves fishing, so—"

"Of course." I smiled at him. "Would you like to fish off my pier or my boat?"

He rubbed his military crew cut and focused sad brown eyes on me. "The pier. I am not allowed to leave your property until they arrest the person who—"

"Sorry." I thumbed at Sophia. "Did she tell you about the big fish we caught?"

A hint of a smile. "She gave me her special bait." He held up a baggie filled with Italian sausage chunks. "And if the fish don't want them, they'll make a good snack."

"Hunter recently caught a big fish with that bait," I said.

"Keep a tight grip on the rod," Sophia warned. "Jett and I landed a couple of four-footers that were vicious fighters—almost pulled us into the water."

He grinned. Five-ten and solid muscle, Jorge towered over Sophia.

Nico playfully socked Jorge's arm. "It would take a very large fish to move him."

He flexed his substantial biceps. "*Sí*, I am a much bigger adversary."

"Yes, but my pier juts into the inlet that connects the Intracoastal Waterway to the Atlantic Ocean. Large fish cruise through there, including sharks." I smiled at Nico, Aldo's handsome bodyguard. His physique was like Jorge's. "Will you be joining him?"

"No, I need to accompany Aldo as he takes his walk around the grounds in about a half hour." He gave me a flirty smile. "Fishing isn't my thing. I prefer catching the eye of a beautiful woman."

If anyone else had said that, it would've sounded corny, but with Nico's dark good looks and sexy accent, the comment was charming.

"Alrighty, let's get you set, Jorge. My gear is in the garage." I led him outside, and Sophia came with us.

We carried a rod and reel, a large bucket, and a tackle box complete with lures out of my garage. Sophia held a baseball bat.

Jorge eyed her bat. "Planning to hit some balls?"

"You'll need this to pound the fish into submission." She held out the bat. "Seriously, if you land a big one, it'll smack you with its fin if you don't knock it out fast."

He shook his head. "I had no idea American women were so violent." He gazed around and lowered his voice. "Last night, Dina Fenton showed me the pistol she carries under her dress in an inner-thigh holster."

"Oh, yeah?" Sophia sounded smug. "I bet that's not all she showed you."

"She's a very forceful woman, but I didn't let her in my room." He frowned. "I was too upset about losing Gaspar. I should've saved him somehow."

We each put an arm around him. "There really isn't anything you could've done. You can't be everywhere at once."

The long pier was where we normally docked the family's one-hundred-and-fifty-foot yacht, but it was empty today, except for the thirty-foot Chris Craft docked on the opposite side. The yacht was being retrofitted with high-tech electronics.

"Kick off your shoes and sit on the end of the pier." I helped him ready the fishing gear. "It's a floating dock, so it goes up and down with the tides."

He settled onto the wood slats with his feet in the cool water. "Thank you, ladies."

"I'll send someone out with a cooler of cold beer and one of those mugs that keeps the contents cold for hours." Sophia laid the bat beside him.

He tipped his ball cap to us as we walked away.

―――――

It wasn't long before some of the guests went for their afternoon stroll. Sophia and I intercepted Dina, Edith, Neville, and Amelia.

I handed the mug filled with cold beer to Dina, and Sophia passed the small cooler with six beer bottles to Neville.

"Please give these to Jorge," I said. "He's fishing from the pier on the north end of the backyard."

Edith glanced in his direction. "I imagine he's feeling low after losing Gaspar."

Sophia nodded. "Yeah, we thought he needed a distraction."

Aldo and Nico joined the group.

Aldo smiled at Sophia. "Care to join us for a turn around the property?"

"I'd love to, darling, but I have things to do. I'll see you tonight." She kissed his cheek.

The group set off on the path to the pier, and we went inside to help Karin set up for the murder mystery dinner. It seemed in poor taste after all the real murders, but it was part of the program, and since all the attendees were stuck here, they elected to continue the scheduled events.

I noted several newcomers. "Looks like the actors have arrived."

Sophia pursed her lips. "This is getting creepy. I can't believe the guests still want to have the fake murder at dinner tonight."

"Yeah, if it was me, I'd lock myself in my room and have my meals delivered until this nightmare was over," Karin said.

"Of course, you would." Sophia winked. "You've got Hunter with you."

We giggled as the actors approached us.

One of the young women asked, "Are there dressing rooms and places for hair and makeup?"

I took her arm. "I'll show you. We have facilities for men and women along the inside wall of the ballroom. You can set up there."

———

The mystery dinner was a formal event, so once everything was organized, I went upstairs and changed into an evening gown. I took the elevator down and found Mike waiting for me in the foyer. He looked dashing in a tuxedo.

He pulled me in for a kiss. "You look hot in that sexy black dress."

"You're not too bad yourself." I took his arm. "I hope we get through this event without any unplanned drama or real murders."

Kelly joined us dressed in a tux. "I checked all the actors' props—no real guns or knives." He paused and listened to his earpiece. "Have you seen Jorge Santos? He left his shoes, all the fishing gear, and the beer cooler on the end of the dock."

I sucked in a deep breath. "I have a bad feeling. We'd better go look for him."

We checked the pier. Nobody was there, but I heard something under the pier bumping against the speedboat. I peered into the water in the narrow gap between the boat and pier and spotted Jorge. One arm was missing.

"Oh, God, there he is!" I pointed.

Mike called it in and asked me, "Do you think this was a suicide?"

"No, and he was too strong for a fish to yank him into the water." I looked down at the body and felt sick. I brushed away a few tears and regained control. "Besides, he was Spain's version of a Navy SEAL, so he must've been an expert swimmer."

Mike picked up the beer mug. "If somebody drugged his beer, he could've been unconscious and fell in."

Kelly grabbed a boat hook from the Chris Craft and helped Mike pull the corpse onto the dock. "What about the missing arm? Looks like it was ripped off."

"A passing shark may have heard him fall and bit off his arm for a taste." I grimaced. "Sharks don't really like to eat humans, so it let him go and moved on."

Mike stared at the beer mug. "Any idea who could've drugged his drink?"

"Oh, God, I hope this isn't my fault. I handed his beverage to Dina and asked her to bring it to him."

Kelly arched an eyebrow. "Why would she want to kill him?"

"Jorge told me she tried to seduce him last night, and he turned her down. It fits with our 'woman scorned' theory about the murders."

Mike rubbed the back of his neck. "Remind me again about that theory."

"All the men who were murdered turned her down, and all the murdered women slept with the men who rejected her."

Kelly shook his head. "Hell hath no fury—"

"I'd better search her room for a knockout drug." Mike strode back to the castle while we waited for the M.E. and CSU.

TWENTY-SIX

I pulled out my cell and called Tim. "Looks like we may have another murder victim—Jorge Santos. Kelly and I are with the body on my pier, waiting for the authorities to deal with it."

"Unbelievable. The murder mystery dinner hasn't even started yet." He sighed. "The property is still sealed, but remind Kelly to have the guards prevent the actors from leaving. I'm handling an event in Palm Beach, so he'll assist you."

"Okay, thanks, Tim." I pocketed my phone and told Kelly what he said.

"Are you going to cancel tonight's event?" he asked.

"No, and I don't think we should tell the guests about this. Better to keep them busy with the mystery dinner than have them freak out about another murder."

"Call Mike, so you're both on the same page, and go back inside. I'll handle things here."

I called Mike as I hurried to the dinner. After he agreed to my plan, I said, "Meet me in the ballroom after you finish searching."

I pulled Sophia away from Aldo's table. "Excuse us a moment." Once we were out of earshot, I told her about Jorge. "We're keeping it a secret for now. No sense in upsetting everyone, and we won't know for sure if it was murder until the crime scene techs test the beer mug and the M.E. performs the autopsy."

"I'll keep a close eye on Dina and make sure she's nowhere near Aldo's food or drinks." Sophia glared in her direction.

"Better watch out she doesn't get near yours either. Remember, if it's her, she killed the women too."

Sophia studied Dina. "You know, I really think she might've done it."

"She seems to be the only one with a plausible motive for all the murders. I hope Mike finds a knockout drug in her room so we can end this."

Sophia squeezed my arm. "Here he comes now. I'll get back to guarding Aldo."

Mike leaned in and whispered in my ear, "Everything good here?"

"We're keeping a close watch on Dina in case she goes after Aldo."

"The person we should be watching is Aldo. I found a small, unlabeled drug-sized bottle of a liquid in his room. The lab's analyzing it now. Nothing in Dina's room."

"She could be framing him. Think about it—she's the one with motives for all the murders." I looked back at Dina. "Aldo had no reason to kill those people."

"None that we know of." He scanned the room. "Has the fake murder taken place yet?"

"No, they usually wait until after dessert is served, and they're serving the main course now."

Mike ushered me to available seats alongside Aldo and Sophia, where we shared a table with Hunter, Amelia, Edith, Neville, Dina, and Aldo's bodyguard, Nico.

Neville looked across at Mike. "Any progress on solving the murders?"

"We've narrowed it down to two likely suspects." He took a sip of chardonnay. "This swordfish is superb."

"Well, spill it, Detective. Who are they?" Neville demanded.

"Sorry, the FBI wants to keep things close to the vest until we're sure which one did it." Mike patted his lips and gave me a side glance.

It was obvious he enjoyed keeping Neville out of the loop. So did I. Besides, we couldn't blab it in front of both suspects.

"Jett, did Jorge catch any fish?" Dina asked.

"I'm not sure." I took a swig of wine. "I've been rather busy."

She turned to Sophia. "Did you see if he caught anything?"

Sophia set down her fork. "No, I was helping the actors set up for this event."

"Well, somebody must know." She looked at the bodyguard. "Nico?"

"I haven't seen him, but he'll stay on the pier until he runs out of beer."

Mike's cell pinged with a text message. He read it and showed it to me.

Unlabeled bottle contained GHB and had Count Aldo Medici's fingerprints on it.

Mike pocketed his phone. "Aldo, Jett, Hunter, I need your help with something." He stood. "Please excuse us a moment, everyone."

Sophia stood. "I'll come too."

Mike put a hand on her shoulder. "No. I need you to stay here and keep an eye on things." He gazed pointedly at the food and drinks. "We'll be right back."

Neville slid his chair back, bristling. "If this pertains to the case, I'm coming."

"It's personal." Mike put his hand on Neville's shoulder. "We'll be right back."

We strolled down the hall and into the music room. Mike closed the door, and we settled on chairs near the windows. Good thing the heavy draperies were drawn. It might've been bad if Aldo spotted the police vehicles parked by the pier.

Mike pulled out his cell, selected a photo, and showed it to Aldo. "Do you recognize this bottle?"

He studied the picture. "No, what is it?"

"It's a tiny bottle of GHB, also known as the date-rape drug, and it renders the victim helpless. It can also be deadly in larger doses." Mike paused. "I found the bottle in your room under the T-shirts in your underwear drawer. Your prints are on it."

Aldo seemed genuinely confused. "I don't understand. Why did someone put it there, and how did they get my prints on it?" He searched our faces. "You don't think I drugged Sophia, do you?"

"No, we think it might have been used for something else," Mike said. "Have you ever seen it before?"

He stroked his chin. "It could've been one of the things I picked up after that purse was spilled on the first day." He sat up straighter. "Do you suspect this drug was used in a murder?"

"It's possible." Mike pocketed his phone.

"Which one?" he asked, looking at us.

"We're not sure which murder yet, but it looks like someone is trying very hard to frame you," Mike explained.

"Can you think of who that might be?" Hunter asked.

Aldo nodded. "The murderer, obviously. I'm not aware of any enemies at this event, but it could be the killer isn't an enemy, and he chose me as the patsy simply because I'm away from my room a lot."

I broke in. "Mind if I ask a question?"

"Go ahead," Mike said.

"Aldo, have you ever been intimate with Dina Fenton?" I watched his eyes for a reaction.

He frowned. "That woman! She's not my type—too forward."

"But has she tried to seduce you?" Hunter asked.

"Only once since I arrived here, but she hasn't had another opportunity. I've been with Sophia every free moment." He glanced from me to Hunter. "Why? Do you suspect Dina is the killer?"

"It's one possibility," Mike said. "If I were you, I'd guard your food and drinks any time she's nearby."

I stood. "We'd better get back or we'll miss the performance."

"Right." Mike stood and opened the door.

"I wonder who they'll pretend to murder," Hunter said.

Aldo scowled. "Let's hope it's Dina."

I hurried down the hall. "I don't want to miss dessert."

We took our seats right before the lights went out. A gunshot followed by screams got my heart pumping.

TWENTY-SEVEN

T he lights were off for about five seconds. When they came on, a female actress lay on the floor with a bright-red bloodstain covering her white gown near her heart. Mike and I rushed over to verify it was the planned fake murder.

He looked relieved after he checked her pulse.

I put a hand on his shoulder and whispered, "Don't ruin it for the players."

He stood and went a little overboard with, "Definitely dead. Who could've committed this dastardly deed?"

An actor stepped forward dressed like a detective from the forties, complete with a tacky raincoat and fedora. "I'm Detective Matt Marlowe, Phil's younger brother," he said with a wink, "and I'll handle this." He thumbed at the body. "Who's the blonde dame?"

A snooty-looking older actor stood and straightened his tie. "That, Detective, is the famous actress, Jean Harlot."

He smirked. "Well, if she lived up to her last name, that could be why she was shot."

The guy standing said, "That's *my* wife you're talking about."

"Give me a break, buddy." The detective rolled his eyes. "You're old enough to be her grandfather."

Mr. Snooty jutted out his chin. "How dare you! I am Sir Nigel Tidsbury of the London Tidsburys, and I own Movie Magic Studios in Hollywood."

"Well, la de da. Now we know why she married *you*. But the important questions are, who was she fooling around with, and who was jealous enough to kill her?" He searched the faces of the crowd.

Everyone at Tidsbury's table turned and looked at a handsome man in his late twenties who said, "I didn't kill her—she loved me." He grinned at Tidsbury. "I starred opposite her in *Love's Deadly Kiss*."

A saucy young redhead said, "Her role should've been mine. I'm a far better actress, but I wasn't willing to sleep my way to the top."

"Now, see here, how dare you impugn my wife's integrity?"

The redhead stuck her nose in the air. "Your wife was a slut, and she deserved what she got."

A mousy-looking woman in her forties wearing thick glasses tried to comfort Sir Tidsbury, and the detective zeroed in on her. "Who might you be?"

"Malinda Goodheart. I've been Sir Tidsbury's personal assistant for the past twenty years." She looked adoringly at her boss. "He's a *wonderful* man."

"A bit smitten, are we?" Detective Marlowe said in a snide tone.

"Humph! I never—" She wiped away a tear.

Mike whispered in my ear, "If I interviewed suspects that way, I'd be fired."

I whispered back, "Who do you think did it?"

He grinned. "The husband—it's *always* the husband."

Sure enough, a few minutes later, Amelia stood and pointed at Tidsbury. "He did it. Sir Tidsbury is the murderer."

A bell rang, and Detective Marlowe said, "We have a winner! Congratulations to?"

"Lady Amelia Ainsworth." She curtsied and took her seat.

Everyone applauded, and Lady Amelia stood and took another bow.

The two FBI agents entered the ballroom.

Agent Taylor grabbed the microphone. "Attention everyone, we're investigating a murder. No one is allowed to leave this room." He scanned the ballroom and spotted the actress in the bloodstained white gown, still on the floor.

He and Agent Barnes rushed over to her.

"Miss, who shot you?" Taylor asked as Barnes called for an ambulance.

She pointed at her fake husband. "He did, but Lady Amelia already solved my murder. You're too late."

"What are you talking about?" Taylor asked.

Mike sauntered over and looked down at him. "This was a murder mystery dinner, and she was the fake victim. I hope you didn't call this in."

Taylor stood and glared at Mike. "*You* told us there's been another murder."

He lowered his voice. "Not her—Jorge Santos, Prince Gaspar's bodyguard, was dosed with GHB and fell off Jett's pier and drowned." Mike poked his chest. "*You* should've paid closer attention to my text. I said the body is already with the M.E."

His face turned crimson. "I, uh, missed that part."

Mike leaned close. "I haven't told these people about Jorge's murder, so don't blow it."

"We'll help you search the rooms for GHB," Taylor offered.

"I already did that and found it." He thumbed at the exit. "Grab your partner, and let's discuss this in private." Mike strode out the door.

The FBI agents followed him to the study, and Taylor closed the door. Before he took a seat, he asked Mike, "Where did you find the GHB?"

"In Count Aldo Medici's underwear drawer, but I think it might have been planted there by the killer. He has no motive for any of the murders."

"You still think Dina Fenton is the killer?" Barnes asked.

"She's the only one with a plausible motive for all the murders, and Medici is rarely in his room because he's spending his free time with Sophia DeLuca," Mike replied.

"Have you interviewed his bodyguard?" Taylor asked.

"Not yet." Mike frowned. "I didn't want the guests to know about Jorge's murder."

"Good." Taylor shot a glance at Barnes. "Find Nico Bernardi and bring him here. We'll interrogate him about his boss."

The two men spent a few minutes discussing Dina while they waited for Barnes to return with Aldo's bodyguard.

Neville burst in behind Barnes and Nico. He snapped, "I demand to be included or you'll hear from the Director of the FBI, and it won't be pleasant."

"Fine, but don't blab anything about this investigation to your buddies," Taylor said.

Once they were seated, the interrogation began.

"Mr. Bernardi, where were you this afternoon while Jorge Santos was fishing?" Taylor asked.

"Aldo wanted to take a stroll around the grounds with some friends." He glanced at Neville. "We joined Dina, Edith, Amelia, and this man. We began the walk after Sophia gave Dina a mug of beer for Jorge. She also handed DCI Wright a cooler of beer to deliver to him on the pier."

"So, Dina could have slipped GHB into the mug when no one was looking," Mike speculated. "Remember, Jorge rejected her last night."

"Or Sophia could've dosed it before she gave it to Dina," Taylor opined.

Mike rolled his eyes. "That's ridiculous. She didn't know any of these people before they checked in, and she has no motive."

"She did it for Aldo," Neville said. "Whose idea was it for Jorge to fish off the pier?"

"Sophia suggested it," Nico said. "She noticed Jorge was depressed and thought fishing might be a pleasant distraction."

"She and her boyfriend have Mafia ties," Taylor said. "Could be Jorge saw something he shouldn't have, and Aldo wanted him eliminated."

"Or the Mob wanted the victims taken out for reasons that have nothing to do with this conference. Think about it. This is the only time they're all together every year." Barnes seemed pleased with himself.

"Right," Taylor agreed. "It's the ideal time to eliminate several high-value targets."

Nico broke in, "My boss would never harm anyone. He's a gentle guy who enjoys wine and women, and I've never seen him talk to anybody in the Mafia."

"How long have you been with him?" Neville asked.

"Two years. He hired me after I completed twenty years in the Italian military."

"You might not know him as well as you think you do," Barnes suggested.

"The Medici family has had ties to the Mafia for more than two hundred years," Taylor explained.

"Any idea how long Jorge worked for Prince Gaspar?" Barnes asked Nico.

"He told me he went to work for the prince a year ago, soon after he finished twenty years in Spain's military."

"A law enforcement agency looking to crack down on Mob activities could've planted him with the prince," Neville suggested.

"And Count Medici found out and didn't want to be exposed," Taylor said.

Mike cut in. "Sounds like wild speculation to me."

"That's why we're in the FBI and you aren't," Barnes said. "Local cops don't look at the big picture."

"Yeah, and don't forget Sophia DeLuca's father was *Don* of the New York Mafia, and her sons run the show now," Taylor said with a smug tone. "She and the count could be working together on behalf of the Italian and New York Mafias."

"Right, don't forget her father, *Don* Calabrese, was from Sicily," Barnes chimed in.

"That's interesting," Neville agreed.

Mike seemed deep in thought. Finally, he said, "It was suggested that all the victims harbored dark secrets that might've resulted in their murders. That could be true. They were all super rich and could've been involved in all sorts of things we don't know about, Mafia or whatever."

Taylor turned to Nico. "If you want to avoid going down with the ship, I suggest you keep a tight leash on your boss and report any suspicious activity to us immediately."

Nico appeared solemn as he nodded.

"And Detective Miller, we expect you to keep a close watch on Sophia DeLuca." Agent Taylor crossed his arms. "We don't care if she's your girlfriend's buddy. It's your job to remain objective and help us nab the killers."

TWENTY-EIGHT

Mike joined me in bed after helping the FBI and Neville question all the guests and staff. He didn't look happy.

I leaned over and kissed him. "How did it go down there?"

"Not good." He sighed. "Everywhere I turn, I keep hitting dead ends."

"Is Dina still the main suspect?" I studied his handsome but tired face.

"She seems like the most probable killer to me, but the Feds are trying hard to blame the Mafia—so stupid." He pulled me to him and kissed me fiercely.

I must admit I enjoyed his attempts to burn off his frustrations by engaging in hot lovemaking with me. Who knew there was an upside to difficult murder investigations?

———

After an early morning romp in the sack, Mike asked, "What's on the agenda today?"

"Mystery panels all morning after breakfast in the dining room. Lunch in the ballroom, followed by a panel on cold cases, a two-hour break, and capped off with a double feature of Hitchcock mystery movies in the media room, *Vertigo* and *Dial M for Murder*. One movie will be shown before dinner, and one after." I pulled on shorts and a T-shirt.

"Anyone other than the guests going?" he asked, zipping up his pants.

"Sophia will be there to ensure Dina doesn't poison Aldo, and Neville will attend to watch the members. As the official hostess, I must go. It'll wrap up around eleven."

"The media room has stadium seating, so sit in the back where you can watch everyone." He buttoned his shirt.

"Any chance you'd want to sit in the back with me and neck?" I kissed him. "Please? It's casual dress night, so you won't have to wear a tux."

"I guess I'd better go and keep an eye on everyone, but no necking." He sat on the edge of the bed and put on his socks and shoes. "We'll save the good stuff for later."

"Drinks and popcorn will be served at the evening movie." I slid my feet into flip-flops. "*Vertigo* is only seventy-two minutes long, so we'll see that one at six and dine in the ballroom at seven-thirty." I gave him a quick kiss. "*Dial M for Murder* starts at nine and finishes at quarter to eleven." I nudged him. "It'll be fun."

"Right, because Mystery Fest has been *so much fun* so far," he said over his shoulder as he sauntered down the hallway.

———

It was 4:35 p.m., and Dina filled the huge clawfoot tub in her private bath with water as hot as she could stand. She would luxuriate in her custom blend of perfumed bubble bath for as long as the temperature remained comfortable. But first, she answered a knock at her bedroom door.

"Is this the whiskey I ordered?" she asked as she accepted a double Bourbon on the rocks from a server.

"Yes, ma'am, Blanton's Black Label Kentucky Bourbon."

"Excellent. Thank you, dear. I'm looking forward to a long, soothing bubble bath and a good book." Dina closed the door and carried the crystal tumbler to her bathroom.

Huh, the bubbles aren't as high as normal. Wonder why?

She slipped off her robe and eased into the hot water. "Ah, this is perfect—so relaxing," she said to herself.

Her glass of Bourbon sat near her Sig P365 micro handgun on a table alongside the tub. She picked up the whiskey and sipped it as she thought about the murders.

So puzzling—no obvious motives, and why kill Gaspar's body-guard? Unless...could Nico be the killer and Jorge figured it out? No, neither bodyguard was at the castle when Gaspar fell down the stairs —unless he wasn't pushed, and the earlier drug overdose made him fall.

Dina took a deep drink and set the glass on the table. The smooth whiskey and hot bubble bath soothed her. She leaned her head back against the tub, the water caressing her upper neck below her chin.

I bet Aldo is the killer. No one ever suspects the sweet, quiet ones, like Aldo...or Amelia. Or could it be the one person everyone assumes is beyond suspicion—DCI Neville Wright?

She picked up the Bourbon and almost dropped the glass with her wet, slippery hand. Her next swallow emptied the double whiskey. Dina returned the glass to the table.

All the victims were foreigners, so the killer could be an American with a secret grudge against them. Aldo or Amelia might be the next target.

She looked up at the small crystal chandelier hanging from the bathroom ceiling. A rainbow of colors danced around the light fixture, and the room blurred.

Dina's muscles suddenly relaxed. She struggled to take a breath as her limp body slowly slid beneath the bubbles.

———

I settled in the top back center recliner where stadium seating provided five rows of six seats. Alfred Hitchcock's masterpiece, *Vertigo*, widely acclaimed as the best movie ever made, began with the eerie opening credits focused on Kim Novak's pupil, morphing into dizzying graphics that ended with the director's name across her eyeball.

Actor James Stewart played an ex-cop who left the force after feeling responsible for the falling death of a policeman who tried to help him when he was hanging from the gutter along the top of a tall building. Stewart's character suffered from acrophobia after that, a trait rumored to be shared by Hitchcock.

As I watched the chilling psychological thriller, I thought it would've been the perfect movie for Mystery Fest had it not been for all the real murders. Even though my seat was only twelve feet above the ground floor, the movie had a dizzying effect. And Kim Novak's dual roles were brilliantly acted. Every scene was filled with imagery and nuance.

If Mike had been beside me, I would've grabbed his hand, but he only agreed to meet me for dinner and the second movie. Sophia and Aldo sat two seats away on my left, holding hands—so sweet, and Nico sat on the right end seat. Almost everyone else sat in the first two rows, not wanting to climb higher.

I spotted Amelia in the front, flanked by Edith and Neville, with three American guests occupying the rest of that row. Six Americans filled the second tier, two sat on the third level, and the fourth row was empty. That accounted for everyone except Dina. Did she decide to skip the first movie?

Everyone in the audience, including me, was riveted by the ever-building tension that climaxed with the shocking ending. No one moved as the credits rolled, stunned by the emotional trauma in the powerful finale. My nerves tingled with adrenaline, and I craved a Scotch even though I never drank whisky.

Best movie kudos for Hitchcock's *Vertigo* had been well earned. And the movie was filmed all the way back in 1958. Apparently, some movies really were timeless.

I ambled behind the guests walking to the ballroom for dinner, allowing me time to recover from the jarring show, especially after so many real murders. Everyone must've felt unnerved because they went straight to the bar after stopping in the restrooms. Looking a bit shell-shocked, they headed for their tables with strong alcoholic beverages in hand.

The bartender handed me my drink, and I turned around and bumped into Mike. "I'm so glad you're here." Hugging him like he was the only life preserver in a raging sea gave me a sense of relief.

He pulled back and looked into my eyes. "Jett, what the hell? You never drink Scotch, and you look rattled. Has there been another murder?"

"No, it's that movie—after everything else, it really got to me." I snuggled against him again.

He squeezed me tightly and kissed me. "I'm hungry. Let's grab some dinner."

We sat at a table by ourselves so we could have a private conversation.

He glanced across the room at Sophia and Aldo. "Has Sophia said anything about Aldo being in deep with the Italian Mafia?"

"No, he mostly talks about his vineyards, favorite wines, and how beautiful Italy is in the summer. She said he's angling for her to fly home with him. Why?"

"The Feds have this crazy idea that Aldo and Sophia are the killers, carrying out hits for the Mob."

TWENTY-NINE

T he guests went up to their rooms to freshen up after dinner, while Mike and I checked that the next movie was ready to show in the media room. At 9:00, we sat in the top row with Sophia and Aldo on our left and Nico on our right. Everyone else sat where they had before, except Neville, who was missing, and Dina, who hadn't attended either movie.

I called Karin. "Has anyone in your wait staff served Dina Fenton?"

"Hang on a sec while I check." Moments later, she said, "One of my servers said she brought her a double Bourbon late this afternoon, and Dina told her she looked forward to a long hot bath and a good book."

"Did she order dinner in her room?"

"No, maybe she fell asleep and will order a meal later."

"Okay, Karin, thanks. I'm with the guests in the media room. We're about to watch Hitchcock's *Dial M for Murder*."

"A server is on the way with popcorn and a bar cart. Oh, and Hunter said to tell you he went home. He was feeling better and getting antsy with nothing to do here. I think he was eager to work on his airplane."

"Too bad for you. When did he leave?"

"Early this morning after I got up to make breakfast for the guests."

"Thanks, Karin. I'll call him later."

Mike nudged me. "Where's Neville?"

"I don't know, but as long as he isn't here, I'm happy." I slid my hand into his.

The opening credits hadn't quite finished when Tim texted me. The message said: *Meet me on the back terrace now and bring Mike with you—urgent!*

I showed Mike the message, and we left quietly. Once outside the media room, I said, "What could be so urgent?"

We hurried outside through the French doors in the great hall and found Neville lying in a broken heap on the terrace. Outdoor floodlights illuminated the corpse.

Tim stood beside the bloody body and pointed up. "Looks like he took a header from his fourth-floor balcony, but the lights are off in his room. Did he seem suicidal to you?"

"Not at all." I looked away from the sickening scene of his smashed head and broken body. "He was hellbent on catching the killer."

"Looks like the killer caught him. Did anyone see him fall?" Mike asked. "One of the guards?"

"Sorry, they weren't looking up at that moment." Tim frowned. "I didn't call it in—figured you'd want to handle it."

"Thanks." Mike pulled out his cell and called the medical examiner and a crime scene unit. He pocketed his phone. "Tim, have your guards keep everyone away from the body while you wait for the M.E. I'll check Neville's room."

I grabbed Mike's hand. "Want me to go with you?"

"No, babe, his room is the crime scene. I can't risk contamination. Go back to the movie and keep an eye on all your guests." He gave me a quick kiss. "Be careful. One of them is the killer."

"Wait, Dina could've done it. She was in her room during the first movie and dinner, and she didn't come to the second movie either."

"Remind me again where she's staying and also where Neville's room is located."

"Dina's room is on the west side of the third floor, one room away from the north end where Klaus was staying, and Neville's room is on the fourth floor, halfway down the east side. There's a carving on his oak door of a Viking head wearing a horned hat."

"Okay, thanks, and don't let on that anything's wrong when you return to the movie. That will give me time to investigate and call in our *friends* at the FBI. I'll see you after the movie." He strode away.

I slipped back into the media room and hurried up the steps to the top row. Nico stood to let me pass, and I settled one seat away from Sophia and Aldo. Everyone seemed riveted to the screen, so it must've been a good movie, but all I could think about was the broken body on the terrace.

I didn't like the snotty little detective, but he didn't deserve to be splattered over my terrace. And a suicidal person wouldn't bother to turn out the lights before jumping. No, the killer wanted the room dark so no one would see him or her shove Neville over the railing.

I hope Mike proves Dina did it so we can finally end this nightmare.

———

As the end credits rolled, I jumped up, moved to the exit, and turned on the lights. I opened the door, and Mike and the two Feds were waiting outside.

"Jett, we have an announcement to make," Mike said.

The Feds pushed past me, and Agent Taylor said, "Everyone remain in your seats. We have news, and it's not good." He waited while the guests settled. "It is my sad task to inform you that Detective Chief Inspector Neville Wright of Scotland Yard is dead. We suspect someone shoved him off his fourth-floor balcony."

The crowd gasped, and Edith and Amelia said in unison, "No, not Neville!"

Taylor continued, "We also found Dina Fenton dead in her bathtub.

We're not sure whether she fell asleep and drowned or someone killed her. We'll know more after the autopsy."

"Could she have killed Neville and then herself?" Sophia asked.

"Initial findings indicate Dina died first, but don't worry. The suspect pool just got a lot smaller." He looked directly at Sophia and Aldo. "We'll catch the killer or killers very soon."

"Soon?" a criminology professor from Harvard said. "There have been eight deaths, and all you can say is *soon*? How many more of us must die before you figure this out?"

"Remain calm, sir. We're close to making an arrest, but for now, procedure requires us to interview each of you." Taylor consulted a list. "Count Aldo Medici, please come with me."

Agent Barnes said, "Mrs. Sophia DeLuca, you're with me."

As Sophia walked by me, I leaned in and whispered, "Be careful what you say. They think you and Aldo are the killers."

"Mrs. Edith Pickering, please accompany me," Mike said.

I grabbed his arm. "Mike, my guests have been in here two hours and need to use a bathroom."

"All right, lead them to the ballroom where they can use the facilities and wait there to be interviewed. And open the bar."

As I led my guests down the long hallway, Lady Amelia clutched my arm. "Jett, I'm worried. The killer seems to be accelerating the murders, and I might be next."

"I'll arrange for a guard to sit outside your bedroom door. Will that make you feel better?" I patted her hand. "I know Neville was a long-time friend, and I'm so sorry for your loss."

"Thank you, dear. I never dreamed I'd lose so many close friends in such a short time. Tomorrow night is supposed to be the conference finale with the formal dinner dance cruise. I was looking forward to a scenic trip down the Intracoastal Waterway, but now Aldo and Edith are the only friends I have left. What do you think will happen?"

"I'll poll the guests and see if they want to cancel the cruise. In any case, I guess everyone will be stuck here until the FBI makes an arrest."

"A trip out in the fresh air might be a nice distraction from all the murders," she said. "I vote we go ahead with dinner on the boat. We need to get away from here for a while."

"All right, if the majority agrees with you, we'll go ahead with the original schedule." I waited while she and the others used the restrooms.

Once everyone was settled with drinks in hand, I asked, "Please raise your hands if you'd like to attend the dinner cruise tomorrow night for the conference finale."

The vote was unanimous. Even with two members not voting because they were being interviewed, there were enough yes votes to override them.

Oh boy, a dinner cruise. What could possibly go wrong?

THIRTY

After such a traumatic night, the guests slept late, still dealing with the deaths of Dina Fenton and DCI Neville Wright. A breakfast buffet was available in the dining room from 8:30 until 11:00 a.m.

Aldo, Nico, and Sophia joined Mike and me for an early breakfast on the back terrace. We wanted to help them avoid being railroaded by the FBI.

The morning was calm and sunny, and the ocean glistened like a placid lake. A hint of a breeze stirred my hair as I sipped my coffee.

Mike broke the silence. "I don't think you're guilty. How did your interviews go?"

"Obviously, someone is framing me, but the FBI doesn't believe it." Aldo frowned. "They assume Sophia is helping me, but our rooms are two floors below Neville's room."

Sophia nodded. "Yeah, they're grasping at straws, trying to pin the murders on us, but nobody saw us on the fourth floor."

"Same for Dina's room on the third floor—no witnesses." Aldo sat back and stirred his coffee. "They're convinced the Mafia wanted all the victims dead, and they used us to carry out the hits—ridiculous."

"Was there any connection between the Mob and the people who were targeted?" I asked.

Aldo frowned. "Possibly. Edmund headed a massive government campaign to eliminate organized crime in Great Britain, but that included Russians, Serbians, and a host of others, not just the Italian Mafia."

"His task force didn't affect you, did it?" Mike asked.

"The Ministry of Commerce suspended my license to export wine to the UK until a thorough investigation was conducted." He sighed. "My family had connections with the Mafia in Sicily and Naples beginning in the 1800s, as did many royals and noble families. But that was long ago. Personally, I've never had any dealings with mobsters."

"And because my father was *Don* of the New York Mafia, the Feds assume I'm active in the organization, which I'm not and never was." Sophia looked at me. "You know my sons run the family business now, but I stay out of it, always have."

"Ask Dominic or Marco if the Mob ordered hits on the victims here," I suggested.

"Don't ask them on the phone—the Feds likely have it bugged," Mike warned.

"I'll invite Gwen over for a chat on the beach and explain the situation. She can call Marco. He'll remember her from a few months ago. She can arrange for him to meet Sophia somewhere on the Intracoastal. We'll take my speedboat, and he can rent one."

Sophia groaned. "I don't know—my boys aren't gonna be happy about this."

"Yeah, but if the FBI arrests you for murder, your sons will go ballistic—we're talking scorched earth," I said. "And they'll blame me because you live here."

Mike squeezed my hand. "Let's not get all worked up. There's no hard evidence implicating Sophia, and all the evidence against Aldo was planted."

He looked at Aldo. "You're an intelligent man. You'd never keep things used for the murders in your room or leave your fingerprints on them. This is clearly a frame-up."

"But who is doing this and why?" He patted Sophia's hand. "Sorry to put you through this, my darling."

"It has to be someone at this event." I searched his face. "Who would want all those people dead?"

"What if Aldo is just the most convenient scapegoat, and the killer has nothing against him personally?" Mike asked.

"I can't imagine sweet Amelia being involved. The victims were our friends." Aldo frowned. "That leaves twelve Americans, and I don't know any of them well."

"Could there be a dark secret from long ago that has finally caught up with you?" I was thinking about the séance and the books that hit Neville's head.

Aldo's face blanched. "No…it can't be that. It was fifty years ago and had nothing to do with anyone at this event."

Mike's voice hardened. "Tell us anyway."

He sighed and glanced at Sophia. "I was twenty and engaged to be married. My rival was a sore loser and threatened to destroy my fiancée with filthy lies. Back then, a woman's reputation was everything."

Sophia reached out and took his hand. "What happened?"

"He challenged me to a pistol duel at dawn, winner takes all."

"Did you accept?" Mike asked.

"*Sì*—he said it was the only way to resolve things. He'd stop his threats if I won."

"Did your fiancée know about the duel?" I asked.

He nodded. "Celia was terrified I'd be killed and she'd be forced to marry him."

"That must've been awful for both of you." I patted his arm.

Mike drained his coffee. "What happened to your rival?"

His eyes moistened. "He missed…I didn't…one bullet straight into his heart."

"Were you charged with murder?" Mike asked.

"The Italian police reported it as a shooting accident." He shook his head. "They look the other way for members of the nobility."

"What about the dead man's family?" Sophia asked. "Did they threaten you?"

"No, our Seconds agreed it was a clean kill. All the rules were followed." He patted her hand. "You must understand—any objections would have dishonored him and his family."

"The way I see it, he brought this on himself, and you have nothing to feel guilty about. You were protecting your woman." She kissed his cheek. "You're a hero."

"I may have done the right thing, but I'm not proud of it." He hung his head.

"Think someone at this event is related to the guy you shot?" Mike asked.

"Nico and I are the only Italian guests, and I checked his background before I hired him. His family has no ties to my past."

"What if one of the Americans is a distant relative to your dead rival?" Sophia asked.

"No, my darling, the members of this organization are thoroughly vetted. No such connection exists, I assure you."

"I hope my son can shed some light on what's happening here." She looked at me. "Call Gwen."

THIRTY-ONE

I slipped Marco DeLuca's phone number to Gwen during our stroll on the beach, and she arranged for him to meet her, Sophia, and me on the Intracoastal near the Riverwalk in Jupiter at 3:00 p.m. The plan was he would take his private jet to the Stuart Airport, accompanied by a couple of goombahs, and rent a Cigarette boat.

All very stealthy and nowhere near the Feds.

———

At noon, I dined at a table in the ballroom with Edith and several guests while a local expert entertained us with a talk on new ways to recover DNA at crime cases. I paid close attention to the speaker, thinking the information might help me in my new career as a private investigator.

After the luncheon ended, Edith asked, "Jett, would you please meet privately with Amelia and me somewhere quiet for a few minutes?"

"Of course. I'll show you to the music room. It's soundproof." I led them down the hallway and into the room with the grand piano and tall windows showcasing the sea. Royal blue draperies adorned the leaded windows, and matching velvet covered the mahogany-framed sofas and armchairs.

I closed the heavy oak door behind us and waited until everyone was seated. "Is this about the murders?"

"No, dear. This is about a gift that must be witnessed." Amelia pulled out an official-looking paper, signed it, and passed it to Edith. "She is my witness to your gift and this document which verifies its provenance." She waited until Edith signed the document, then passed it to me along with her gold lion's head cane. "The eyes are ten-carat diamonds, and the head and base are almost solid gold."

My hand tingled when I held the cane. "Lady Amelia, I'm honored, but I can't accept this. You take it with you everywhere, and besides, you need it for support." I handed it back to her.

"Jett, dear, I've never needed this to help me walk. It's more like a trusted companion, which I insist you accept now as a token of my esteem."

"I don't understand—why now and why me? I hope it's not because you expect to be murdered like the spirits warned."

"Well, no, but I'm not getting any younger, and I have no children —never married. Long ago, after my sister was killed in a hit-and-run accident, I canceled my wedding and dedicated my life to seeking justice."

She leaned forward. "I help the Met solve cold cases, and I write mystery novels that always end with the criminal getting what he deserves." She glanced around. "You live in this historic home with over a century of family history, and it's obvious you appreciate and revere the heirlooms preserved here."

"That's true, but still, why would you want to part with your precious cane?"

"This is more than a pretty accessory. It's an historic artifact over four hundred years old which originally belonged to James I, the first king of England and Scotland—he ascended the throne in 1603." She stroked the lion's head.

"This cane has served me well for almost fifty years, and now I believe you need it more than I do. You see, legend claims it imbues its owner with an almost supernatural insight." She chuckled. "Unfortunately, mine has since been diminished by age."

She grasped my hand. "Jett, I believe you share my keen desire for justice." She handed the cane back to me. "Before I came here, I read about how you solved your parents' murders."

My hand tingled again as I held the artifact. "You're right about my desire for justice, and I could certainly use some insight into solving the Mystery Fest murders." I admired the intricate features of the extraordinary cane made of hand-carved mahogany with inlaid gold filigree and an intricately molded gold head and paw that had withstood four centuries. "Thank you, Lady Amelia. I'll treasure it always."

"I have one request."

"Anything for you, dear lady."

"In the unlikely event that you have no children, please bequeath the artifact to the British Museum."

"That's a promise, and I always keep my promises."

We stood, and I hugged her. "Thank you for trusting me with this." I held the beautiful work of art.

"I'm counting on you, Jett." She checked her watch. "We'd best get on or we'll miss the panel on serial killers."

I walked them out and headed up to my room with my new treasure. My closet held a hidden firearms vault, and I locked the special cane inside. Was it my imagination, or did it emit a pale, golden aura in the dark cabinet?

As I headed downstairs, I wondered when the "almost supernatural insight" would kick in. I wanted to catch the killer, and Amelia implied she was counting on me to save her life.

––––––––

I left word with the guards that we were taking a quick ride on the Intracoastal in my vintage, thirty-foot Chris Craft to clear our heads and check nautical conditions for the formal yacht party scheduled to depart from my pier at 7 p.m. Luckily, the FBI agents hadn't arrived when we sped away at 2:15 p.m. They planned to accompany us on the dinner cruise and spy on Aldo and Sophia.

It was a beautiful day as we cruised up the Waterway, careful not to leave a wake in residential areas, which was most of the trip. Also, we kept a sharp lookout for Manatees, the gentle giants known as sea cows, who lived in Florida waters.

On arrival, I pulled the throttle back to idle in the middle of the wide channel, the Riverwalk buildings towering along the waterfront to our east, and the huge Indiantown Road Bridge looming above us to the south. Small waves lapped at the hull in a gentle breeze.

Gwen pointed north. "That flashy Cigarette speedboat has to be Marco."

When they were close enough, we waved, and they turned toward us, the deep rumble of their engines growing louder. Moments later, they cut the power and coasted alongside our varnished mahogany speedboat, the reddish-brown wood glistening in the sunlight.

Sophia and I boarded Marco's boat in case mine was bugged. Gwen stayed behind, and we didn't speak until we were far enough away. Our cell phones were off.

Sophia hugged her son. "Thanks for coming on such short notice."

I recognized the refrigerators with no necks—Sal and Joey, who had accompanied Marco to Valhalla back in March when Sophia had been in peril. Sal shut down the engines, and we drifted.

"Hi, guys. Good to see you again." I was nervous, not sure how Marco would react to our situation, but positive he wouldn't like it one bit.

Sal smiled and said, "Jett," and Joey gave me his usual blank look.

Marco, thirty-six, single, and a dark, handsome Italian, pulled me in for a hug. "Hey, Jett, you're looking as gorgeous as ever. I hope you're keeping Ma out of trouble."

"I'm trying my best." I kissed his cheeks, attempting to stay on his good side.

He sat between us. "Okay, Ma, does the big emergency have anything to do with the murders at Jett's castle?"

She hesitated and looked at her feet.

He glanced at me.

I looked at my feet.

"Oh, geez, Ma, you're giving me gray hairs already." He tapped the sides of his head. "See? You did that." A few silver hairs decorated his temples.

I touched his arm. "Marco, we had nothing to do with the murders, and we have no idea who the killer is, but the FBI is hellbent on blaming your mother and her new boyfriend."

"Dom and I were in South America this past week. We didn't know about the murders or we would've rushed down here. I found out this morning from Gwen."

"I don't suppose there's any chance they were Mafia hits?" I asked.

"Believe me, I'd know if the Family was targeting guests in your castle. Why do you ask?"

Sophia turned to him. "Because the FBI thinks my boyfriend and I are carrying out hits for the Mob."

His eyes narrowed. "Since when do you have a boyfriend, and who is he?"

"He's Count Aldo Medici from Italy, a nobleman from a very old family." She looked into her son's eyes. "I really like him, Marco. It might even be love."

He stared at her, momentarily speechless. "Ma, the Medici are a centuries-old royal family connected to the formation of Cosa Nostra in Sicily in the 1800s. We revere them. How can I help?"

I jumped in. "All the targets have been extremely wealthy, high-profile VIPs from Europe and Great Britain, except the Spanish body-guard, a Scotland Yard detective, and a Texas oil heiress. Most of them belong to an elite club, Mystery Lovers International, and they're at Valhalla for their annual conference. It's the only time all of them are in the same place at one time."

Sophia nodded. "That's why the Feds think they're targeted hits. The killer has been framing Aldo, and the FBI suspects us because we have Mob connections in our families, and we're dating."

"After Gwen called and told me about the murders, I made some calls. The Mafia isn't involved and would be very upset if anything bad happens to Count Medici." He studied us. "There has to be another motive, and the killer must be a pro, or he would've been caught by now." He paused. "I'll have my people take a hard look at the American guests, bodyguard Nico Bernardi, and that author, Lady Amelia Ainsworth. I'm betting it's one of the Americans, but we'll check everyone." He asked me, "Have the Feds cleared your household staff?"

"Yes, they're clean. I feel like all the crimes are connected, but I can't figure out how or why yet."

Sophia clutched his hand. "How will we communicate without the FBI knowing?"

Marco nudged me. "Give me your lawyer's name and number. We'll hire him and use him as our intermediary—attorney/client privilege. No problem."

I wrote down the info and glanced at my watch. "We must get back. The final conference event is a formal dinner cruise tonight. Hopefully, we'll get through it without another murder. Local police, the FBI, and private guards will watch everyone on the boat."

"You girls be careful." He hugged me and then his mother. "I love ya, Ma."

"I love ya too, darling boy."

In minutes, we were back onboard my Chris Craft headed home.

THIRTY-TWO

A gents Taylor and Barnes waited for us as we pulled up to the pier. They didn't look happy. I tossed Taylor a line.

"Where did you go?" he asked, as he incorrectly wrapped the rope around a cleat. Typical landlubber.

"We wanted to get away for a few hours and do something cheerful —we love boating." I checked the fenders hanging on the dockside and secured the lines.

"You're going on a four-hour boat cruise tonight." He glared at us.

"This was different—sunshine and salt spray." Sophia stepped onto the floating dock and smoothed her shorts. "Tonight, it's a formal affair aboard a giant yacht. It won't even feel like we're moving."

Gwen arched an eyebrow. "I do hope you're not going dressed like that, Agents."

They looked down at their black suits and ties with white shirts.

Barnes asked, "What's wrong with this?"

"All the men will be wearing tuxedoes, even the local cops. But if you don't mind embarrassing the FBI, go as you are." Gwen gave them a disapproving look. "Gotta run. I want to look perfect when Clint and I board the yacht."

"Wait—*you're* going on the dinner cruise?" Taylor asked.

"My date and I are Palm Beach Police Detectives, and we agreed to help Jett keep watch over the Mystery Fest guests." She turned and strode away.

"Detective Miller and another Banyan Isle Police officer will also be aboard, along with four private security guards I hired," I said. "Excuse us. We need to get ready for tonight."

Sophia and I made a beeline for the castle and away from the pesky Feds.

————

The security guards and law enforcement officers wore shoulder holsters under their tuxedo jackets, except Gwen, who had an inner-thigh holster and side slits in her long dress so she could quickly reach her handgun if necessary.

Gwen boarded wearing a sultry red silk gown, and her date, the tall, dark, and dashing Clint Reynolds, looked like a young version of Pierce Brosnan in a James Bond tux. I hoped they'd enjoy a romantic evening with no drama.

It looked like the FBI agents had decided not to join us, but then they rushed up the gangplank in ill-fitting formalwear rentals.

"Agents Taylor and Barnes, glad you could make it." I suppressed a smirk.

Mike assured me I didn't need a firearm with him at my side, and he warned Sophia not to carry one with the Feds watching her every move. He and I remained at the gangway amidships and greeted the guests.

The one-hundred-foot party boat had a main-level dining room and piano bar, a galley and staff cabins belowdecks, and a top deck encircled by a railing and open to the sky. It was decorated with party lights, had tables at both ends, and a dance floor in the middle with a bandstand beside it.

"Lady Amelia, I love your rose silk gown." I smiled warmly, and Mike helped her aboard.

"Thank you, dear." A mere five feet tall, she leaned close to me. "Have you received supernatural insight from my gift?"

I bent down, my five-inch stilettos making me almost six-foot-two, like Mike. "I'm afraid not, Lady Amelia. Sorry."

She looked up at me. "The thing is, for the lion's head cane to work, you must carry it with you."

"Oh, darn, I have it locked in my gun safe."

"That simply won't do, dear. Its energy can't reach you from inside a vault."

"Understood, and I will remedy that as soon as I return to the castle."

"Good. I'm counting on you, Jett." She strolled into the dining room.

Next to board was club president, Edith Pickering, and her husband.

"Fabulous navy gown, Edith, and it's good to see you, Roland."

He took my hand. "I remember you, Jett. You're the kind lady who saved my life a few months ago."

Edith smiled and took his arm. "Yes, dear. Now come, we're holding up the line."

Mike shot me a sideways grin and squeezed my waist. He mimicked my comments to the women, whispering, "Jett, I *love* your low-cut electric-blue gown. It matches your eyes." He nibbled my ear.

I giggled. This night might be fun after all.

Soon, everyone was onboard, and most of us were seated at the long dining table.

The huge yacht was perfect for only twenty-eight passengers, counting all the conference guests, law enforcement officers, and security guards.

The captain took us south toward Miami, past all the mansions, despite the numerous drawbridges we'd encounter. As we motored beneath the tall Blue Heron Bridge connecting Singer Island to the mainland, we enjoyed a sumptuous dinner with choices of Peking duck, Chilean sea bass, or *boeuf bourguignon*. Several wines were offered to pair with the dinner choices, and everyone seemed to be having a good time.

No drama.

Nico sat beside Aldo, keeping an eye on his food and wine. Tim and Kelly were all business, doing a thorough search of the boat while the other security guards patrolled the dining deck. Local law enforcement officers enjoyed dining with us while keeping watch with the two Feds seated at either end of the table.

Everyone seemed to be on their best behavior as the wine flowed and laughter rippled through the room. The steady distant hum of the engines had a soothing effect that implied safety, and the guests began to relax and let their guard down.

A large assortment of desserts was offered, along with digestifs such as cognac, Armagnac, limoncello, and the delicious dark-brown liqueur, nocino, from Italy.

Feeling light and cheerful, the guests made their way to the top deck where the balmy night air had a refreshing effect. The band played popular tunes for the senior crowd, and soon the dance floor was filled with happy couples.

Lady Amelia took me aside. "Jett, I've enjoyed getting to know you, and you're welcome to visit me in England anytime. I have a lovely home in the Cotswolds with plenty of room for guests. Feel free to bring Mike or a friend with you."

"Thank you, Lady Amelia. My friend in the red gown, Gwen Pendragon, is half-English, and her uncle is the Duke of Colchester. We'll visit you both next time we're in England."

"I'd love that, dear. I'm acquainted with Clive and the late Duchess. I noticed your friend is wearing an ancient brooch Elizabeth used to wear." She patted my back. "Now go and dance with your handsome boyfriend."

I gave her a hug and pulled Mike out for a slow dance to "Smoke Gets in Your Eyes."

He whispered in my ear, "Everything okay?"

"So far, so good. Everyone seems to be having a good time." I nuzzled his neck.

The captain gently reversed the engines for a moment to stop our forward progress as we waited for a drawbridge to open. The boat maintained its position as Mike held me close and guided me ever so slowly around the floor. I rested my head on his shoulder, enjoying the moment.

A shrill scream pierced the placid night.

I turned toward the outcry and heard a loud splash.

THIRTY-THREE

Aldo stood at the railing looking shocked, and Tim and Kelly dived in after a rapidly sinking woman wearing a pale rose gown.

Lady Amelia.

Mike grabbed a life ring and tossed it to Tim after he surfaced with Kelly and the victim. They put her arms through the floatation device and towed her inert body to the fantail.

We rushed below and arrived aft as the men laid Amelia on the deck. Her rescuers began CPR, but she didn't respond.

Kelly looked up at us. "Nothing. Maybe she was dead before she hit the water."

I bit my lip, fighting back tears. "I can't believe she's gone. I should've saved her."

"Could've been a heart attack or a slow-acting poison that took effect right before she fell in." Tim lifted her wrist. "Mike, look, she's clutching something in her right hand."

Mike grabbed a linen napkin and used it to pry open her hand. A torn piece of cloth that looked like a tuxedo breast pocket lay in her palm.

Agents Taylor and Barnes arrived with Aldo. Taylor noticed his jacket pocket was ripped off and spied the cloth in Amelia's open hand.

"You killed her, Count Medici. That cloth proves it." Taylor pointed at Aldo's torn tux and the fabric in her hand.

"No!" Aldo insisted. "I tried to save her, but she went over the rail so fast I couldn't stop her."

"This is the last straw. The evidence for all the murders points to you." Barnes cuffed his wrists behind him.

Taylor said, "Count Medici, you're under arrest for multiple murders." He recited his Miranda rights.

Sophia ran up to them. "He's innocent. Amelia's fall was an accident—too much to drink. Let him go."

Barnes grabbed her wrist. "How do you know?"

"I was in the ladies' room on the dining deck. She hit the water right after I left the bathroom—saw her through the window." She poked Barnes. "The thing is, she looked limp—no struggling. That's not normal."

Taylor glared at her. "Go on."

"She looked like she was already dead."

Barnes cuffed her wrists behind her back. "You poisoned her for him, didn't you?"

Sophia's eyes were filled with contempt. "No, I didn't, and when Aldo and I are proven innocent, you and your buddy will never work in law enforcement again."

He dragged her to a chair. "You're going to jail with your boyfriend."

"I'll get you a good lawyer, Sophia. Don't worry." I fought back tears, frustrated that I couldn't protect my dear friend, who was also like a mother to me.

"These two Feds are the ones who should be worried." She glared at them. "Their careers will be over, and they won't be able to hide behind their badges."

"Think about this, Mrs. DeLuca—Florida has the death penalty." Taylor smirked. "The Mafia can't save you."

The captain turned the boat around, and we docked at my pier at

10:20 p.m. The passengers had to wait until the medical examiner removed the body, and the Feds interviewed everyone. My guests finally got to bed around midnight, except poor Aldo and Sophia. They were locked in holding cells at the county jail.

I stood on my back terrace with Mike and called my family's corporate lawyer, Niles Lockwood. His oceanfront home was a few doors down from mine. "Niles, sorry to wake you, but this is urgent."

He yawned. "It must be for you to call after midnight."

"My dear friend, Sophia DeLuca, and her boyfriend, Count Aldo Medici from Italy, have been arrested for murder and taken to the county lockup. I'm certain they're innocent. Find them the best criminal defense attorneys in the country, and ask them to schedule a bail hearing tomorrow."

"I'll make some calls and get back to you later in the morning."

"One more thing—expect to hear from Sophia's sons, Marco and Dominic DeLuca. They live in New York, but one or both may come to Florida to help their mother. They want you to represent them so you'll have an attorney/client relationship."

"Understood. I'll take their call."

"Thank you, Niles." I pocketed my phone and snuggled onto Mike's shoulder.

He held me close. "Don't worry, sweetheart, we'll find a way to clear them. Somebody framed Aldo, and we must figure out who and why."

"I know one thing for sure. This has nothing to do with the Mafia."

He took my hand. "Let's get some sleep. There's nothing more we can do tonight."

"I feel terrible Amelia died, and I hate the thought of Sophia sitting all alone in a cold, dark jail cell." I fought back tears as I started up the staircase with Mike.

———

The next morning, my guests gathered in the dining room for a final breakfast. FBI Agents Taylor and Barnes came in and returned everyone's passports, including mine.

Taylor said, "You're all free to go wherever you wish, but you might have to testify at the murder trials, which will be months from now. We're sorry we had to keep everyone here until arrests could be made. On behalf of the FBI, we'd like to thank you for your cooperation."

The agents nodded at me and walked out.

I closed the dining room door behind them. "Ladies and Gentlemen, we've all been through a terrible ordeal and suffered many losses. I respect you all as crime experts, so if you ever think of anything that might help solve these murders, please let me know."

My eyes swept the group. "You know Aldo. He's an intelligent man who would never keep evidence in his room if he was the killer. Nobody in your club is that stupid. He was obviously framed, and I don't want the real killer to get away with all the murders. I'm sure you don't either, so please stay in touch."

They nodded their assent.

The Harvard professor said, "This is by far the most puzzling case we've ever seen. If you solve it, please share your findings with us. We'll do the same for you if we come up with something useful."

"Thank you. I wish this could've been a better experience, and I'm sorry if my home played a part in this nightmare. I wish you well." I opened the door and walked them out.

Every guest checked out before 10:00 a.m., like they couldn't leave fast enough despite going to bed so late the previous night.

My beloved home, Valhalla Castle, would never live this down. It would forevermore be known by names from the news media: House of Horrors, Crime Castle, and Murder Mansion. At least my parents and ancestors weren't around to see this tragic legacy unfold.

Mike had to leave as soon as we got up so he could change clothes and deal with a mountain of police paperwork associated with the murders.

And I had to find a way to save Sophia and Aldo.

THIRTY-FOUR

I felt alone as I sat on the back terrace steps and hugged my dogs. They sensed my mood and kissed my cheeks. Everything seemed hopeless. I dreaded meeting Marco with the news about his mother.

A gentle tap on my shoulder made me turn around. Hunter reached down and pulled me up for a big hug.

"Don't worry, we'll get her back. I promise." His words reassured me.

My cell dinged with a text. It read: *Meet me on Peanut Island.* The message was from an unknown number—Marco.

I turned off my phone. "Switch off your phone and come with me. We're going for a boat ride."

I left my dogs with Karin, and Hunter and I took the Chris Craft south past the Blue Heron Bridge to Peanut Island, a manmade island near Singer Island. We docked at the long pier and walked past the empty Cigarette boat tied nearby. Marco and his muscle waited for us at a picnic table on shore.

"Hey, guys, you remember my uncle?"

They smiled and shook his hand.

"Of course. Good to see you, Hunter. My ma loves you," Marco said.

"And I love her." He sighed. "We have to find a way to get her out of this."

"I talked to Niles Lockwood this morning. He said Ma is in the county jail, and so is Count Medici. What the hell happened?"

Hunter frowned. "I wasn't there." He glanced at me.

I faced Marco. "Everyone was on the top deck, dancing and enjoying the view." I told him everything. "The Feds are claiming Aldo pushed Lady Amelia Ainsworth overboard, and she tried to save herself by grabbing his breast pocket, which ripped off in her hand."

"What do you think?" Hunter asked.

"The autopsy isn't in yet, but two things seem to contradict the Feds' assumption—the shocked look on Aldo's face and both Sophia's and Kelly's claims that Amelia seemed dead before she hit the water."

"You said Ma was in the bathroom when the Brit took a header," Marco said.

"Sophia told us she came out in time to see Amelia fall past the window—said her body looked limp."

"Anything else?" Hunter asked.

"Tim thinks she either had a heart attack or may have been given a slow-acting poison that took effect while she was beside the railing—made her fall overboard and killed her before she hit the water."

"We'll know more after Mike gets the autopsy results," Hunter said. "If there's no water in her lungs, they can't say she died because Aldo pushed her."

"Lockwood said top criminal defense lawyers will be at their bail hearings midday at the Palm Beach County Courthouse." Marco narrowed his eyes. "I'll have a car waiting outside. When they get bail, I'll spirit them away to Sicily in my jet."

I shook my head. "The FBI has their passports."

He chuckled. "Jett, my dear, they're the kind of *famiglia* that don't need passports. Once they get to Italy, the Feds will never get them back."

"Could be they won't be granted bail for that very reason, plus the fact it was nine murders. And the crimes were against high-profile citizens from several countries." I brushed away tears. "Their governments will be out for blood."

Hunter put his hand on Marco's shoulder. "Don't do anything crazy if they're refused bail. There's no case against your mother. It's all innuendo and suppositions that can't be proven."

"Yeah, and Aldo's lawyers will argue he was obviously framed," I said, trying to sound positive.

Marco frowned. "That torn breast pocket will be hard to explain— makes it look like she clutched at him as he shoved her overboard."

"And she was an international best-selling author beloved by millions," Hunter reminded us. "Public opinion will demand justice."

Marco pounded the table. "If Count Medici is innocent, who the hell killed all those people? Has anyone uncovered a motive?"

"That's the big mystery, but I promise you, we'll figure this out. I need a little time to get a fresh perspective."

"If not, you can visit Ma in Sicily." Marco stood and pulled me in for a hug. "You've got my burner number. Keep me informed."

Hunter and I waited at the picnic table while the three Mafiosos sauntered back to the Cigarette boat and zoomed out of the Palm Beach Inlet for a cruise up the coast to Stuart.

———

I was allowed to deliver clothes to Sophia and Aldo so they wouldn't have to appear in formal wear. When I visited her jail cell, she put on a brave face.

"Those FBI agents will be lucky to serve burgers at the Golden Arches after we're proved innocent." She hugged me. "Don't worry, Jett. We'll have the last laugh."

I held back tears. "I'll be at the courthouse this afternoon, and hopefully you'll get bail and come home with me." As I walked away, I hated the sound of her jail cell locking with a loud metallic clank.

This can't be happening. I must save her.

One of the lawyers brought Aldo his clothes so they could talk again before the bail hearings at 2:00 p.m.

———

I waited anxiously with Hunter in the courtroom as the prosecutors, attorneys, and defendants assembled. Aldo was scheduled to appear first.

My uncle squeezed my hand. "Don't worry. These lawyers are the best."

After hearing, "All rise," I watched the judge enter and settle behind his massive desk front and center. We were instructed to be seated, and the proceedings began.

Aldo's legal team claimed he was "a nobleman, a model citizen, and a pillar of his community with no criminal record, that there were serious issues with the evidence against him, and that he should be granted bail while his defense attorneys work to have the charges dropped."

The prosecutor said, "This man has been charged with nine murders—eight citizens of foreign countries, most of whom were successful, well-known leaders in business or politics, and one prominent American. The defendant's vast wealth and organized crime connections make him a major flight risk, and his many crimes make him a danger to the public. I request that bail be denied."

One of Aldo's lawyers jumped up. "Objection. No proof of my client's connection to the Mafia has been offered, and the murder evidence is circumstantial."

"Overruled. Given the heinous nature of the crimes and the extensive loss of life, combined with the defendant's considerable resources, I agree he's a flight risk, and the public must be protected. Bail is denied, and Mr. Medici will be held in the Palm Beach County Jail until his trial is concluded." The judge pounded his gavel, and that was that.

No bail for Aldo. I prayed Sophia would fare better, and Hunter gave me a side hug.

She was brought in, our eyes met, and I waved. Her lawyers painted her as a model citizen and asked that I be allowed to testify about her exemplary character.

"Miss Jettine Jorgensen, please take the stand."

I came forward and was sworn in.

Her lawyer asked, "Miss Jorgensen, how long have you known Sophia DeLuca?"

"I met her six months ago after I advertised for a dog nanny. She moved in the next day and has become my house manager and close friend."

"And have you ever known her to participate in Mafia activities?"

"No, in fact, she moved to Florida once her sons were grown so she could get away from all that. She was living in an affordable retirement community for people fifty-five and over before she moved to my home."

"So, not the sort of neighborhood a wealthy Mob mother would choose." He looked at the judge. "Nothing further."

The District Attorney stood. "I have a few questions. Isn't it true your friend, Mrs. Sophia DeLuca, is the daughter of the late *Don* Francesco Calabrese of the New York Mafia?"

"Yes, but she never had anything to do with the family business, which is typical of most females born into that situation."

"Oh, really? Isn't it true she shot and killed an intruder in your home, and later, she shot and killed the accountant for a drug cartel in Miami?"

"The first incident was self-defense, and in the second one she was defending my life and hers from a man intent on killing us." I glared at him. "She was found blameless in both cases."

"Her skill with a firearm doesn't sound like an innocent Mafia wife who had no connection to the family business."

"Objection!" Sophia's attorney yelled.

"Sustained," the judge ruled.

"No further questions. Your honor, I'm requesting bail be denied based on Mrs. DeLuca's romantic connection to the accused murderer, the fact that she was on the premises for every murder, she's charged with assisting the killer, and she has strong ties to the New York Mafia."

The judge scrutinized Sophia. "I'm inclined to agree with the prosecutor. Bail is denied, and Mrs. DeLuca is remanded to the Palm Beach County Jail until the completion of her trial."

I gasped like I'd been gut punched. This was a disaster.

Hunter squeezed my hand.

Oh, God, what will her sons do?

THIRTY-FIVE

We exited the courthouse, a black limo pulled up, and someone inside opened the rear passenger door. I recognized Sal, and we hopped in.

Marco sat out of view of the door. Hunter closed it, and the car moved into traffic.

"Ma isn't with you, so I'm assuming the bastards denied bail." He balled his fists.

"She's been remanded to the county jail until her trial is completed. Same for Aldo." I fought back tears.

Marco patted my hand. "No worries. I'll see that she's protected while she's inside."

Hunter interjected, "Her lawyers told us the case against her is weak, and they'll work hard to have the charges dropped." He paused and glanced at me. "Uh, he said the prosecutor would drop the charges today if Sophia agrees to testify against Aldo and gives them evidence to prove his guilt."

"But he's not guilty," I blurted.

Marco took my hand. "Are you absolutely sure about that, Jett?"

I hesitated. "There's no way I can be one hundred percent certain until I catch the real killer."

"Then we should advise her to take the deal." He shrugged. "It'll be several months before his trial. In the meantime, Ma will be free, and you can look for the guy who killed nine people."

"There's one big problem—Sophia will never agree to it," Hunter said.

"That's true. I think she loves Aldo." I sighed. "Oh, God, what if he really is guilty, and the evidence in his room was a double bluff?"

Marco shook his head. "No way a killer would take that chance. He'd destroy the evidence."

"Okay, so that proves he's innocent, right?" I asked.

"Except for the torn breast pocket," Hunter said. "That one's hard to explain."

"Where's your car parked?" Marco asked.

"We're in the parking garage across from the courthouse," I answered.

"We'll drop you by your car, and I'll talk to Ma's lawyers about getting the charges dropped—see if we can get her to turn State's evidence."

Hunter nodded. "I'll talk to her."

"And we'll do our best to figure out if somebody else is the killer." I leaned over and kissed Marco's cheek before I left the limo.

———

My dogs greeted us after Hunter and I arrived back at the castle.

"Unc, I can't thank you enough for giving me Pratt and Whitney. They always cheer me up." I asked them, "Who wants to play frisbee?"

Both dogs barked and twirled around, doing their happy dance.

We took them into the backyard and tossed the discs. The fresh air and fun activity helped distract us and lift our spirits.

We returned to the terrace, and Gwen was waiting for us.

She hugged me. "I heard the judge denied bail. Poor Sophia. Is there anything I can do?"

I shrugged. "I don't know. Everywhere I turn, I keep hitting dead ends. I feel like I'm missing something crucial, but I can't think what it might be."

"Think back to the dinner cruise and try to remember everything Lady Amelia said to you." Gwen squeezed my shoulder. "Could be a clue in something she said."

I thought back and felt a jolt of energy as I remembered her comment about the cane. "Lady Amelia said the lion's head cane she gave me would give me almost supernatural insight, but that its energy couldn't reach me while it was locked inside my vault."

Hunter patted my hand. "I suggest you go and get it."

"She said it's four hundred years old and originally belonged to the first king of Scotland and England. Maybe if I do some research on it, I'll learn something helpful."

Gwen gave me another hug. "You do that, and I'll keep my ear to the ground at work in case something breaks in Sophia's case. Let me know if you find anything." She hugged Hunter and bid us goodbye.

He waved and turned to me. "Is there anything I can do to help you?"

"I might need your help later if I find something. For now, why don't you go home and work on your airplane? I know that relaxes you."

"All right, but call if you need me." He gave me a hug and sauntered away.

I looked at my dogs. "Come with me, my darlings. We're on a quest."

Pratt and Whitney followed me up four flights of stairs to my bedroom suite. I opened my vault and took out the ancient cane. My fingers tingled as I held it.

I grasped the gold lion's head and used the cane as a walking stick while descending the secret stairway from my room to the study. The dogs ran ahead as I followed the winding steps downward. The cane made a thump sound each time it hit a step. I'd heard that sound before as spirits led me down to the study and showed me *A Strange Case of Nine Murders*. Would they let me read the book this time?

I entered the study and laid the cane on my desk. The door to the hallway was closed, and a cold wind swirled around me as I grabbed the Chinese mystery novel.

I asked, "Are the answers I seek in this book?"

The book flew out of my hands and landed in its spot in the bookcase.

"I guess that's a no." I sat at my desk and switched on the computer.

It wasn't long before I found info on King James I, who took the throne of England and Scotland in 1603. After scrolling through pages of historical information, I found a mention of his favorite belongings. Photos of the cane were included, but not many details. Only that legend claimed it imbued its owner with supernatural insight and that it held many secrets.

Maybe the clues I need are in the four books that hit Neville during the séance.

I jumped up, pulled the four mystery novels from the shelf, sat at my desk, and flipped through the pages, searching for something relevant. A cold breeze whipped past me again. As I started on the second book, the third book flopped open and stayed that way. I grabbed it and read the page.

Holy cow! The murderer used a weapon hidden in his cane.

I stared at Lady Amelia's unusual cane. Could this be the key to everything?

———

I called Hunter, Gwen, and Mike and asked them to meet me in the castle. A lot was riding on this. Lives were at stake.

They were due at 4:00 p.m. The two detectives would be my official witnesses, and my uncle and I would use our combined *Aniwaya* intuitions to discover hidden secrets.

Mike arrived first and pulled me into his arms. "You found new evidence?"

"I'm hoping it will exonerate Sophia and Aldo, and I want you to get all the credit. I know how the Feds treated you during this investigation. I'd love to see you one-up them." I kissed him. "And it'll be good for your career."

"Yeah, if I was an FBI agent, I'd show them a better way to work with police detectives."

Gwen and Hunter walked in together.

I greeted them and said, "Ready to roll?"

"Let's do this," Gwen said. "Where do we start?"

"My study. I have everything ready." I led them down the hallway.

Mike and Gwen settled across from Hunter and me. The gold lion's head cane lay on the desk between us.

"Before we start, there's something you all should know," Mike said. "The full report from Lady Amelia's autopsy was released today. She was dead before she hit the water—arsenic poisoning. The M.E. thinks a liquid form of it was added to her drink. It only takes one-eighth of a teaspoon to be lethal as a liquid, and she would've died about twenty minutes after ingestion."

"Proving she didn't drown or die from the fall," I said, staring at her cane.

"Yeah, but here's the shocker: Amelia had an inoperable brain tumor that would have killed her anyway."

"Whoa." Gwen sat back. "Did Amelia know she was dying?"

"The M.E. contacted her doctor in the UK, and he said she'd known about it for almost a year." Mike ran his hand through his hair. "Her doc said he checked her again right before she flew here for Mystery Fest, and she was fully aware she'd die soon."

I touched the cane and yanked my hand back like it had given me an electric shock.

Hunter put his arm around my shoulder. "Jett, what the hell?"

"Touch it—you'll see." I pointed at the ancient artifact once possessed by a king.

He tentatively touched the lion's head, pulled his hand back, and touched it again. Arching an eyebrow, he looked at me. "Is this a trick?"

"No, I promise. Let's try touching it together and see what happens." I reached out in unison with him.

The instant we made contact with the cane, I felt a rush of dark energy, and the faces of every Mystery Fest murder victim flashed through my mind like they were in a spinning kaleidoscope.

I pulled my hand back and turned to Hunter. "Did you see anything?"

"Yeah, everyone killed at the conference spun around in my head, and black energy surged through me." Hunter frowned at the cane. "This thing has bad mojo."

Gwen tapped the desk. "Time out. What are you two talking about?"

"We felt negative energy because I think the cane holds dark secrets that must be released." I scanned the length of it. "I realize now this was meant to be a clue, but I missed it."

Mike crossed his arms. "Are you saying this fancy walking aid is going to give us the killer's name?"

"It might give us the who, the how, and the why. That's why I asked you and Gwen to be official witnesses. You should video this to verify everything we find is from this cane."

Mike pulled out his smartphone and started the video recording.

I pulled on latex gloves, lifted the cane, and studied the gold lion's head. I tried twisting it, but it wouldn't budge. Inspiration hit me, and I pressed both diamond eyes simultaneously. The head released, and I found myself holding a lion's head attached to a dagger with dried blood on it. "This could be the weapon used to stab Klaus." I set it in front of Mike. "The lab can check the blood for his DNA."

I picked up the hollow cane and peered inside. "There's something in here." I upended it, and rolled-up documents dropped out followed by a lace handkerchief wrapped around a ring.

"Whoa, that's Natalya's black widow ring." I picked it up and showed them. "And Amelia's initials are embroidered in gold thread on the white cloth."

Mike handed his phone to Gwen. "Continue the video." He pulled on gloves and unrolled the pages. "Jett, these are vellum copies of original blueprints for Valhalla. They have the Danish architect's signature, and look, two sections have been highlighted." He showed them to me.

"This shows *two* secret passages—the one I knew about that connects to the study and another one at the other end of the castle that connects to the ballroom. It goes all the way up to my parents' bedroom."

"Wasn't that where Amelia was staying?" Gwen asked.

"Yes." I stared at the blueprints, stunned.

Hunter nudged me. "Does this mean Amelia was the killer?"

"If so, she wouldn't leave us wondering why and how. She was a famous author. There must be more here." I studied the gold lion's foot.

The paw had five toes with claws on the ends and a royal seal engraved underneath on the footpad. I pressed the seal, and the center toe popped off. It contained a flash drive.

I held it up. "They didn't have these four hundred years ago. Amelia must've modified the foot."

"Fire up the computer and plug it in," Mike said. He dragged his chair around to me, and Gwen pulled her chair next to Hunter.

We all had front-row seats as I opened the document. It was titled *The Mystery Fest Murders* by Lady Amelia Ainsworth.

It began with the author's note: I wrote most of this earlier and finished it at Valhalla Castle. This book is a true story and a confession to nine murders, including my own. Ten murders, if this manuscript isn't found in time, and the State of Florida executes Count Aldo Medici for my crimes. I had ample reasons for the murders and will explain how I accomplished each one.

My apologies to Jett Jorgensen for dragging her, unknowingly, into my crusade to right many wrongs before my death. I hope she and my many fans will forgive me, and that in time, history will remember me as a noble instrument for justice served.

THIRTY-SIX

I grabbed Mike's wrist when he reached for the flash drive. "What are you doing? We've gotta read her manuscript."

"This is evidence in a serial murder case, and more importantly, it might exonerate Sophia and Aldo." He turned and looked at me. "You *do* want them released from jail as soon as possible, don't you, Jett?"

"Let Jett copy the manuscript onto her computer first," Gwen said. "We'll stay and read it while you enter the lion cane and its contents into evidence."

"This is big." Mike rubbed his chin. "I won't jump to conclusions. Amelia could be lying or be an accomplice to the murders. The facts must be verified before I blow the whistle, and Gwen, I need you to accompany me and confirm chain of custody."

"All right, and I'll make sure *you* get credit for solving the case instead of the FBI," Gwen said.

"You can count on Jett and me to study every word while you log in the evidence and see if it matches Amelia's account," Hunter said. "We want Sophia free, and we understand it's important to do this right."

"And remember, Mike, that cane and the contents belong to me." I saved the document on my computer. "I expect everything returned once the case is closed." I pulled out a blank page. "List the cane and its contents here and sign it."

Mike handed me the paper and pocketed the flash drive, ring, and handkerchief. He picked up the cane after reinserting the missing toe into the paw and the rolled-up vellum into the hollow stick. The lion's head with the dagger was inside an evidence bag, which he also took. "I'll be at my office." He gave me a quick kiss, looking more excited than he had in years, and he and Gwen left.

Hunter and I sat in front of the monitor. The manuscript was a full-length, 70,000-word book, and the timeline started half a century ago when Edmund and Amelia became engaged.

I elbowed Hunter. "To save time, we should skim over the story and focus on the parts that detail the why and how of each murder."

As we paged through the book, it turned out Edmund had cheated on Amelia, and Amelia's sister, Roberta, had caught him. After the infidelity, he pleaded with Roberta not to tell. He vowed undying love, but she suspected it was more likely that he wanted Amelia's money and position to aid his political aspirations. She waited almost a week, carefully considering the consequences, and then told her sister everything.

That night, Roberta was killed. Amelia knew her hit-and-run death wasn't an accident—no skid marks to show braking. Edmund didn't know Roberta had told her about the cheating, and Amelia never let on that she knew the truth. She was certain he killed her sister, but she couldn't prove it because Aldo gave Edmund a false alibi, and Edmund claimed his damaged car had been stolen before the accident.

Amelia wrote: I was never sure if Aldo knew about the murder or if he thought he was helping a buddy avoid getting caught for cheating on his fiancée. And there was also the matter of Aldo killing his rival in a pistol duel. I decided to leave his fate in the hands of Almighty God and Jett Jorgensen. If God meant for Aldo to live, Jett would discover my manuscript in time.

I scrolled down: As for Edmund, I ended our engagement and waited for justice to prevail. Instead, he rose through the political ranks, destined to be our next prime minister. I couldn't let him get away with killing my sister, and since I was fated to die soon anyway, Mystery Fest presented the perfect opportunity to execute those that I knew had escaped justice, starting with him.

Edmund's murder had to be violent, and once I knew where the next Mystery Fest would be held, I had months to plan for his demise and all the others.

I researched Valhalla Castle, designed by a Danish architect over a hundred years ago. The architectural firm still existed, and I visited their offices in Copenhagen. They thought I was researching huge old residences for a book I was writing, and I was allowed to examine the original blueprints for Valhalla, along with ones for two other castles and several magnificent mansions. I photographed Valhalla's blueprints and had them printed on vellum later so they would fit inside my cane.

Those plans allowed me to discover two secret passages. I won't list them here for Jett's sake, but I requested the suite where one of them could be accessed. I also studied recent photos of the castle with all its furnishings, including the Viking weapons mounted on the wall in the great hall.

A quick trip to a museum for Viking artifacts allowed me to discover I could wield a battle axe. Next, I arranged to carry an antique guitar to a friend in the States. On arrival at the castle, I wore white cotton gloves and wandered around, holding the guitar case. I slipped inside the great hall, took out the guitar, and slid it under a sofa. Then I lifted the battle axe off its mounts and hid it inside the guitar case.

While Jett was busy downstairs, I entered her suite and carried the battle axe down the secret passage where I left it behind the hidden door to the study. My friend was due to pick up the guitar soon, so I retrieved it and waited outside. In minutes, the guitar was in its case inside my friend's car, and no one suspected a thing.

Earlier, Fiona sat beside me inside the airport limo on the way to Jett's home. She laid her cell phone on the seat, and I sent a text from her phone to Edmund, asking him to meet her in Jett's study at 7:00 the next morning.

I entered the study a few minutes early that morning and retrieved the weapon. I left the bookcase door partially open to draw his attention and hid behind a large statue. When Edmund arrived, he walked straight to the open bookcase, and I sneaked up behind him and swung the axe into his head. After gazing at his corpse, I took the secret passage upstairs, changed clothes, and joined everyone in the great hall.

Hunter shook his head. "That was cold. She must've really hated him."

"Yeah, unlike the sweet lady she seemed." I scanned further and found this: Lucky for me, the surprising results of a séance held in the study after Edmund's death added a supernatural element to my plans. The spirits gave everyone a major clue by hitting Neville's head with four mystery novels, each involving multiple murders. Although unplanned, the séance helped me by creating apprehension among those marked for death.

"I've always heard it's the quiet ones you have to watch out for, but who would ever suspect a demure little old lady?" Hunter asked.

"She certainly fooled me." I quickly jotted the details of Edmund's demise on a pad and continued reading the chronicle of murders, skimming over several pages.

Scotch Whisky Heiress Fiona Campbell was next. According to the author, Fiona murdered her father and her husband. Amelia knew this because she confessed it to her at a previous Mystery Fest after drinking too much whisky. Her father's and husband's estates netted her millions.

Amelia wrote: I suppose this would be a good time to mention I brought all the necessary poisons with me, disguised as harmless cosmetics and medicines. One such poison was a cartridge of liquid nicotine identical to those used in Aldo's vapor pens. I also retrieved an empty vial with his fingerprints on it from his room.

During breakfast, I poured the nicotine into Fiona's espresso while everyone was distracted. After she was seated in the tent for the polo match, I dropped an empty cartridge covered with Aldo's fingerprints beside her chair. An hour later, she was dead.

I stared at the monitor, stunned.

Hunter gently leaned into me. "Hey, it's dinnertime, and I'm hungry. Let's call the kitchen and order something."

"Right," I agreed. "We can keep reading while we eat." I picked up the house phone and dialed Karin in the kitchen.

"Let me guess, you and Hunter are hungry."

"You read my mind."

"I thought you might want food so I made grilled ham, cheese, and tomato sandwiches. I'll bring them to the study along with chips and a pitcher of iced tea."

"No wonder Hunter is crazy about you." I laughed. "We'll see you soon."

Ten minutes later, she wheeled in a cart with all our goodies, including some freshly baked chocolate chip cookies for dessert.

Karin glanced at the monitor. "Find anything interesting?"

THIRTY-SEVEN

After eating, we skimmed over several pages and stopped at Baron Klaus von Helsig's murder. Amelia claimed he was a serial killer responsible for deaths all over Europe.

She figured he killed at least thirty people—two in each of the past fifteen years after attending annual Mystery Fests. Her private investigators had amassed a mountain of circumstantial evidence against him, but she couldn't get anyone to prosecute him. They feared him because he was too rich and powerful.

Amelia wrote: Killing Klaus was easy—he was heavily medicated after his ordeal in the plane crash, and the drugs made him sleep soundly. His room was directly beneath mine, and a secret passage led to an entrance in the back wall of his closet.

I sneaked into his room late at night and stabbed his heart with the dagger hidden in my cane. He woke for an instant, looked into my eyes, and died. Before leaving, I shut off his oxygen and unlocked his balcony doors and entry door to confuse investigators.

"She made it sound so cold and simple, as if it were only a fiction scene in one of her books." I shuddered. "It gives me chills, knowing it's all true."

Hunter sipped iced tea. "Let's find out how she killed the Spanish prince."

We scanned several pages about the conference and social interactions and stopped where Amelia wrote: Prince Gaspar Borbón was next to die because he murdered his pregnant young girlfriend after she refused to have an abortion. Gaspar and his bodyguard, Jorge Santos, threw her off his yacht. Many of the women in Mystery Lovers International suspected Gaspar killed her.

I paid a visit to his yacht crew while he was away playing polo. The second mate witnessed the murder but was too afraid to testify. He recounted the details in exchange for ten thousand dollars and the promise I wouldn't go to the authorities. He said there was no hard evidence anyway. No matter, I had my own plans.

Aldo made everything easy by sleeping in Sophia's room. The day before Gaspar's death, I stole a large quantity of Xarelto pills from the bottle on Aldo's nightstand. (I was originally going to use my blood thinners, which were a different brand.) I crushed the pills into a powder, and later, slipped them into Gaspar's whisky while he was dancing.

The next afternoon, after the blood thinner had plenty of time to take effect, I descended the stairs with Gaspar and tripped him with my cane. He tumbled down the marble steps and stopped in a twisted heap on the second-floor landing. While he suffered from massive internal bleeding, I hurried back up to the fourth floor and took the elevator down. I was already in the great hall when Dina discovered his body— a lucky coincidence that made her a suspect.

I stopped reading. "Wow, I mean, I know the victims did bad things, but Amelia seems so heartless. The nobility is adept at hiding their feelings, so I never suspected that the victims weren't her dear friends. What a shocker!"

Hunter agreed. "I kind of understand why she killed them, but I'm amazed she was able to remain so detached. Who's next on her hit list?"

I scrolled through several pages. "The Russian oligarch, Natalya Petrov."

Amelia wrote: Natalya murdered all four of her husbands and became richer with each death. I know this because I quizzed her about unusual murder methods she learned in the KGB, hoping to use a few in my books. She was deep into a Vodka bottle and described killing her husbands with prussic acid sprayed into their nostrils while they slept. She also admitted to coaching Fiona on using it for her murders. I played along and agreed to keep her secrets.

It seemed fitting to use Natalya's favorite murder method on her, so I procured a small spray bottle of prussic acid, disguised as a lipstick tube, and brought it with me to Valhalla Castle. The first day, while we waited in the great hall, I spilled my purse beside Aldo. He picked up several items that I wanted his fingerprints on and dropped them into my open handbag. The fake lipstick was one.

That evening after Gaspar's death, Natalya was distraught. I dropped a sedative into her drink during dinner, so she'd be sound asleep later. She turned in early, and I waited until midnight to sneak into her room via the secret passage. I wore my cotton gloves and was careful to hold the spray canister in a way that wouldn't smudge Aldo's fingerprints. After delivering the lethal dose into her nostrils and stealing her spider ring, I dropped the canister on the floor so it would be found after the body was discovered.

Another nail in Aldo's coffin. I'll never know if he survived my frame job, but I trust that God will ensure justice.

Hunter recapped, "So far, she planted Aldo's nicotine vial beside Fiona, used his blood thinners to kill Gaspar, and left the sprayer with his fingerprints on it by Natalya's bed. That's diabolical."

"Well, she was an expert at planning murders in her books, so this wouldn't have been difficult for her to conceive." I grabbed a cookie and took a bite.

"This is more riveting than any fictional murder mystery," Hunter said. "I want to know how she killed Jorge. Keep scrolling." He scooped up a handful of chips.

I found where Amelia wrote: Prince Gaspar's bodyguard, Jorge Santos, was next by a happy convenience, and I already explained why he had to die.

He was fishing off the end of Jett's floating pier, and our little group of strollers was asked to bring him a mug of cold beer and a beer cooler. Dina carried the mug, so I distracted her for a moment and poured GHB into the beer. Later, the drug immobilized his muscles, and he fell into the water and drowned. The shark that ripped off his arm was a bonus. After our stroll, I planted the little GHB bottle in Aldo's room.

More nails in Aldo's coffin. The evidence against him was mounting.

"Whoa, her comment about the severed arm showed how much she detested Jorge for helping kill Gaspar's pregnant girlfriend." I washed down my cookie with iced tea. "I'm seeing a very different side of Amelia in these pages. Writing so many murder mysteries jaded her."

"Are we done with the murders?" Hunter asked. "I lost count."

"Nope, we've got three to go—Dina, Neville, and Amelia." I took another sip of iced tea and scrolled to the next murder in the manuscript.

Amelia wrote: Next to die was Texan Dina Fenton. As with Fiona and Natalya, after she drank too much at one of the Mystery Fests, I cajoled her into admitting she killed her husband. She wanted to be free and not share all the millions their oil wells earned. I let her think the secret was safe with me, a woman who had sworn off marriage.

During a two-hour break after the afternoon panel on cold cases, I stopped by Dina's room before she filled her bath, and we discussed the recent murders. I made the excuse that my room was too far away and asked to use her toilet.

While I was in her bathroom, I mixed powdered ketamine into her bath crystals. The hot bath water would help the drug enter her bloodstream through her skin. In minutes, her muscles would go limp and allow her to sink beneath the surface and drown. And that is exactly what happened after I left her.

I scrolled ahead past the movie viewing and stopped where Amelia wrote:

Our group was served dinner in the ballroom after *Vertigo* ended. We had a brief break after dining, and I stopped by Neville's room and told him I spotted a murder weapon from my balcony. I suggested that the dagger would be easier to view from his balcony because it was closer. I even had him turn off all his lights so he could see outside better in the dark with a few ground lights on.

As he leaned over the railing for a closer look, I shoved him with all my might, thrusting him over it. He went headfirst down to the terrace in an instant, never having time to react because my actions were so unexpected. Rushing inside before he landed, I slipped into the hallway and took the elevator down to the first floor. I joined everyone in the media room for the second movie, giving me an alibi.

My readers are no doubt wondering why I murdered DCI Neville Wright of the famed Scotland Yard. I had assisted him on several cases, but over the years, he became obsessed with his career. He cared more about closing cases and getting promoted than he did about fairness and justice. He coveted the position of Detective Chief Superintendent and was close to achieving his goal.

The promotion was between Neville and a man with several commendations and a scar from a bullet wound. His rival had saved a group of Londoners from a terrorist attack. Not wanting to appear inferior, Neville cornered a Muslim man with suspected ties to Al Qaeda, shot him dead at close range, and used a street pistol he'd brought with him to make it look like the man shot him first. He had the dead man hold the gun and fire it against Neville's side. The wound was merely a graze, but it bled profusely.

A notorious snitch he had used in the past witnessed the murder and made Neville pay him twenty thousand pounds not to tell anyone. For an additional ten thousand pounds, he told me instead. I bided my time until the conference in Florida. It was fun watching Neville agonize over trying to solve the murders at Valhalla Castle before I seized the opportunity and shoved him over the balcony.

"Geez," Hunter said. "I'm glad I wasn't on her hit list."

After several pages, Amelia wrote: My death was scheduled for the final night of Mystery Fest during the dinner cruise down the Intracoastal Waterway. My brain tumor would've killed me soon anyway. I preferred to choose the time and place of my demise, and so I carried a small bottle of liquid arsenic in my handbag. After dosing my wine, I tossed the empty container into the water. The poison took about twenty minutes to cause death, so I timed it while I'd be on the top deck near Aldo.

Right before my poisoned wine took effect, I pulled Aldo aside by the railing and ripped the pocket off his jacket. I screamed, and clutching his pocket, threw myself backward over the railing before he could grab me. At least, I hope that's what happened. Obviously, I wrote this account before my death, so I have no way of knowing exactly how it turned out. Chances are, afterward, Aldo was arrested for all the murders, including mine.

I killed eight people in the name of justice and executed myself for those murders and the possible future execution of Count Aldo Medici. It is my hope that Jett Jorgensen discovers this manuscript, along with the blueprints for Valhalla Castle, the ring, and the hidden dagger. I want the world to know the truth. And if God wills it, the manuscript will be found in time to save Aldo. If not, may he rest in peace.

Justice has been served.

THIRTY-EIGHT

One week later, Sophia and Aldo appeared before a judge, and Mike testified about Amelia's written confession and the contents of her cane. The judge examined the new evidence and dropped all charges against them.

Sophia's sons, Dominic and Marco, sat on either side of me as we watched the court proceedings.

Dominic DeLuca, an older version of Marco by four years and head of the family, leaned close to me. "You found the stuff and gave credit to your boyfriend, didn't you?"

I nodded. "This could give his career a big boost, and I especially enjoyed upstaging the two Feds."

"You're okay, Jett." Dom whispered, "You ever need anything, call us."

Moments later, we all hugged Sophia, and the men shook hands.

Aldo and Sophia hugged the longest.

Aldo said, "We've been through a lot together, and all the bad stuff was a result of my connection to Amelia and Edmund. For the record, all those years ago, I thought I was helping Edmund cover up a one-night stand so his wedding could go ahead. I never knew he killed Amelia's sister with his car."

"Of course, you didn't, sugar buns." Sophia gave him a kiss.

Dom and Marco seemed mortified.

Dom said, "Ma, ya can't call Count Medici sugar buns. It's undignified."

Aldo smiled. "I like it—makes me feel like a young stud."

She grinned. "See, boys, he likes it."

"I think you and I deserve a romantic getaway." Aldo took her hand. "My dear Sophia, will you accompany me to my *palacio* in Florence? You'll be treated like royalty."

She turned to me. "Can you manage without me for a while, Jett?"

"Yes, of course. Italy is beautiful in the summer, and you deserve a break after your jail nightmare." I hugged her again. "I'll miss you."

"I'll miss you too. Now let's get back to Valhalla so you can help me pack. I want to look good for my sweetie." Sophia grabbed Aldo's hand.

———

The next day, I waved goodbye to Sophia and Aldo as they boarded his private jet. She'd only been home one day before they left for Italy, and I missed her. She had become such a big part of my life.

I needed Mike, but he was busy dealing with the aftermath of one of the most notorious murder cases in American history. Lauded for solving the Mystery Fest Murders, he spent the next few days in the spotlight doing interviews for television and the press. We finally managed to spend the night together four days after Sophia's release from jail.

After a tender night of lovemaking, we woke in each other's arms.

Mike pulled me closer. "There's something I need to tell you."

"That sounds ominous. Is everything okay?"

He nodded. "A slot opened up in the next FBI class at Quantico, and thanks to your help with the murder case, I've been offered the position." He grinned. "I'm going to be an FBI agent, something I've always wanted, despite those rude Feds from Miami."

I hugged him. "Congratulations! When do you start training?"

"That's the thing. I'm flying out today. Class starts tomorrow morning."

"You're leaving *today*?" I sat up. "When will you be back?"

He hesitated. "The course takes twenty weeks."

"But that's five months," I protested. "Will you get some breaks for visits?"

"The training is very intensive, but once I graduate, I'll come home and pack."

"Pack? Shouldn't that be the time you unpack?" I didn't like where this was headed.

"Babe, after I complete training, I'll be one of their most junior agents, so forget Florida." He sighed. "I'll probably start somewhere like North Dakota or Wyoming."

"So, this is it? You're leaving me?" I bit my lip, desperately trying not to cry.

"We'll have a few days after I return home." He took my hand. "Don't forget you left me to spend six years in Navy Intelligence."

"Not true—I fully intended to see you as often as possible during my service, but *you* ghosted me. You ignored all my calls, texts, emails, and letters. *You* left me, and now you're doing it again."

"Jett, baby, this is for my career. We'll figure it out and find a way to make it work." He kissed me. "Let's have breakfast together before I leave."

My world was imploding. First, Sophia left with Aldo, and now Mike was leaving me for the FBI. *I don't deserve this.*

We shared a silent breakfast, followed by what might have been our last kiss.

———

Mike had been gone a month when Gwen commiserated with me over a bottle of merlot. "If it's meant to be, he'll come back to you." She shrugged. "You might even cross paths with him during one of your P.I. cases after he's an FBI agent."

"My interactions with the Feds don't usually go well." I swirled my wine.

"On another subject, what did you decide about Lady Amelia's cane?"

"I gifted it to the British Museum in London, minus the contents, of course." I stared into my wine glass. "After all, it's a four-hundred-year-old artifact that belonged to one of their kings."

"Uncle Clive will love that you did that, and it should earn you goodwill from the British people."

"The news reports praised my generosity, which should help after all the bad press from the murders here." My mind drifted back to my absent lover. "Any news on Mike's replacement?"

"The town council asked me to serve on the selection committee. The islanders want someone who understands our lifestyles, so we chose a guy from a prominent family in Boston."

"Tell me about him," I refilled my glass. "I need a distraction."

"He has a BS from Boston College and a Masters in Criminology from Harvard. His wife died two years ago, and he's looking for a fresh start in a warm climate."

"Sounds like a good candidate. Anything more?"

"We did a video chat via Zoom. He's thirty-two and quite a hottie —blond hair, blue eyes, six-two, and super fit. He plays tennis, golf, and polo—thought the Wellington polo fields were a big plus."

"A widower, huh?" I sipped the wine. "Any children?"

"A seven-year-old boy." Gwen drained her glass. "A British nanny helps him with the child-rearing, and once they're settled here, he'll hire a live-in housekeeper/cook."

"Sounds like he comes from money."

"He inherited a bundle from his wife." Gwen glanced at her phone. "I'm late. Clint will be waiting next door." She air-kissed me. "Must dash."

Five minutes later, my doorbell boomed Wagner's "Ride of the Valkyries." I opened the door to a handsome man with blond hair and intense blue eyes.

"Good evening. I'm Detective Blake Collins with the Banyan Isle

Police." He flashed his badge and scrutinized me. "Are you Miss Jettine Jorgensen?"

"Yes, and please call me Jett."

I invited him inside, we shook hands, and I felt an ominous tingle that reminded me of Amelia's cane. Was my *Aniwaya* intuition warning me again?

"Follow me." I led him through to the great hall. All the Viking weapons were once again hanging on the wall. "Have a seat, Detective. Can I get you a drink?"

"No, thanks, and call me Blake. I wanted to meet you for an informal chat." He sat in a leather armchair and studied me.

"Welcome to Banyan Isle, Blake." I sat across from him and noticed his imposing, muscular physique. "I hope you found a suitable home."

"I bought a house three blocks from here. The movers will unload tomorrow and have all the furniture in place before the nanny arrives with my son."

Pratt and Whitney came barreling in from a run in the backyard with Karin. She followed them inside as they bounded over to me.

"Sorry, Jett. I hope we aren't interrupting." She smiled at the blond Adonis.

"Not at all, Karin. I'd like you to meet our new police detective." I introduced Blake, and he stood and shook her hand.

She responded with a silly grin and left us. My dogs turned and stared at him, but they didn't wag their tails.

"These are my Timber-shepherd pups, Pratt and Whitney." I stroked their fur as they remained focused on him.

He smiled and settled in the chair. "My son has a three-month-old German shepherd named Hans. He's quite a handful—so much energy."

"If you ever need a dog sitter, we love puppies, especially German shepherds, and he'd have fun playing with my dogs. They're seven months old."

"I'll keep that in mind." He cleared his throat. "My visit today is mostly because your home has a reputation for being murder central." His eyes burned into mine.

"That's a new one. I've heard Crime Castle and Murder Mansion."

"My point is I do things by the book. I understand my predecessor was your boyfriend and may have allowed you certain liberties. I'm giving you a friendly warning that won't be the case with me. I run a tight ship."

"Geez." I rolled my eyes. "It's not like I enjoy finding murder victims."

"You must admit the body count here has been unusually high during the six months you've been home."

"True, but most of the deaths had nothing to do with me."

"Good to know." He glanced around the room. "I understand you served six years in the Navy, and now you're doing your P.I. apprenticeship." His intense gaze seemed to bore into my soul.

"I want to help people get the justice they deserve."

He arched an eyebrow. "That's commendable, but you don't really need a job."

"The same could be said for you."

He smiled. "I went into police work to solve crimes and protect people."

"My work as a P.I. accomplishes the same thing. Two serial killers are no longer a threat because of my efforts."

"It seems we have a lot in common."

Something about him unnerved me, and my dogs didn't like him, which was a major red flag.

He noticed a book on the table beside him and switched gears. "Do you enjoy mysteries?"

"Yes. I have an extensive collection in my library."

He grinned. "I'm a big mystery fan."

"Which one's your favorite?"

"You probably never heard of it. It's an obscure Chinese novel titled, *A Strange Case of Nine Murders*."

AFTERWORD

Banyan Isle is a fictitious residential barrier island in Palm Beach County on the east coast of South Florida, north of Singer Island and south of Juno Beach.

Beach polo is real, and the author has enjoyed watching polo exhibitions played on the public beach on Singer Island, Florida.

The Bücker Jungmann biplane described in the book is real, and the author has owned and flown the rare antique aircraft.

Jett's Timber-shepherd puppies, Pratt and Whitney, are based on the author's dogs who enriched her world for fourteen wonderful years.

ACKNOWLEDGMENTS

First and foremost, I thank my Lord and Savior, Jesus Christ, for my many blessings.

Although I know how to do most of the things Jett does in the story, I always get a second and third opinion on the action scenes in case I forget to include something important.

Thanks to George Bernstein and Peter Schlosser for advice on the fencing scene.

Many thanks to retired airline captain, aircraft mechanic, and vintage airplane restorer Jeff Rowland, who is always willing to share his expertise with me. He was a big help with the most effective way to extract the passenger from the crashed biplane.

Thanks to my advance readers Vicky Edwards, Mary Lou Benvenuto, and Robert Metz. I truly value your opinions.

As always, a heartfelt thanks to my treasured critique buddies Fred Lichtenberg and George Bernstein.

And thank you to my excellent editor, Suzanne Berglind, for a job well done.

DEAD RECKONING

A JETTINE JORGENSEN MYSTERY, BOOK 4

Hunter Vann, Mom's tall, dark, and handsome younger brother, was an airline captain who also owned a flight school and aircraft maintenance facility. I agreed to replace him on a student cross-country flight with a teenage girl who had a crush on him.

Hunter introduced us. "Kerri Lyon, meet my niece, Jett Jorgensen."

We shook hands, and he said, "Jett's been flight instructing for nine years. She was a Navy Intelligence officer and now works as a private investigator." He smiled. "I need a word with her while you do the preflight inspection, Kerri."

He took me aside. "Your P.I. mentor, Darcy, called while you were riding your Harley here. Muffy Murdoch went missing from a night-club last night. Her friends filed a police report, but they want you and Darcy to find her."

"I remember Muffy from my charity ball. Should I go now?"

"No, Darcy said it might be nothing. She'll look into it while you help my student complete her 'old-school' dual cross-country flight first."

———

Kerri landed the 1940 Piper J-3 Cub at our first stop, and we refueled. With no radios or navigation aids, not even GPS, the next leg would be more challenging. We took off and navigated at 3,500 feet using a compass and dead reckoning, which involved a known starting point and factored in airspeed, wind, landmarks, and the airplane's heading —a skill used long ago.

Normally, I wouldn't fly over the Everglades, but no landmarks made that portion of the flight more challenging for my student. I allowed her to drift off course for learning purposes.

Big mistake.

The engine in our vintage, tandem-seat airplane made a loud bang, black smoke billowed out, oil splattered the windshield, and the propeller seized.

Kerri yelled into the battery-powered intercom, "The engine's blown! What should I do?"

The cockpit was dead silent, except for the whisper of air rushing past.

Adrenaline supercharged me as I pulled off my headset and looked back over my shoulder. "Remember your training. Check left and right, make a gentle turn while maintaining best glide speed, and search for a place to land."

Seated behind me, she yanked off her headset, and her voice shot up two octaves. "A place to land? There's just a scary swamp with gators and snakes."

"Look out the side windows for a road or a clearing."

I pulled out the portable radio to call in a mayday, but before I selected the frequency, we collided with a flock of pelicans. One smashed through the windshield, and its bloody carcass hit my chest and fell on my lap, knocking the wind out of me.

A second pelican slammed into my right hand and shoulder, jarring the handheld radio loose and dragging it past me to the floor behind my seat. The bundle of bloody feathers flopped around between Kerri's feet. She screamed, opened the side window, tossed out the bird, and realized her mistake.

"Jett, I accidentally threw out the radio!"

"Calm down." Wind whipped my long hair as I tossed out the first pelican and yelled, "I've got the airplane." The controls felt mushy. I looked out the side windows and spotted damage to the leading edges of both wings.

"Kerri, pull your belts tight. The collision damage shortened our glide capability. We're going down fast."

I pulled out my cell phone and called my uncle. "No signal."

Turning right, I spotted a narrow opening in the trees and brush.

"Do you see it? A dirt rectangle."

"It looks super short," she cried. "Think we can make it?"

"It's larger than a basketball court, the approach end is clear, and we're in a Cub." I scanned the area on the way down, searching for a road, but none existed.

Alarm bells rang in my head as I realized the only access to that tiny strip was by air or water.

We descended through 500 feet in what had become a sluggish glider.

Her voice quavered, "Are we going to crash?"

"I've got this," I assured her, knowing the Cub had a low landing speed.

My concern was who we might encounter while waiting to be rescued.

As we neared what looked like an oversized helipad, I spotted a pier and a narrow path leading to the landing site.

Kerri kept reasonably calm despite being only sixteen.

"Brace yourself." My heart hammered my chest as I leveled off at a faster-than-normal speed ten feet above the marsh, and our main wheels skimmed the brush.

We were sixty feet from the edge of the hard surface.

As we glided to the helipad, a stout branch speared the aft left side, ripping open the plane's fabric-covered fuselage. Our sudden drop was cushioned by hot air rising from the crushed coral surface. We bounced once and rolled to a stop a foot from the end.

I glanced back at my wide-eyed student. "Kerri, reach back and switch on the Emergency Locator Transmitter."

She unbuckled her seat harness, turned, and cried, "It's gone!"

———

Available in Paperback and eBook from Your Favorite Bookstore or Online Retailer

ABOUT THE AUTHOR

S.L. Menear is a retired airline pilot. US Airways hired Sharon in 1980 as their first woman pilot, bypassing the flight engineer position. The men in her new-hire class gave her the nickname, Bombshell. She flew Boeing 727s and 737s, DC-9s, and BAC 1-11 airliners and was promoted to captain in her seventh year.

Before her pilot career, Sharon worked as a water-sports model and then traveled the world as a flight attendant with Pan American World Airways.

Sharon has enjoyed flying vintage airplanes, experimental aircraft, and Third-World fighters. She has flown many of the airplanes in her Samantha Starr Thrillers featuring a woman airline pilot and in her Jettine Jorgensen Mysteries.

Sharon's leisure activities included scuba diving, powered paragliding, snow skiing, surfing, horseback riding, aerobatic flying, sailing, and driving sports cars and motorcycles.

Her beloved Timber-shepherds, Pratt and Whitney, were her faithful companions for fourteen years, and they produced eight darling puppies. While living in Texas, Sharon enjoyed riding her beautiful black and white paint stallion, Chief, who kept her mother's mares happy, fathering several adorable foals.

Sharon lives and writes on an island in South Florida now. She is an active member of Mystery Writers of America, International Thriller Writers, Sisters in Crime, Florida Publishers and Authors Association, and Florida Writers Association.

Sharon can be contacted at...

www.slmenear.com

 facebook.com/slmenear

 x.com/%20SL%20Menear

instagram.com/slmenear